FAKE
fiancée

WALL STREET JOURNAL BESTSELLING AUTHOR
ILSA MADDEN-MILLS

Monica —
Charlie loves you...

Ilsa
xoxo

Fake Fiancée
Copyright © 2017 by Ilsa Madden-Mills
Little Dove Publishing

ISBN-13:978-1542779302
ISBN-10:1542779308

Cover Design:
by Hang Le

Model:
Jack Greystone

Photography:
Glenn Mackay

Editing by:
Rachel Skinner of Romance Refined

Interior Design & Formatting by:
Christine Borgford, Type A Formatting

FAKE fiancée

They say nothing compares to your first kiss,

But our first kiss was orchestrated for an audience.

Our second kiss . . . that one was REAL.

He cradled my face like he was terrified he'd f*ck it up.

He stared into my eyes until the air buzzed.

Soft and slow, full of sighs and little laughs,

He inhaled me like I was the finest Belgian chocolate,

And he'd never get another piece.

A nip of his teeth, his hand at my waist . . .

And I was lost.

I forgot he was paying me to be his fake fiancée.

I forgot we weren't REAL.

Our kiss was pure magic, and before you laugh and say those kinds of kisses don't exist,

Then you've never touched lips with Max Kent, the hottest quarterback in college history.

Three months . . .

Two hearts . . .

One fake engagement . . .

SCARS
ARE
wings

chapter ONE

Sunny

A WARM SUMMER night.

Music on the radio.

A young girl driving a red Mustang convertible.

It sounded perfect—only the evening was humid as hell, the radio was stuck on a stupid gospel station, and the car, well, it was stolen.

Chewing on my nails, I debated on pulling off to the side of the road and putting the top down, but this wasn't a pleasure ride. Obviously. I had to get out of Snowden, North Carolina before I lost my nerve to run away.

An image of my father loomed. He'd pop a blood vessel when he discovered I'd not only stolen his car but also most of the money from his wallet. I pictured his barrel chest and the way his thick fingers clenched when he was angry. He'd be grabbing his Bible and snapping his belt up. If he found me, he'd—

Stop.

I shook myself, focusing on Atlanta, Georgia. I had family there on my mom's side, people my father refused to talk to. I'd be safe . . .

For the hundredth time, I checked the rearview mirror and saw nothing but black highway, pine trees, and mountains. No one was following me, and I hadn't met a car in half an hour. I could almost imagine I was the only person alive in the world.

I fiddled with the radio station to find something besides gospel. I got nothing but static. Suddenly a raccoon dashed in front of me, and I swerved.

Wrong move.

The tires locked and the car went into a tailspin. I froze up, helpless as I was pressed against the seat of my Tilt-A-Whirl. A thud. Screeching metal. The car ground to a halt against a guardrail that lined a narrow bridge.

Shit!

I ran shaking hands over my face and the rest of my body. I was injury free except for my chest aching from the seatbelt catching me. No airbag had gone off and the engine was still running. *Thank God.* Maybe if I made it to Knoxville, I could ditch the car and buy a bus ticket to—

Everything went to hell.

The car lurched forward with a groan that sent chills up my spine as the guardrail gave in to the weight of the front end. My world tipped and then froze again. I could see the murky lake below rippling in the moonlight. I recoiled in my seat, willing the car to not move another inch.

It didn't work.

The Mustang slipped down the rocky side, nose-dived off the edge, and slammed into the water below. I screamed the entire way down, my hands like a vise around the steering wheel.

This wasn't happening.

It was.

I clawed at the seatbelt and unlatched it, but when I went to open the door, it refused. Water pressure blocked my way out.

Dosomethingdosomethingdosomethingdosomething . . .

The smell of algae surrounded me as water seeped in from the floorboard. It crept up my legs, my chest, my chin. I scrambled away from the cold but there was no escape. I took one last gulp of air as the vehicle sank below the surface, water gushing in through the soft top. Light as a feather, the car drifted down several feet and settled on the bottom of the lake.

Silence.

I watched my blond hair float around my face.

I looked around at the watery darkness.

The car should be pressurized.

I could get out now, right?

God, I didn't know.

I was only seventeen.

I didn't know anything about anything!

I tugged at the door handle again. Nothing.

I tried to roll down the window, but the electric wasn't working.

Break the windows!

I positioned my legs on the glass and shoved.

Stomped.

Beat.

I was never getting out.

Dizziness.

Panic.

My chest burned.

My nails scrabbled at the vinyl top of the vehicle. Searching for a tear. Anything.

I closed my eyes and wished myself out of the car. I even wished myself back home in that shabby house on the side of the mountain.

God, please.

Bubbles came out of my mouth.

IwasgoingtodieIwasgoingtodieIwasgoingtodieIwasgoingtodie . . .

Then I heard it—a tap, then a scratching sound. My eyes flew open.

The top of the Mustang moved. A small hole appeared and then grew bigger.

My heart surged.

Someone was there.

Someone was tearing into the car with a knife.

Everything went black.

CONSCIOUSNESS CAME SLOWLY, dragging me along in bits and pieces.

Something warm touched my lips, and I coughed as pain rippled through my throat and chest. Hands turned me on my side and water gushed out.

I struggled to suck in precious air as my eyes cracked open.

Where was I?

Who had saved me?

I was lying on a shore with sand, cattails, and wild grasses. Mountain evergreens lined the perimeter.

But that wasn't what got my attention.

A young man—or angel—huddled over me. I blinked, zeroing in on him. Even wet he was handsome with a jaw that was wonderfully chiseled, lips that were lush, and broad shoulders that looked as if they could hold the weight of the world. Water lingered on his way-too-long-to-be-real black lashes. Even in my state of shock, I recognized he was flawless.

Heavy breathing escaped his lips, and I gingerly touched my own. He'd kissed me.

It's called mouth-to-mouth, you hillbilly.

"I thought you were dead," he said as if he could barely believe I wasn't. He rubbed his face briskly, pushing wet hair out of his face. "Was anyone else in the car?"

"What?" I croaked. My brain hadn't caught up yet.

He stumbled as he stood and weaved on his feet. "Wait here. I'll try to get them—"

"N-no," I whispered, reaching a hand out to stop him. My voice was ragged. "Just me."

He came back and collapsed down next to me, eyes searching my face in the darkness. "You hurt?"

I shook my head. I didn't think so. If I was alive, I was okay. Images of the wreck flashed in my mind. Being trapped. The dark water. A shudder racked my body, and I made a guttural noise in the back of my throat I'd never heard before.

He gathered me in his arms, his hand palming my scalp. "I've got you. You're safe. Shhh." His neck smelled male and spicy, and my fingers dug into his shoulders to pull him closer. We stayed that way for a while, and after my shivering stilled, I eased back and glanced up to the bridge, noticing there weren't any other cars.

Where had he come from on this dark and lonely night?

He'd braved the water to cut me out, and the average person wouldn't—couldn't—have done that. If he hadn't been *here* in this exact spot when I'd gone over, I'd be dead and swimming with the fishes.

No one crosses our path without a reason. I believed this.

"You sure you're okay?" He pushed hair out of my face, his voice incredibly gentle.

I nodded. "Thank you."

We locked eyes, and a spark zinged from my head to my toes. One, two, three moments passed, and something—I couldn't tell you what—fell gently into place. In the space between my near death and waking up, is it crazy to say I recognized him even though I didn't *know* him? How is that even possible?

A siren wailed in the distance, pulling me back, and I visibly flinched as fear swallowed me again. The cavalry was on its way—police or an ambulance. Either way it all led back to my father and his rules. And I wasn't going back. Ever.

Rolling out of his arms, I stumbled to my feet, grasped a nearby pine tree to steady myself, and scoured the dark forest beyond the lake. There was a town a few miles from here; maybe a phone. I grimaced as pain shot through my leg, and I touched it, finding a three-inch gash on my inner thigh. Blood dripped. It wasn't a main artery, but I'd need to get something on it. It would probably leave a scar—another one to add to the list.

I whipped off my T-shirt, thankful I wore a bra as well as a camisole. Pulling on the neck, I ripped the Snowden High School Lions shirt into two pieces, my strength a heck of a lot stronger than I'd anticipated, probably from the high that came from nearly biting the dust. I dabbed the gash with one of the pieces then used a clean corner of it to wipe the tears from my face. The other piece I tied around my leg.

"That looks bad," he said softly, coming closer to me with his eyebrows drawn in tightly. For the first time I noticed he was practically naked, wearing tight black briefs and nothing else. He must have ripped his clothes off to dive in. A Viking of a man, he stood well over six feet tall, his body perfectly sculpted with well-defined muscles.

Up close, I watched a droplet of water drift down his chest to his six-pack abs. I sighed. God had been using his A game when he'd created my hero.

Part of me was . . . excited. I'd never seen an almost naked guy.

I tore my gaze away from him and looked around at the picturesque shoreline and how the moonlight shimmered on the lake. *Maybe I was dead and this was heaven?*

The sirens inched closer, the high-pitched sound crawling up my spine.

I took a step backward, further into the woods, my foot crunching on the sound of pine needles and fallen leaves.

"Don't run, please," he said, raising his hands up hesitantly. He studied my face. "I know you're scared, but I won't let anyone hurt you. I promise."

How did he know I was running?

Because you look like you just stole something, stupid.

I chewed on my bottom lip, contemplating what to tell him. Not the truth—that was for certain. "You didn't see me here," I went with, my voice still scratchy. "You never pulled me out of that car."

"Why?" His brow knitted again. "People will be worried about you."

"Please—just don't tell them." Desperation rang in my tone as I tried to convey to him everything I didn't have time to explain.

"Wait," he said, his warm hand brushing against mine, but then he let it fall to his side, a confused expression on his face as if he didn't know what to make of me.

I was confused as well. And scared. Yet in the middle of those tumultuous emotions, I was drawn to him. My body hummed with an acute awareness of our proximity, and my heart thumped so loudly that

I pressed my hands to my chest. I was sure he could hear it.

What was this thing between us? *Adrenaline? Lust? Destiny?* I didn't know.

But I did know he sent a buzz straight to my heart.

I wished the moon had been bright enough to see the color of his eyes.

I wished I knew his name.

I wished . . . I wished fate would bring us together again, some other time, some other place.

But not today.

With one last lingering look at his face, I turned and ran into the woods.

chapter TWO

Three Years Later

Max

MY ALARM BLARED and I reached over to click it off.

God, it was early. I rubbed my temples, wishing I'd passed on that last shot of celebratory tequila.

Welcome back to Leland University, I muttered under my breath.

A naked female body jostled into mine, and I froze, distinctly remembering going to bed alone.

I jumped up and yanked my jeans on. "Who the hell are you?"

A brunette raised her head up, eyes like road maps. Nice.

"Shit," I groaned, recognizing one of the groupies who hung around the football team. At least when I'd had a girlfriend, they'd left me alone.

"Sierra, silly. I come to all the home games, and sometimes I watch you practice."

"How'd you get in?" I asked.

Coming more awake, she propped herself up until her tits popped out from the covers. "Felix picked the lock last night . . . said you were a grouch and needed to get laid."

Felix—all around asshole and second-string quarterback. We'd had a small party last night and he must have showed after I crashed. I cracked my knuckles. He was messing with me. Again.

Freshman year, he'd put a black rat snake in my car and I'd nearly hit a tree when that damn thing wrapped itself around my leg. Just last year, we'd had a brawl over my ex in the locker room, and I'd broken his nose. That shit was supposed to stay between the team, but somehow the media got a whiff and my temper had been called into question—when he was the bastard who'd started it. I suspected he'd been the one to leak the story to the news.

Did I mention he was dating my ex? Yeah. It was screwed up.

This year, I had to keep my fists down and my head in the game because this was going to be *my* year.

"Did we have sex?" I scrubbed my face, then looked around for condom wrappers.

"You passed out," she huffed, a peevish expression on her face. "Which is sad. You *are* my favorite player. I even had your number put on a jersey. I sleep in it every night."

In other words . . . *I have our relationship all planned down to me getting pregnant.*

"You were amazing at the scrimmage," she continued, her gaze lingering on my crotch. "Three touchdown passes . . . a hundred yards rushing. You're going to win the Heisman this year." She bit her lip, pumped her hips like she was having an orgasm, and moaned. "I can feel it, Max."

I couldn't deny I wanted the Heisman like a man in the desert wants a tall glass of water—but I had other things to take care of first.

I grabbed her phone off the nightstand. "What's your code?"

"Why?"

"Because I'm not stupid." My gaze was hard as nails.

She poked her lip out. "Why are you being so mean? It's my phone, not yours."

"If there's nothing to hide it shouldn't matter if I check out your photos, huh?" My lips tightened as I dangled the phone.

She confessed the code. Sure enough she'd taken several selfies of me stone-cold passed out. She'd arranged my hand on her bare boob and snapped pics of her kissing me. She'd pulled down the covers and snapped a pic of me in my black athletic boxers and a pic of her hand wrapped around my cock. I swiped to the last pic, one of her licking the tiger tattoo on my bicep. *Fuck.*

Nausea simmered under the anger. Shit like this sent me over the edge. If I hadn't found these, they'd be posted all over social media or possibly sold to some magazine—and my chances at a Heisman would be pulverized.

And wouldn't Felix just love that?

After deleting the pics and tossing her phone back, I strode to my bedroom door and flung it open. "Time for you to get out."

"I'll text you later," she said as she sat up on the bed to pull on her underwear and pants.

"I won't respond."

"I don't care. I just like knowing you know I'm thinking about you. I picture you seeing my text and smiling. It'll make your day better. Like a little ray of sunshine."

Psycho. I gritted my teeth. "Trust me, I don't think about you. I don't even know your name."

"Sierra."

"Fine, *Sierra*," I growled. "Just because you slept in my bed and did a cock selfie with me doesn't mean jack. I don't do groupies."

Her lips curled in a half-smile. "I don't give up that easily." With a little wave she stumbled out the door.

Yes! Finally. I slammed it shut behind her, the noise reverberating through the house.

Eminem blared in the background as I flew around the room, getting my ass in gear for my Anatomy and Physiology class with Professor Whitt. I wanted to get an early start today, especially since he was one of the hardest teachers on campus. After taking the fastest shower ever, I threw on loose jeans, a V-neck navy blue Leland shirt, and leather flip-flops. I swept my long hair up in a quick man-bun. I hadn't cut it since my mom died three years ago.

With a swift gait, I strode in the den and saw my roommate, Tate, standing in plain view of the street from the bay window, his hair a rat's nest as he scratched his junk in his Union Jack boxers. An overly hairy blond giant originally from London, he was the first string wide receiver and my best friend since freshman year.

I clicked the light on. "Morning," I called out, biting back a grin as he covered his eyes.

"Bugger off," he muttered and dropped down to the couch. "Never let me drink tequila again—at least until next weekend." He leaned his head back, mouth flapping open.

I slapped him on the shoulder. "Last night was our last hurrah, dude. Football has officially begun." As a senior and the head quarterback, I was the captain on our team, and it was my job to make sure we all stayed tight. Living and breathing football would be all I'd do for the next few months.

I wandered into the open kitchen area to scrounge for food. It was a small room, but sufficient for two athletes who did the majority of their eating in the athletic cafeteria on campus. We'd just moved out of the dorms and into the rental house this summer, and I dug it. The house itself, like many on the west side of campus, was built in the seventies and needed a shit ton of updates. We'd actually gotten one of the nicer ones thanks to my dad, who *knew* people.

The Formica countertop was littered with empty pizza boxes and beer cans from our celebration of the scrimmage. I rounded it all up and chunked it in the trash. Tate didn't care too much about keeping the place clean, but I did. A blueberry muffin that had somehow not been eaten this week caught my eye and I snatched it, devouring it in two bites. I grabbed a protein drink from the fridge and chugged it. I felt wound up. Antsy. Like something was about to happen.

A staccato knock came at the door.

"Bro, can you get that? I'm cleaning up," I called from the kitchen.

"I'm a fragile flower," he moaned. "Can we just ignore it?"

Fine by me. I grabbed my backpack, my laptop, and notebooks. Where were those new pens I'd gotten? I scurried around, opening the drawers under the counter until I found the new pack of fine-tips and stuffed them in.

The knock came again, and a chick's voice came through the wood of the door. "Hello, I know you're there. I can see both of you through the window." An exasperated sound came from outside, and I may have heard the creative insult *jock-ass.*

I cocked my head. Not Sierra's voice. Thank God. I made a *meh* noise and opened the fridge to grab a Gatorade. Which one did I want, the blue or the original . . .

A loud plop came from the porch. Was our unwanted visitor stamping her foot? I smirked. She could stamp all she wanted. I was sick to death of girls showing up here expecting to get a signed autograph—or suck me off. I didn't stick my cock in girls I didn't know. I wasn't my father.

A grumble came from behind the door. "I'm calling the cops in five seconds if this door isn't opened. One, two, three, four—"

Cops?

That got my attention. I slammed the fridge shut. I did *not* need the cops over here.

If this was another groupie . . .

I went to the door and flung it open.

chapter
THREE

Sunny

MY ALARM BLARED and I reached over to click it off.
The glare of the sun hitting my blinds woke me. I scrubbed at my face and squinted as I pried my eyes open.

Welcome back to Leland.

I stretched, loosening tight muscles that had washed every dirty crevice in my new rental house the day before. I'd even pulled down the weird mallard duck wallpaper in the den. I felt accomplished and ready to tackle the day, even though I had Professor Whitt this morning *and* my stupid-jock-ex would be there.

I turned my head to check out the time again and met the beady gaze of a huge brown spider that sat next to my head on the pillow.

My scream pierced the morning silence, the sound ricocheting off the walls and probably waking the old lady who lived down the street. Of course the spider didn't like this. He skittered off my pillow and down between the cracks of the headboard.

Shuddering in revulsion, I bolted out of bed, stumbled over last night's shoes, and promptly stubbed my big toe on the wooden dresser. I yelped, fell to the floor, and poked at the red-hot pain that was my appendage. *Only me.* And only on the first day of class. Ugh.

I eyed my bed accusingly, willing the spider to come out and face what he'd done. Dammit. Now I'd have to sleep on the couch for the rest of the semester.

My phone rang, and I limped over to scoop it up. My bestie Isabella was on the ID.

"Morning, Sugartits!" she sang into my ear.

I winced. "Please. I haven't had coffee yet."

"Can't help it. I had sex last night, and it was *phe-nom-e-nal.*" She drew the last word out and made a crazy *meow* sound at the end. I held the phone out from my ear to lessen her sound effects.

"Imagine that," I said wryly. "Who's the lucky guy?"

She rattled off some boy from the Tau house she'd met at a back to school party. She described him in vivid detail, right down to the piercing on his privates.

"You think I'm a slut, don't you?" she asked after a few moments.

"Of course not." *Because that's what friends say.*

She kept chatting, clearly in the mood for socializing, even though I could hear customers in the background of the local Starbucks where she worked. How she didn't get fired, I had no clue.

"I bet he has a buddy," she added.

"Don't they all?"

She harrumphed in disgust. "You need to hop on over and meet that sexy neighbor of yours. *Hello, Mr. Quarterback.* I bet he's got some backfield in motion. I bet you could *score* with him. Heck, I bet he knows how to ball—"

"Stop," I said. "I don't do athletes anymore. It's a hard rule. And if it had been my choice, I wouldn't have rented a house across the street from him."

"Hello, have you seen how wide his shoulders are—without the pads? *Day-um.*"

I heard a slurping sound and pictured her sucking down a latte or a steaming mug of hot chocolate. "What are you drinking?"

"Caramel Macchiato."

I cursed. I loved that drink.

"I'm also eating a raspberry white-chocolate muffin. It's delicious. There's this amazing cream cheese in the middle of it—"

"I hate you. I really, really do." Sweets were my thing, and the image of a muffin made my belly grumble. Not surprising since my dinner last night had consisted of a peanut butter and jelly sandwich—'cause it was cheap and pretty much all I'd had in the house.

Padding to the kitchen with the phone pressed to my ear, I came to a dead halt in front of the stained coffee maker I'd inherited from my grandmother Mimi when she'd upgraded. My heart dropped. I'd forgotten my grocery run last night. I wailed.

"What's wrong?" Isabella asked.

"*Dammit.* I was so tired last night, I forgot to stop at the market." I pressed my forehead against the coolness of the fridge and banged it. "I don't have any coffee, there's a giant spider under my bed, my ex is going to be in class, and my toe is falling off. I'm gonna die!"

"God, I love the way your voice gets extra Southern when you get upset. Do I need to come over and give you a pep talk?"

"Maybe."

She cleared her throat. "You're Sunny freaking Blaine and you always have your shit together. You've paid your own way through college. You're not Italian yet you make the meanest lasagna in the whole state of Georgia—maybe the world. You don't care what people think, case in point: yoga pants *are* your dress up clothes. You drink coffee like I shoot tequila. You once stole a car. You are a badass mama jama, and I'd be your lesbian lover in a heartbeat if I went that way—and if you went that way. I'm so jealous of your blond hair that I dream of shaving you bald—"

"Now it's weird." I smiled even though she couldn't see me. "I feel better, though. Lunch at Hotdog Haven soon?"

"Yeah," she said around her chews. "I'll tell you about frat boy's big wiener."

I groaned. "Thank you for that parting image."

We said our goodbyes, and I got off the phone and limped to the bathroom. A small room with an antique claw tub, it had a certain eclectic charm with pale blue walls and a myriad of rainbow and unicorn decals leftover from the previous renters. I hadn't the heart to take them all down. The biggest one, a white unicorn, was stuck right next to the mirror over the sink. With a glittery pink mane and long eyelashes, he was fit for a princess—so unlike my own childhood. Perhaps that's why I kept him.

I sent him a nod. "Morning, Charlie. Let's hope this day doesn't get any worse."

It did.

After wrapping my toe in a waterproof Hello Kitty Band-Aid, I put my long hair in a bath cap and hopped in the tub, which had been modernized with a shower head on the wall above it and a shower curtain on an oval rod hanging from the ceiling. I turned the water temp to hot and just stood there, gut churning. Today I was facing Bart for the first time since we'd broken up.

Later while I was brushing my teeth, I glanced out the window next to the tub and saw a disheveled brunette bounce out of Mr. Quarterback's door, stumble off the porch, and fall in the azalea bushes. I snickered. She crawled up, brushed herself off, and weaved along the sidewalk, obviously still trashed as she dug in her purse for what I assumed were her keys. She was the second girl this week who'd done the walk of shame from *his* house. The brunette finally made it to her BMW, got in, and cranked it up. Gunning the engine, she lost control and sideswiped my poor Camry parked on the street.

My mouth plopped open, and my forgotten toothbrush fell to the floor. I'd just paid the clunker off this summer!

She threw her car in reverse and backed up, scraping along the side of my car, making me cringe at the sound of grinding metal. Then she sped off.

Fuck! I stared up at the dingy popcorn ceiling and blinked my tears away.

And so it begins. The football player and I were finally going to meet.

I was going to murder him.

chapter FOUR

Max

THE GIRL ON my porch was livid.

I studied her, taking in the wild white-blond hair that draped over a wrinkled shirt with *Pizza is my Soulmate* printed across the front. A pair of black yoga pants clung to her lean thighs. They'd seen better days according to the hole at the knee. I quirked an eyebrow, my gaze leisurely as it roved across her nice tits, all the way to her pink toenails and then back to her flushed face. Simple, no makeup, and barely together. Not the usual kind of girl who knocked on my door.

Yet . . .

My heart jumped.

I knew her.

I shifted through memories of countless girls I'd met—and screwed—at Leland.

Had she been in one of my classes? Had I met her at a party?

Nope. I got nothing, but I couldn't erase that feeling of goosebumps, like a ghost was blowing on the back of my neck.

Her eyes flared as she took in every inch of me. Heart-shaped lips parted in surprise. Guess she hadn't expected a six foot six badass.

"Who are you?" I said curtly. Direct. I had shit to do.

Smoky gray eyes blinked, looking uncertain. A range of emotion skittered across her face, from anger to amazement to complete and utter confusion. "I—I'm your new neighbor. I moved in last week." Her voice was thin and reedy as if she couldn't breathe.

Great. Another psycho.

I vaguely recalled a truck backed up to the porch of the sagging house across the street. "Yeah? What's your problem?" I said, popping a smirk and slipping into my *I'm cool* mask. I wore it a lot in public. When you'd gotten to the level of success I had, everything you did was open for scrutiny. I played everything as if someone was watching—or I tried to. "Mad because you weren't invited to our party last night?" I asked, leaning against the doorjamb.

She rubbed her forehead and continued that dazed stare.

Those fucking goosebumps came back.

"Uh, hello?"

She blinked rapidly. Clearing her throat, she shook herself, swallowed, and smiled tightly, seeming to gain her equilibrium. "I don't really party. It's the skank I'm here about."

"Skank?" I asked, rearing back with a frown.

From the doorway, she swept intelligent eyes over me and Tate on the couch. "That's right. Which one of you has a girlfriend that left here a few minutes ago—who was obviously intoxicated, by the way. She slammed into my car. And if you don't give me her details, I'm going to notify the police." A look of urgency came to her face. "But for right now, I'm hoping for a ride to class. It's really important that I not be late."

Girlfriend? Neither of us—*oh shit . . .*

"Didn't I see Sierra leaving your room?" Tate asked me, scratching his bare chest. "Have to admit, she seemed a wee trashed."

I cursed, blew out a breath, and slumped against the doorjamb. Tate was the one who encouraged the groupies. He liked them to do his homework, make his bed, wash his car; they were his personal maid service.

Neighbor Girl looked suitably disgusted, a smidge of *I should have known it was you* on her face. "Nice girlfriend. What are you going to do about her ruining my car, Mr. Quarterback?"

The spitfire knew who I was—which wasn't surprising.

"She's *not* my girlfriend. No doubt, she'd love for me to be her baby-daddy—"

She held a hand up. "It's a bit early to get squeamish."

Tate snorted in the background.

"She broke into *my* room," I huffed. "I woke up and there she was all bare-assed and ready, but nothing happened."

"I bet," she muttered.

Why was I explaining this to her?

I rubbed my scruff. Most girls would be tripping over themselves to ingratiate themselves with me. Trust me, it gets old fast when you don't know if a girl likes you for *you* or if she just wants to be with you for the money and fame that's sure to be part of your future.

I should have been more upset at her throwing a kink in my day, but for some reason I was more amused than chagrined. Perhaps it was the Hello Kitty Band-Aid on her toe. My lips twitched. "You're kinda prickly, aren't you?" And pretty.

"Not usually."

"Then it's just me?"

"Just you, Quarterback."

I was stumped. Here was a girl who couldn't stand the sight of me, and I had no clue why—well, except her car was ruined. Still. It was an odd experience to have a member of the opposite sex disliking me on sight. "Look—"

Tate let out a groan and pushed himself up to standing. "You're both ruining a perfectly good hangover with all this bloody banter." He grinned. "I'll run you to class, love. Just give me a sec to put on my trousers."

What the hell? He didn't have a class until noon. Why would he—

Oh, I got what was going on. I saw that glint in his eyes as he checked her out. He thought Neighbor Girl was hot. Dude had more notches on his bedpost than he could count.

I waved him away. "Take a seat. You're probably still loaded." Turning back to her, I said, "Sierra really did that much damage?"

She nudged her head toward the street. "See for yourself. I can't open the door, much less drive it."

I stepped out to the porch and considered the vehicle in question, a late model Toyota sedan with a smashed driver's side door. The window had burst, and glass glittered in the road. Gouges raked down the entire length of the vehicle. I whistled.

What the hell had Sierra been thinking?

How had I not heard that from inside the house?

Probably because I was in the shower with the music cranked up.

I walked back in and took a more appraising look at Neighbor Girl, and she stiffened. She acted tough, but it was just that, an act, judging by the lip biting and twitchy hands that kept plucking at her backpack. She was oddly nervous.

"It's pretty bad, but I don't think it's totaled. Just cosmetic," I said as I tried to find something positive to say about her poor car. I didn't know Sierra well, but I'd seen her at practice before, usually pulling away in a sleek little convertible. I didn't even think she was a student here. I exhaled. *Shit, shit, shit.* I was responsible for this. I should have noticed she was still drunk. "Let me find Sierra later today and I'll ask her to call you."

"And if that doesn't work out?" She crossed her arms.

"Then I'll take care of your car. Somehow." Was I seriously going to cough up the money to pay for this girl's car to be repaired if Sierra didn't come through?

Her brows knitted, surprise on her face. "Wait, that's too much. I didn't mean for you to pay for my car. I just came over to find out her name—and maybe bitch a little because it's a big day for me and now everything is falling apart. But *you* didn't hit it; the lunatic did. The police can deal with her—"

"I'll do whatever needs to be done." Which really meant I didn't want the cops sniffing around here. *Girlfriend of Max Kent Involved in Hit and Run* would be the headlines whether it was true or not. The media would run with it and Coach Williams would flip his lid. No thanks. I rubbed my forehead. "Damn groupies. I wish they'd leave me the hell alone."

She mulled that over, her nose scrunching up. "So you *really* didn't have sex with her."

"Swear. She's been with half the team. I wouldn't touch that with a ten-foot pole."

"He hates easy tail," Tate chimed in from the couch. He propped his feet up on the coffee table, watching us with interest. He indicated me with a nod, like we were members of some Hot Guy Club. "He's an alpha, love—like me. We like to work for it. I'd work for you." His gaze roamed over Neighbor Girl lazily, with an intent that was so obvious I half-expected porn music to play in the background.

Seriously? I gave him a look that said *back off.*

Wait. Why did I care?

I glanced back at Neighbor Girl, and the earlier palpable tension between us had eased somewhat although I could tell the jury was still out on if we were going to end this on a happy note. A grimace crossed her face as she checked the time on her phone. "Okay, we can deal with this later. I have to go."

Thank you, baby Jesus.

She played with the bottom of her skirt.

We just stood there. Staring.

The air around us thickened, becoming charged with electricity.

Sometimes in the middle of a normal day, a life-changing choice is thrown in front of you. Right then, you're one decision away from a completely different existence. You decide your future even though you aren't even aware you're doing it. Your choice might result in finding love or death or winning the fucking lottery—you don't know.

Was it like that with this chick at my doorstep?

Losing my mom made me think about that kind of shit all the time. One minute she'd been there—and then she'd been gone.

"I really need a ride to class," she said, pulling me back. She gave me a sheepish look. "I have Whitt first thing and he's a jerk."

Oh, right.

I cleared my throat and focused. "Sure, I can get you to class. And thank you for coming to me before you called the police." I tilted my head. "Maybe this little incident brought us together for a reason."

"Like what?"

"Like we should go out," I said, my voice growing husky. "I can make it up to you."

She flushed. "You mean like have sex with me? I'd rather have a car."

My lips twitched. Again.

"I don't hang out with jocks," she added. "It's a rule. Nothing personal."

I shrugged. "I'm an athlete—not a jock. Big difference."

"Not to me, Quarterback," she said curtly.

I grinned. Her snippiness didn't faze me. It amped me up like I was staring down a blitz and had to throw a Hail Mary to win the game.

I took a step back and snatched up my backpack off the floor. I slung a casual arm around her shoulders, much like I would any girl I was friends with.

"What are you doing?" she asked, giving my arm a bewildered glance. I noticed she didn't pull away though.

"We're leaving. Let's get you to Whitt's class. I'm assuming that's Anatomy and Physiology?"

She nodded.

"I'm in the same class." I grinned, broader this time. "Coincidence or destiny?"

Her mouth parted, a puff of air escaping as she stared up at me.

And what did I do? I stared right back at her, feeling a whole lot of *déjà vu.*

Her body brushed against mine, and I caught a whiff of her scent . . . vanilla with a hint of lemon. It was different. Fresh. Sweet.

I glanced down at her full pink lips, wondering how they'd feel pressed against mine.

Fuck no. Forget that.

Focus on football.

Right. No hooking up with Neighbor Girl. The season had just begun, and I didn't need a girl mucking up my year. Been there. Done that.

I tweaked the tiny line of freckles across her nose. "Hope you like listening to Snoop Dog, Blondie."

chapter FIVE

Sunny

BLONDIE?

Please. Kill me now.

How easy did he think I was? *Let's go out. I'll make it up to you.* Yeah, right. He wanted to bone me and then kick back and watch *me* do the walk of shame . . . not going to happen.

I wouldn't be the next girl stumbling around in his azalea bushes.

Yet, I couldn't deny the absolute pure truth between us.

Ignore that, I told myself. So I did. I slammed the door on those feelings, stuffing them in the part of my brain that kept anything with the power to hurt me locked up tight.

He wasn't who I thought he was. Not really.

I let out a sigh as we walked out the door. His irreverent attitude reminded me of my ex, and if there's one thing I'd learned at Leland, it was that super star athletes were not to be trusted.

He was much bigger in life than I had imagined. Of course, I'd seen pics of him in his uniform on television for a big game, and sometimes I'd catch sight of him on the quad, usually surrounded by teammates or girls, but we'd never come face-to-face. He was popular and way out of my social circle.

I'm a plain and simple girl who kept my head down—even more so after my mom had died when I was sixteen. My father had made it his mission to make sure I didn't turn out like her. A strict preacher, he'd yanked me out of public school to homeschool me after she passed. No more singing lessons. No more friends—or boys. He wanted me home and under his thumb. He'd managed to hide that dark side from his parishioners, but it lingered just on the edges of his personality.

I saw it every time he looked at me.

He hated me because I wasn't her.

Mimi said it was because I was the spitting image of her, long blond hair, eyes the color of smoke, and an oval face. I even had a heart-shaped birthmark like hers on my right ear. We could have been twins.

Max opened the passenger door for me on a black Land Cruiser—*cha-ching*—and then proceeded to clear out the passenger seat that was stuffed with protein bars, books, and football pads. Besides the mess, the car smelled like him, all alpha male mixed with expensive leather.

I inhaled another whiff, feeling frustrated. Dang. *Why did he smell so good?*

I snuck a quick glance at his well-developed biceps in his tight shirt, taking in the orange and brown tiger tattoo, our school mascot, peeking out from the sleeve. My gaze shifted to his face, and part of me—the crazy part—yearned to reach out and touch his chiseled jawline, maybe run my fingers over his full and pouty lips. I sighed. We may have gotten off on the wrong foot, but holy cow, he was hot.

With a smirk that said he'd caught me staring, he wiped errant crumbs off the seat and gestured for me to sit as if it were a queen's throne. "Here ya go."

"Thank you."

He climbed in the driver's side, popped on a pair of Tom Ford shades, and pulled out of the drive. I tried to act cool, but the truth was I was nervous as heck. I opened my purse and applied a rose-colored lipstick I found in there. I'd freaked when that groupie hit my car, and I pretty much ran out of the house with what clothes I could find. I smoothed down my shirt and raked a hand through my unruly hair.

I probably looked like a deranged person.

You are a deranged person, I reminded myself. *You asked—maybe demanded—Max Kent take you to class.*

In what universe did any of this make sense?

He put his hand on the radio, but instead of cranking up the music like I thought he would, he turned it off. Ocean-colored eyes assessed me.

"So what's your name? Have we ever met before? Class? Maybe a party?"

"Sunny Blaine, and no, I don't even like football. I prefer reading—or chess."

I didn't know a knight from a pawn!

I hadn't read a good book in months!

What was wrong with me?

He laughed. "You must be new. Football's practically a religion at Leland."

"I went to Southwest Community first and started Leland last year. I'll graduate this May," I said. Leland was a private institution with a price tag that boggled the brain. The only way I'd been able to pull off the past two semesters was with an art scholarship and federal grants. Of course there was still the basics to pay, like food and rent—which is why I worked twenty hours a week at the library.

"Big plans after graduation?"

"I love art, so I'm hoping for something in a gallery." I bit my lip, feeling self-conscious about telling him my dream, but it came out anyway. "Someday, I'd like to own a store that sells clothes I designed. Depends on how much money I can save." I shrugged, playing it off. "I'll probably end up working at The Gap."

"Where you from?"

"North Carolina. I moved here a while back to live with my grandmother Mimi."

He shot me an interested glance. "What part are you from? We used to vacation there in the mountains. Pretty place."

"Why the twenty questions?" I asked stiffly.

He shrugged, drawing my attention straight to those ridiculously broad shoulders. "Just making conversation. Why so defensive?"

He was right. Anytime anyone brought up North Carolina, I clammed up. I kept my life before moving to Atlanta tucked away, and that didn't make me an easy person to get to know.

"Sorry. It's just . . ." I sucked in a sharp breath, thinking about the other reason for my rotten mood. "My boyfriend . . . we recently broke up, and he's going to be in our class. We picked out all our classes together last spring." My teeth tugged at my bottom lip. "I dread seeing him. We had the biggest non-breakup ever. No closure."

His gaze shot to me. "That sucks. Been there myself recently. I get it."

"We were supposed to be living together this semester, and I had to find somewhere last minute," I added. "Thank goodness I knew a professor who wanted me to fix up his house while I live there."

"Oh?"

"Just pulling down wallpaper and general repair stuff."

"Sounds like work," he murmured, giving me a once-over, as if surprised.

"Tuition isn't cheap and books don't buy themselves." It was no secret he came from money. Heck, his dad was a famous NFL player turned sportscaster.

"There you go—being prickly," he smirked, but looked oddly pleased.

"It's been a heck of a day, okay? And I still haven't had coffee."

"We can't have that." He whipped the car into the Circle K, told me to wait a minute, and then came back five minutes later with two Styrofoam cups. He tossed sugar and packets of creamer in my lap. "It's not Starbucks, but it'll hit the spot."

My heart flip-flopped when I accepted the cup, cradling it like the Holy Grail. I tore the lid off and inhaled the first sip. Maybe he wasn't a douche like all the other athletes in my life.

He chuckled as he pulled back out to the street. "You should have mentioned coffee was the way to tame you."

"Yeah," I murmured, settling back in the seat. "Muffins and scones work too."

He pulled into the lot behind the Clark Science Building, parked, and turned the ignition off. But for some reason, neither of us moved to get out. He fiddled with his keys, as if he wanted to say something. Then he took off his sunglasses and twirled them around his fingers. He was a live wire, and I couldn't help but follow his every move. A lock of dark hair had come loose from his bun, the chestnut and honey highlights begging for my fingers to push it out of his eyes.

Don't do it, Sunny.

I wanted to fill in the silence, though.

"So your breakup sucked too, huh?" Bianca Something was his ex's name, and their tumultuous relationship had been the talk of campus last year. The sports media had even mentioned their crazy back and forth a few times. Heck, I'd witnessed them arguing once on the quad. I'd been coming around a tree when I saw them facing off, plain as day that they were having a huge fight. As I'd watched, she'd thrown a book at his head and yelled obscenities. He'd stormed off with his fists clenched.

A shadow crossed his face. "She screwed up my game last year. Can you believe she still throws herself at me when her boyfriend isn't around?"

"Want me to kick her ass?"

He laughed.

I laughed.

And we stared at each other.

Okay, the staring thing was getting weird as heck. But I couldn't stop—and neither could he. Heat grew in his gaze, and I felt my own body responding. Melting.

Get out of the fancy car, Sunny. Mr. Quarterback is dangerous.

"Wait," he said as I moved to open the door. His hand touched my arm, lingering down to my wrist. My heart thundered. Good grief. I was as weak as a baby kitten.

I clenched my fists.

Keep your panties on, Sunny. Don't. Fall. For. The. Quarterback.

My brain briefly noted that a football player was the only athlete I *hadn't* dated. In high school, before I'd left to be homeschooled, it had been a scorching hot basketball player who could run down the court fast as lightning. At Southwest it had been a lean volleyball player with the softest kisses. Then it had been Bart, my latest, who was a sexy baseball player well on his way to the majors this spring. I sighed. The truth is I had a horrible, horrible thing for them. Call it opposites attract or whatever, but athletes were magnets to my heart, and once I let them in, they obliterated me.

"Yeah?" I studied his face, taking in the perfection of each feature.

He reciprocated the appreciation, his gaze skating over the V of my shirt just enough to make my nipples harden. Stupid nipples.

"Do you feel this *thing* between us? Like a connection?" he murmured and then scoffed a little under his breath as if the idea was ludicrous.

"No," I lied.

"Really? The moment I opened my door, something strange happened." He gave me a self-deprecating shrug. "That is, unless my girl radar is completely off the rails."

I laughed, but then quickly sobered.

Why would the King of Leland Football be interested in me?

He was like . . . this famous football star that the entire university—heck, the entire state of Georgia—adored.

I mean, don't get me wrong, guys hit on me sometimes when I went out. I have long blond hair and nice boobs, but I wasn't anything special. My nose was a little too long and my cheekbones a little too broad to be considered a conventional beauty. I rarely wore makeup except for lipstick and mascara, and I wasn't big on dressing sexy unless you counted skinny jeans and flats.

A black jeep whipped into the parking spot next to me and my breath caught.

"Someone you know?" Max asked.

"My ex." The anxious feeling I'd woken up with grew in the pit of my stomach.

"You dated Bart Morgan, the pitcher of the baseball team? Huh.

Maybe that's why you look so familiar. Maybe I saw you at the athletic banquet last year?"

I nodded.

"He's why you don't date athletes?"

"He's why I'm not dating *anyone*. All I want is to graduate and get out of here. I don't need anyone but myself."

"Ah. He played you," Max said.

"Like a banjo."

Bart exited his car, grabbed his book bag, and took off for the sidewalk. He never even glanced in our direction.

My face flamed at the memory of how I'd trusted him even though Isabella had warned me he had a reputation. I twisted my fingers into my hair, tugging on it.

Max's eyebrows furrowed, and he pulled my hand out of my hair. "Hey. What happened between you two?"

I fidgeted, realizing that Max had been watching and scrutinizing my reaction to Bart.

"Sunny?"

Maybe it was because it was the first time I'd heard my name on his lips or maybe it was the scathing look he'd sent Bart's back as he walked away—but whatever it was, I let myself sink back into the car.

"He . . ." My voice trailed off as I recalled his birthday party. It had been a warm night last spring, and I'd been exhausted after working my shift at the library. Excited to see him after his busy week of games and being on the road, I drove straight to the baseball frat house without calling him first. I found him at the back of the den, lying on a couch with his hands down another girl's pants—in full view of everyone at the party. And totally oblivious I was standing there. Gaping at them.

He'd been such a LIAR.

Oh, baby, I love you.

Oh, baby, you and I are meant to be.

I chewed on my lip. "He was with another girl . . . I watched them . . ." I paused, remembering the humiliation.

"Want me to kick his ass?"

I half-smiled. "No."

"You still care about him?"

"I shouldn't. Do you still care about Bianca?"

"She's going to be in our class." His face hardened.

My mouth opened. "No way."

"Way."

I shook my head. "Aren't we just a bunch of losers?"

He thought about that for a moment. "I hate losing—at anything." A light dawned in his eyes. "I have an idea. Let's walk in that class like we're together and blow their fucking minds."

I started, even more so when he reached across and grabbed my hand.

"What do you mean?" I didn't disentangle our hands, though.

He edged closer to me, his face earnest. "Let's show them we've moved on—to bigger and better things. What do you say about being my pretend girlfriend for class today?"

What?

Was he nuts?

I shook my head to clear the fuzzies. "Slow down a minute. Are you—gay?" *How horrible.*

He sent me a *get real* look. "No. I'm just feeling unsure this morning—not an emotion I'm used to. I'd like to walk in there and show her that I've met someone special. Start the semester off with a bang."

"Are you serious?"

A wicked grin curled his lips. "Why not? Let's screw with them."

My thoughts raced, grasping at a reason to say *no*. I couldn't find one.

He had offered to fix my car if the groupie didn't pan out. He'd even stopped and gotten me coffee. Plus, it would be nice to waltz past Bart with the most popular guy on campus next to me.

Normally, I'm the least impulsive person ever, but what could possibly go wrong if I pretended to be his girlfriend?

Nerves and excitement flew over me. "Let's do it."

chapter
SIX

Max

W E STOOD WAITING for the elevator, Sunny a good two feet away. Her expression was composed, yet I sensed nervousness. She'd been quiet since we'd agreed to do this, and I hoped she wasn't regretting it. The idea of a fake girlfriend was growing, taking root in my head.

"I don't have a disease," I teased, poking at her arm, trying to get her to relax. At this point, no one was going to buy it.

She considered me with a serious expression. "Whatever. I've heard about your reputation with the ladies. Love 'em and leave 'em seems to be your motto."

"Meh. That was freshman year when I was stupid." I grinned. "Maybe sophomore year too—but I'm clean as a whistle. Just had a complete physical."

Her gaze shot to the crotch of my jeans and then to the wall. She swallowed. "Nice to know. I'll file that away under my *Things to Know*

About Max Kent folder—which I'll never use."

I grinned. "And no one's going to believe you're into me unless we play it up, which means I'm going to have to kiss you before we walk into class," I said.

"Kiss?" she squeaked, her eyes big as she faced me.

Yeah. That had gotten her attention.

I nodded. "The elevator doors are going to open in front of a hallway full of students. Most people haven't talked to me or seen me all summer besides my teammates and, trust me, all eyes will be on us. We want them to think we're in love. We want them to think that I can barely keep from screwing you right here."

She gaped at me. "You're insane. I didn't agree to this just so you could make out with me."

I splayed my hands out. "I won't do anything you don't want me to. I'll kiss you so good, you won't be able to kiss another guy for an entire year without thinking about me."

She shook her head in disbelief. "*Pffft.* Do you even know how cocky you are?"

"Won't deny it. I am Max Kent."

She blew out a loud breath like this was the last place she wanted to be. Was it just me that bugged her? I *was* intense and hard to handle—mostly on the field, though.

Don't be an idiot, Max.

Everything isn't about you. Put yourself in her shoes. Her car's just been demolished, she's braced to see her ex, and a guy she doesn't know just asked her to put on a show.

"What's it gonna be?" I asked, tapping my fingers against my thigh, oddly anxious.

"Fine, you can kiss me, but no boob squeezing or crazy stuff."

I nodded. Fine with me. I could keep it light. Public displays weren't my thing anyway since I kept my life as private as I could.

But I couldn't stop myself from teasing her. "Most girls would kill for that, ya know," I said with a grin.

"I'm not most girls."

The elevator arrived and we stepped on, thankfully alone. Brushing my hands across her shoulder, I eased her backpack off and set it next to mine on the floor.

"You ready?" I asked, inching into her personal space.

Her chest rose and she nodded.

She was a stranger to me, yet I had no qualms as I touched her neck, tracing the lines of her throat and the shell of her ear. She wasn't that pumped up pretty like some girls with their makeup and crazy eyebrows; no, she was lovely, with creamy skin and hair the color of straw and cotton mixed together. I dug it.

And that orchestrated kiss idea? A gimmick—*partly.* I just wanted to kiss her.

She looked at me with big gray eyes and my breath hitched. Gray didn't do them justice; they were a soft smoky color with pale blue lines that feathered around her pupils like lightning. And her lips? I'd noticed them first thing. They were plump and symmetrical, the sweet indentation on the top calling my fucking name.

I swallowed. "You ready?"

"You already asked me that," she said a bit breathless.

Oh. Yeah.

Without moving away from her, I pressed the button for the sixth floor.

I leaned down and kissed her. She tasted like honey and sugar, and I wanted more—but not with her standing like an android, hands limp at her side.

I ran my nose up her neck and licked the tiny heart-shaped birthmark on her lobe, making her shiver. "Kiss me, Blondie."

"Rule number one: don't call me *Blondie.* It's unimaginative, plus it was Bart's thing."

"Done." I cupped her face and took her mouth again, this time more insistent, sweeping my tongue inside to explore her—but Bart's face loomed in my head. I barely knew him, and the cheating boyfriend story wasn't a new one in the college scene, but something about the vulnerability in her eyes made me angry.

She brushed her tongue against mine, her hand going to my waist and tugging me closer.

I forgot about Bart.

Shit. I forgot everything.

Heat went all over me.

Our hips gravitated toward each other as if we'd done this before, and what had started out as a first date kind of kiss turned into something else entirely. My hand slid into her hair to get a better angle, deepening the kiss until it was a full on make-out session. I hitched her leg up until it curled around my hips. She moaned, her hands sliding down to squeeze my ass. My skin sizzled, and my cock hardened, ready to—

The elevator door opened on our floor, but our lips stayed fused as my hand kept the door from shutting on us. I wanted everyone to see this. I pressed one more kiss to her swollen lips and eased back. Her gaze was low and heavy. Mine had to be the same. If I had my choice, we'd march out of this elevator, find a corner in a dark classroom, and fuck each other's brains out.

It was tempting.

But I couldn't. Not with my neighbor. It was bad to mix pleasure with girls who lived next door. Only an idiot would do that.

She let out a shaky breath, her chest rising and falling. "Don't . . . do that . . . again."

"I won't." I totally would—hypocrite that I was.

I laced our fingers together and escorted her out of the elevator.

Several people with raised eyebrows watched us as we exited the elevator, cruised down the hall, and entered Dr. Whitt's class. A couple of guys nodded at me, their eyes following Sunny as we passed. A few sent me appreciative nods.

She's mine. Keep your hands off.

"Wait." I got out my phone and pulled her off to the side. "We need a pic to commemorate our one day affair."

She winced. "I look like I'm ready for bed, and I didn't even get to straighten my hair—"

How could she not know how lovely she was? "You're gorgeous, Sunny. Say it."

"You're gorgeous, Sunny," she deadpanned.

"Come on, say it like you mean it."

She shook her head. "No. It's not true. I'm a six, maybe a seven when I put on eyeliner, maybe an eight if I use a push-up bra."

I sent her a grin. "We're not going to class until you say it."

"I'm gorgeous," she snapped. "Happy?"

"Yep. Now smile." I held the phone up for a selfie, licked her on the cheek and snapped the pic. *Boom.* "Once I lick you, you're mine," I said softly.

Her cheeks pinked, and I knew where her mind went. I pushed that thought away and sent the pic to all my social media accounts. Let the groupies get a look at that. Maybe they'd leave me alone for a week or so.

A few seconds later, we bumped into Bianca.

I'd at least expected to find a seat before the drama started.

She saw me and lit up like a Christmas tree. Petite with huge boobs and a tight ass, she was the kind of girl who demanded you look at her. The low-cut clothes she wore, the bright red lipstick, the way she raked her cat-like eyes over you like she wanted to eat you, all of it added up to a chick that craved attention and got it. Her exotic, flowery scent slammed into me, and I felt my body tensing, remembering how my sheets had smelled like her for weeks even after I'd washed them.

I glanced over her shoulder for Felix. Fucker wasn't there. Guess he wasn't taking this class.

She smiled, her brown gaze refusing to leave mine, one of the tactics she used to ignore the girls I was with. "Long time no see. How was your summer?"

"Awesome. How's Felix?" My voice was sharp.

"Fine," she said, reaching out to touch my shoulder. "Uh, maybe we can talk after class. I have a lot to tell you."

"No thanks."

She sighed, her hand dropping down to rest across her chest as a wounded expression flitted across her face. "Okay. I deserve that, but you have to forgive me someday. Please. I'm sorry for . . . everything."

Everything? She'd tried to trap me into marrying her.

Someone bumped into me to get to a seat, and I looked around, re-alizing we'd been stopped too long and were impeding the traffic. Other students sidestepped around us to get to their seats.

Shit, shit, shit. I wasn't handling this well. I should be the first one to walk away. I should—

Sunny wrapped an arm around my waist and leaned into me. She couldn't make it any plainer that I was *hers*. I relaxed.

"I'm sorry, have we met? I'm Sunny, Max's new . . ." she stumbled a bit, but managed to push out, "girlfriend."

"Bianca," she retorted, "his *ex*-girlfriend." She turned back to me, her eyebrows raised. "I didn't realize you were dating someone."

"I don't have to keep you updated," I said curtly.

She sniffed at Sunny dismissively, assessing her casual shirt and flip-flops. A tiny curl formed on her lips. "Not your usual, Max." She flicked her hair, a glint of malice in her gaze. "I'll be sure and tell Felix you said *hello*."

My hands clenched, remembering how he'd picked my lock. "Better yet, tell him he's a cocksucker who can't throw a decent pass. Maybe he should tryout for cheerleading."

She laughed low under her breath and waltzed off, making me fume. My emotional reaction was what she craved.

"Let's go," I said to Sunny.

She nodded and followed me as I headed toward two seats midway back from the podium. "Well, that was uncomfortable," she said, sending me a side-eye. "Now maybe she'll leave you alone for a bit. That *is* what you really want, right?"

My lips flattened. "I am done with her."

"Uh-huh."

"I am."

Yet, I couldn't deny there's something about a girl who shits on you that always makes you wonder where you went wrong.

We got out our books just as Ryn, an offensive lineman, took the seat behind me. A huge Asian player from California, he was a destroyer on the field.

I introduced him to Sunny, and when he asked how we'd met, I froze. I hadn't planned on concocting a story, but I fumbled around and ended up telling an elaborate story about how we met at the Phi Alpha toga party last spring. Famously known as one of the craziest parties of the year, it was the first thing that popped in my head, but I wasn't even sure I'd been at that particular one.

" . . . we ended up kissing in the bathroom at the party, and when I saw her again this summer, we started dating."

Total BS.

"Where did you meet this summer?" he asked.

I blinked. Lying was harder than I thought.

Sunny jumped in. "At the Orion Coffee Shoppe on Third Street. They have the best lattes and chocolate croissants in Atlanta. He spilled his water on me—*I mean, who drinks water in a coffee shop?*—and the rest is history." She smiled broadly and fluttered her eyes at me.

Two thoughts hit me at once. First, Sunny was a great actress. Second, I had never heard of this coffee place—but obviously she liked it. I made a mental note to find out where it was.

"Dude. That's awesome," Ryn said, sending me a knowing glance. "You deserve someone good after Bianca."

Yeah. The entire team had seen how she and Felix affected my game.

I felt a malevolent gaze on me, like someone wanted to shove a stick of dynamite up my ass. I flicked my eyes one row over and found Bart's eyes on me.

Well, well, well. First Bianca and now the douche-canoe.

I straightened in my chair. Hell, I was tempted to blow him a fucking kiss—but I had to keep my temper in check. Football demanded it.

He jerked out of his chair and made his way over to us.

chapter SEVEN

Sunny

T HE GUY WHO'D broken my heart was walking straight to where I sat. A handsome, All-American type, I'd met Bart at the library when he'd been on the hunt for a book about Jane Austen for a research paper. I fell for him immediately. He was a sexy athlete who read books and could talk about interesting authors. Duh.

He'd probably read up on Cliff Notes before our dates.

I inhaled a deep breath. *Prepare thyself for drama, Sunny.*

He halted in front of my desk. His usually perfectly styled auburn hair was in disarray as if he'd recently raked his hand through it. Long on top, he wore it in a dramatic swept back fashion that reminded me of Edward Cullen. It had been a little joke between us—Bart, my sparkly vampire.

Sparkly liar, I reminded myself.

I did my best to keep my face calm. But seeing him up close, taking in his chiseled jawline and the lean body that had been my first, made a knot rise in my throat. Sadness mingled with hurt swept over me. We'd never had closure. Not really. I'd simply walked out of the party and never spoken to him again. Since that day, he'd left me over fifty voicemails and had sent me hundreds of texts. I'd never listened or read a single one. Once you've seen betrayal with your own eyes, there's nothing left to say. I had too much pride to listen to his excuses.

Last year, it had taken me three months before I was ready to go all the way with him, and the first night we'd had sex, he'd been gentle and kind. By six months into our relationship I was planning a future with him. I'd follow him to whatever team he got called up for.

Then he started pulling away . . .

"You kissed him," Bart pointed at Max in disbelief, "at the toga party? When we were dating? That's interesting since I recall you saying you had to study that night. You'd been cheating on me the entire time."

I replayed Max's story back in my head. *Oh.* Bart thought I'd kissed Max before he'd cheated on me. My teeth clamped together. *How dare he?*

I shrugged, feigning coolness.

He came in closer, and Max stood, his body straightening to his full height, towering over everyone, Bart included. "Watch it. I don't like how close you're standing to Sunny."

Bart turned to glare at him, his ears red, a clear sign he was angry. He shoved his fingers into Max's chest. "Mind your own damn business."

Max's face turned into a block of ice. Ominous and cold. I imagined that was how he looked at the defensive players whenever they lined up on the field. "I'm not letting you yell at my girl."

"Your girl?" Bart sneered, throwing his hands up. "You don't even know her. And for your information, I'd never hurt Sunny. Can't say the same about you." He looked pointedly at Max's clenched fists. "You're the one who likes to fight," he said, obviously referring to the altercation between Max and Felix last year.

"That's right. Now get back to your seat before I shove my fist in your face," Max said softly, his eyes narrowed.

"I'm not afraid of you, asshole—"

"Everything okay back there?" Professor Whitt had walked in and was staring at them from behind wire spectacles. He frowned and adjusted them, his eyes darting from Max's face to Bart's.

"Yes, sir," Max said, but never took his gaze off Bart.

Neither of them moved.

"Sit down," I hissed, directing it at both of them. They were acting like petulant children fighting over a toy. And Max and I weren't even a real couple! *Insanity.*

Thank goodness, Bart stalked back to his seat.

"I can fight my own battles with him," I whispered to Max as he sat back down. "Don't do that again."

He ignored me, his lips pressed together, his movements sharp yet tautly controlled as he took out his laptop, letting it plop loudly on the desk.

Okay. Fine. He was angry. I got that. *But why?*

I focused back on unpacking my things, feeling as weak as a wet noodle.

Whitt got down to business calling roll and laying down the law about tardiness and absences. Inwardly, I groaned. I'd done my best in here last semester, but after I'd missed a few days when Mimi had gotten her knee surgery, it had been impossible to catch up. As a person in the arts, science and math were my kryptonite.

The room got quiet. Everyone was staring at me.

"Miss Blaine . . . you with us today?" Whitt said.

"Yes." I straightened in my seat.

"Good." He nodded at me and sent me a small smile. With dark wavy hair and a nice face, he was good-looking for an older guy. I'd heard he was actually a nice person, just ridiculously hard.

"Welcome. Let's hope you pay attention this semester. Tell me, Miss Blaine, what organ is the most important in the human body?"

Crap! He didn't waste any time.

I flipped the pages in my textbook, skimming over the material he'd assigned through email last week. My anxiety shot up. Maybe instead of pulling down wallpaper I should have read my assignment. "The heart?" Sounded good.

"Why?" he asked.

I chewed on my bottom lip. *Think, Sunny, think!* "It pumps blood and provides nutrients. We can't live without it. It's the center of our—"

"Wrong. We *can* live without it with a heart transplant." His finger landed on Max. "You. Mr. Kent. What's the most important organ?"

Max adjusted a pair of tortoiseshell glasses he'd slipped on at some point, looking suave and cool as if the altercation with Bart had never happened. "The brain, sir. It controls vision, hearing, smell, balance, learning, memory, and a few things I'm sure I've forgotten. It communicates by using neurons, and it's estimated we have billions."

My mouth gaped. It dawned on me that Max wasn't exactly the dumb jock I'd imagined.

Maybe there was more to him . . .

Nah.

"Nice answer," Whitt replied.

Max paused, his eyes gliding over to mine. "But back to the heart—Miss Blaine makes a valid point."

"How so?" Whitt asked, crossing his legs as he leaned against the podium.

The entire class looked from Whitt to Max to me. It felt as if the entire room hushed to hear what he had to say.

Max cleared his throat. "The heart may not be the control center, but the brain is nothing without oxygen that the heart supplies. They rely on each other—it's a relationship of sorts. Also, metaphorically speaking, the heart *is* the seat of the soul and our psyche. After all, it is the organ that falls in love."

Whitt chuckled. "Love has nothing to do with our heart."

"I disagree." Max sent me a leisurely look, sweeping over my face. "When you first meet someone special, your heart reacts. It flutters or jumps or something. It's like it recognizes its other half." He dipped his head, appearing a bit embarrassed by the admission.

I didn't buy it. Not for a hot minute.

Wistful sighs came from the girls around me. Maybe even a couple of guys.

" . . . so romantic . . ." someone murmured from the back of the room.

" . . . you can have my heart anytime . . ." said another.

Oh, please.

I lifted an eyebrow at Max. *You are so full of shit,* my eyes said.

You know you want me, his eyes replied.

"Player," I whispered under my breath.

He just grinned.

chapter
EIGHT

Max

I FOLLOWED SUNNY out of class, grabbing her hand before she stepped into the stairwell. I wasn't ready to let her walk away. An idea was niggling at me.

"Wait. Let's talk a minute. I have a proposition for you."

She turned toward me, a harried look on her face as she shuffled her backpack around. "What's up? Oh, and nice acting in class. Half the girls are in love with you now."

"Just half?"

She glared. "Fine. Probably all of them."

"But not you?" I asked.

"Sorry, but your little show was impervious to my hard heart."

I shrugged noncommittally. Class had been a show, but pretending was what I did best. I pretended that losing my mom hadn't slayed me my freshman year. I pretended that my dad was the best guy in the world. I pretended that Bianca hadn't hurt me last year.

I pushed those thoughts aside.

"Okay, this is going to sound nuts, but maybe we could continue our little charade about dating?" I said. The idea had taken root in class, and the more I thought about it, the more stoked I became.

"Why would you want to?" she sputtered.

"It's simple. I want the Heisman, but with all the rumors about me fighting last year with Felix—it's a long shot. The award isn't just about achievement and skill. It's all hype and to get hype you need a feel-good story that resonates with people. Maybe finding a serious girlfriend and falling in love could be *the story* that tips the voters over." I paused. "Heck, we could even go all the way and say *fiancée*. The reporters would eat up that romantic shit—just like that classroom did."

Her mouth opened. "Fake fiancée? Falling in love? What is this . . . a Hallmark movie?"

"We could be the best damn Hallmark movie ever made, Sunny." My voice was dead serious.

"And what do I get?"

I leaned in closer, feeling drawn to her, inhaling her sweet scent. "A thousand bucks. You're always working. You need money, right?"

A little puff of air came from her parted lips. "I don't know. This seems crazy. You're crazy."

Maybe I was—but football was everything.

"I'm just focused—it's what it takes to be the best. Plus, it's not *just* the Heisman. You could keep the groupies off my back. And Bianca. Hell, I could have the best season of my life—and all because I have a pretend girl next to me . . . one that I don't really have to invest a lot of work in. See? It sounds like the perfect plan."

A long exhale came from her as she took her eyes off me to focus on the students milling past us to head to the stairwell. I watched her face with keen interest, looking for a chink in her armor, some way to convince her that this was a spectacular idea. She chewed on her bottom lip.

"I'll even help you study for this class. I am a pre-med major, you know. And . . . I can put in a good word for you with Whitt. He loves me," I said in a sing-song voice. "Come on. You know you want to. I'm fun and hot. You'd be so popular—"

She held her hand up. "I get the picture. How long will we have to—you know—be together?"

"They announce the finalists the first week of December, so that's around three months, give or take. We could come back after Christmas and say we'd broken up. You can even say you broke my heart. Easiest thing ever."

She mulled that over. "Don't you have a girl you could ask—like someone you already have on the hook?"

"It's got to be you. I trust you."

"Why?" Her brow wrinkled.

"I don't know. Maybe it's because you've got guts enough to stand up to me." I carried on, rushing through the words, making it sound easy. "There'd be minimal obligations—of course. We'd have to be a couple in public—maybe attend some frat parties together or have lunch at the Student Center. Nothing crazy."

She frowned. "I don't get out much. I bake cookies and watch sitcoms. I'm nothing like Bianca. I can't be all girly and stuff."

"I don't want to be with anyone like her," I said rather sharply. "It's football season anyway. I go to class, train, and play. I'll be gone some weekends for the away games. We can keep appearances to a minimum. Besides, the less people see us, the less likely they'd know we're fake." I shrugged. "Just, if we do this, don't fall in love with me. I don't want anything serious."

"Trust me," she said with steel in her voice, "that won't happen."

"Good."

"Good."

My lips curved up at her snippy tone. "So what's the answer?"

She pursed her lips and thought. "Five thousand—and it's just *girlfriend*. None of this fiancée stuff. It sounds complicated—class was already a mess with Bart—plus

I don't want to lie to my grandmother."

Why did I feel disappointed?

Not at the money part, but the fact that I couldn't get a bigger commitment out of her.

Whatever. Take what you can get.

"Fine. Girlfriend it is, then."

She sent me a nod, her face set as if she'd made up her mind. "It's a deal. You've got yourself a fake girlfriend until December."

I sent her a smooth smile as we shook hands, not impervious to the zing when we touched. I *was* attracted to her—obviously—but I was determined to not ruin a good thing.

No groupies.

No Bianca.

No drama.

Just the Heisman and my future in the NFL.

We talked a bit more as we walked down the stairs, our steps in sync as we came out the metal door to the lobby. I felt good about this. Confident. Sunny would be perfect for the outsiders looking in. She wasn't a rich girl. Hell, she worked. She didn't have a volatile temper like Bianca, and she was nice, except for when she was being prickly, but my gut knew that was her defense to protect herself from jerks like me.

She was on her way to another class, and I had one on the other side of campus, so we parted ways. Before I thought too hard about it, I brushed my lips against her cheek before she walked away. Why not? It's what a boyfriend would do and looked good if anyone was paying attention.

She accepted the touch and then walked away from me in those tight yoga pants. Her ass was perfectly round and the way she swiveled her hips with just the right amount of sass . . .

I thought back to that off the charts kiss in the elevator.

It was going to be tough to keep things between us platonic.

You have to, Max.

I pivoted and headed to my next class, willing myself to focus on football. I was going to ignore the odd connection I felt with her. It was for the best anyway. I couldn't get attached to her. My entire career depended on it.

chapter
NINE

Sunny

A FEW HOURS later, I'd finished two more classes and walked home. Hot and sweaty from the four blocks, I was grouchy and a bit off kilter from the thing with Max.

I set my books down on the rickety kitchen table, grabbed a soda from the fridge, and sat down to play back my morning.

For some insane reason, I'd agreed to be his girlfriend.

I hadn't been able to tell him no.

Why did he have to be so damn irresistible?

The entire time he'd been talking to me in that stairwell part of me was trying to keep my eyes off his flawless face, another part of me was trying to convince myself to run like hell, but it was the money-hungry part of me that won the battle. I could cut back on my hours at the library. I could check in on Mimi more. Heck, I could study. I might even be able to save some of it for after graduation.

If he wanted to throw it away, who was I to say no?

You don't really know him, Sunny!

Did I need to?

It's not like he and I would be emotionally involved. He'd made it clear he wasn't looking for a real relationship.

And asking me to be his fake fiancée? He certainly knew how to get my attention, but I had my limits to deception—mostly because of my grandmother. Mimi was all I had as far as family and lying to her made me feel ill. It was going to be hard enough when I told her I had a boyfriend. I couldn't tell her he was fake. She'd be equal parts disappointed in me for debasing myself for money and hurt that she couldn't provide more for me.

Forcing thoughts of Max back in that locked box, I went outside, kicked my broken car in frustration, and called an Uber to take me to Mimi's. I saw her every Monday afternoon before work, and a ruined car wasn't going to stop me.

I arrived at her assisted living apartment complex and walked to the back where the pool and hot tub were. She waved me over from a patio table, shoulder-length dyed blond hair blowing in the wind. At sixty-five, she was spry and had piercing gray eyes that could cut right through you. Laser eyeballs, I called them. The residents vied for her attention, and according to her, she'd had "relations" with several of the single men.

I plopped down next to her and stretched out my legs. "You'll never believe what happened today, Mimi."

"I hope you won the lottery." She showed me her flip-flops. "I need to add to my collection. Mrs. Barnes in 2B has been bragging she has more pairs than me."

"Well, we can't let that happen." I pulled out the cushy flip-flops I'd picked up last week at Wal-Mart. "Check these out. They have bumble bees on the straps and the bottoms are made from a yoga mat."

"Well done, grasshopper." She tucked them down next to her and poured me a glass of tea from the pitcher on the table.

"I don't know why you love those so much," I said, nudging my head at the ones she already had on.

"'Cause Mr. Wallis said I have beautiful feet, and I should show them off."

Mr. Wallis was an old boyfriend in the apartment complex who was currently dating Mimi's archenemy, Mrs. Barnes in 2B.

"Isn't he the one with the foot fetish?"

"Maybe." Her eyes flashed to a tan gentleman in a red speedo who was at least eighty. She nudged her head at him, her voice low and conspiratorial. "Ricky's my latest. He's from New York City—darn liberal, of course. He snores loud enough to wake a bear from hibernation, but his pecker still works—at least for two minutes. He's a frisky one, that one. Maybe a keeper."

I bit back a grin. "I can't keep up with you. I thought you were dating Mr. Sully in 3A? You said he brought you flowers every day. And he has a nice vacation house in Boca."

She waved that idea away. "Meh. He got too attached—and sometimes he'd get on these long tangents about sailing. The man is crazier than a dog in a hub-cap factory when it comes to boats. All he talks about is rudders and nautical miles. The only rudder I wanted was the one in his pants. Plus, I do not want to spend the rest of my life floating on some ocean in the middle of nowhere. There's sharks there, and I can't even swim!" She took a breath. "Tell me about your news, hon."

I inhaled a deep breath, preparing for the crazy storm that was about to land on my head. "I have a boyfriend too . . . Max Kent."

She slammed down the glass of tea that had been on its way to her mouth, and she bounced in her chair like a kid. "*The* Max Kent, the football player from LU?"

I grimaced. "None other."

Her palm pressed her chest like Fred in *Sanford and Son* when he'd fake a heart attack. "I can't believe it. You waltzed in here all cool and calm like you didn't have a care in the world. Why wasn't that the first thing you told me! Lordy, you *did* win the lottery." She settled back down, her chest rising rapidly. "You're not pulling my leg, are ya?"

I threw my arms up. "I swear you love football more than you do me."

"He's hotter than a red jalapeno, Sunny!" She fanned herself. "He moves like lightning, and not all quarterbacks can run, let me tell you. Some just stand there like grumps and throw the ball—but not him. Nope, he's got some speed on him. He's the whole package. I'd like to know the size of his rudder . . ."

"Mimi," I shook my head. "Don't even go there."

She giggled.

"This calls for a celebration." She reached in her beach bag she'd brought down and pulled out a flask. I watched her pour a healthy amount into both our glasses. Mimi was a bit of a hippy and a free thinker when it came to me. If she had a beer, she offered me one. If she was having sex, she didn't hide it from me. Truthfully, she was more of a friend than a parent figure, but by the time I'd arrived at her doorstep three years ago I'd been done with anything that had to do with the word *parent*.

She sat back. "Go on. Take a sip. And then I want all the details on how you met."

I sputtered at the taste, getting a whiff of strong alcohol. "Um, it's . . . good."

"It's a Long Island Iced Tea. Got the recipe off the internet. I googled it." She lifted her glass as if to say *cheers*. "The internet has nothing on this old woman."

I giggled. "You always know exactly what I need, Mimi."

Her face changed, the lines around her mouth deepening as she frowned.

I set the drink down carefully. "What's wrong?"

"Your father called."

A breeze fluttered, cooling us off in the September humidity. Laughter came from the people playing checkers at a nearby table, and somewhere from one of the open windows I heard the drone of a gameshow. *The Price is Right? Family Feud?*

It didn't matter—because she'd brought him up.

A small shrug shifted her frail shoulders. She cleared her throat, her eyes swinging to my face and then back to her tea. "I hadn't spoken to the man since the day your mama left here to marry him, so there's no love lost between us, but he asked me to give you a message, and I will."

"What is it?"

"He's dying."

My chest froze. "From what?"

"Cancer."

One of Mimi's sisters had passed last year from bone cancer, and I'd seen her at her frailest. My father was a big man, and I couldn't imagine his frame bent by weakness. I tossed myself further back in the seat, desperately analyzing how I felt, but there was no answer. I was a mixed-up bag of emotions when it came to him.

I hated him. I loved him.

He was the only immediate family I had.

Yet, after my wreck when the police had dragged the lake looking for my body, I'd never volunteered I was alive. Not until I turned eighteen. Mimi had supported me in that decision because she'd seen the marks on my back.

The beginning of my family's demise had started when my brother had been delivered stillborn. Born five years after me, his grave was in the Blaine family cemetery in Snowden. A framed photo of him had sat on my mother's nightstand, a tiny boy wrapped in a blue blanket, his lids tightly shut. His name had been Lincoln, and although my parents never discussed him in front of me, I'd hear their hushed voices through the thin walls at night. Most of those conversations would end with my mother crying, the sound muffled as if she pressed her face into a pillow.

Mimi nudged my arm gently. "Forget all that. I've told you, and that's all we have to say about it. Let's focus on the good news. Tell me about Max. Is he as handsome as he looks on TV?"

I smiled rather absently and rambled off an answer, but my thoughts were scattered somewhere in the mountains of North Carolina, remembering a family that had broken my heart.

chapter TEN

Sunny

FOR THE TENTH time, I checked my appearance in the small compact in my purse. My hair had been styled until it was straight, my makeup was minimal except for pink lipstick and mascara—but my hands were still shaking.

I was freaking out. I shoved the compact back in my purse and zipped it shut, analyzing why I was so antsy.

Was it being in close proximity to Max again?

Or was it the deception itself?

Both.

It had been five days since our little agreement, and tonight was our first official night out as a couple. Of course it had to be at a place where I wouldn't know anyone—a football party.

I stood in front of the door—the one I was supposed to be knocking on—and sucked in a sharp breath.

I could turn around and call the Uber to come back and get me.

I could go home, bake some chocolate pie, and draw up some T-shirt designs.

Or . . .

I could go in there like a boss and show these people I was worthy of an Oscar.

Think of the money, Sunny. You need it.

He hadn't written a check yet, though. I could always back out right now.

No.

I shook my arms and stretched my neck, psyching myself up, prepping for a long night of being Max Kent's arm candy. Batting my eyelashes and summoning my inner groupie, I stared at the wooden door and practiced. "Hey, baby. I've missed you." I did a delicate finger wave. "I love you, Maxie-Pooh."

"In the great scheme of things, Maxie-Pooh isn't that bad. I've been called worse," a deep voice murmured from behind me.

Caught.

Mortification swept over me. I spun around on the sidewalk to see Max and Tate, both clad in jeans and blue Leland shirts that clung to their sculpted chests. They towered over me, one dark with glossy hair that swung around his shoulders and the other slightly smaller with a headful of sandy blond hair.

"Yeah," Tate said, grinning. "Jock-ass is my favorite, though. I think you're going to make me laugh a lot, new girlfriend."

"You can call me Sunny." I felt the blush rising up my cheeks. "Just so you know, I don't always talk to myself."

"Glad to know I'm not dating a loon," Max replied.

"Nope. Those only pick the lock to your room," I said smugly.

"You can pick it anytime," was his quick comeback.

I blushed. Again. "Speaking of crazy, have you found Sierra?"

The grin slipped off his face. "No. I didn't have a number for her—*because I don't encourage her*—but I managed to get it from one of the other players. I texted her but got no reply. She's not a student here, so I haven't been able to track down her home address yet." He rubbed at his temple.

"I'm sorry about her. You know, you could have ridden with me tonight instead of insisting on taking an Uber."

He had texted me earlier in the day to see if I wanted to catch a ride with him, but keeping it professional meant the less time we spent together alone, the better. "I'm fine."

"At least let me pay for it," he said.

"No." He'd already done enough with offering to fix my car if Sierra didn't pull through. In fact, yesterday he'd called a garage to come pick it up and give him an estimate.

"Is this our first disagreement?" he asked, an amused look on his face.

"First of many, I bet," Tate murmured just as a cute redhead opened the door and called for Tate to come inside. By the eagerness on her pretty face, I imagined she'd been standing by the window waiting for him to show.

"I'll catch you two later. My lady awaits." He gave us a little grin as he brushed past us to the girl waiting on him.

"Is that his girlfriend?"

"For the moment. He flits from girl to girl. Not exactly a paragon for committed relationships."

I thought about Bart. "Typical."

He ignored that, his eyes coasting over me and lingering appreciatively. I'd worn a soft pink fuzzy sweater. Ultra feminine and cropped so that it showed a sliver of my stomach, it was something I imagined a girlfriend of his might wear. When I'd worn it around Bart, he'd barely kept his hands to himself in public. It was also itchy as heck.

I tugged at the hem, pulling it closer to my gray skinny jeans. I should have worn one of the shirts I'd made. At least I wouldn't have felt so self-conscious. It was rather tight across my chest, probably because I'd tossed it in the dryer when I should have let it hang dry.

"You look nice," he said softly.

"Thank you." I stared at his mouth. I still wanted to touch his lips.

"You're welcome." He let out a little laugh. "We sound like we're on a first date."

"We are!"

A considering look came over his face. "That's a problem. Everyone in that room needs to think we've been dating since this summer."

I lifted my hands, feeling exasperated. "Well, I'm not kissing you on the lips again, so don't get any ideas. Once was enough." I sounded a bit like the virgin who protested too much, and I snapped my mouth closed from saying anything else. It wasn't that I was a prude. I'm not.

Kissing him was a dangerous game. His lips tasted like forever—and they weren't.

He tossed an arm around me. "Just follow my lead."

We walked in the door and took in the crowded party. People milled around the house chatting and talking while music blared in the background. A few couples were headed upstairs to the bedrooms, and it didn't take a genius to figure out why.

Everyone seemed to look at us, especially girls who sent me envious glares. Yeah. I understood that. I'd gotten those looks with Bart too. I stiffened, and I guess Max picked up on it. He focused on me, and I caught the barest hint of vulnerability on his face. "Yeah, everyone's watching. They always are. Truth is, I only have a couple of real friends—the rest are just sharks waiting for me to fuck up. Just smile and wave and walk on."

"Like this?" I did an exaggerated version of the Miss America wave.

"Exactly like that." He tapped my nose, a lot like he had that first day we met. "Thank you for coming, Sunny." His voice was low and husky and my body softened, drawn toward the warmth of his as we walked to a makeshift bar in the kitchen.

I liked this side of him. Protective. *Real.*

I glanced up at him. "So, every single thing you do with me tonight will be fake?"

He grabbed two cups of beer from a guy manning the bar and handed me mine. He took a long sip and stared at me over the rim. His lashes lowered. "Isn't that the point?"

"Right. Of course." I swallowed down a gulp, needing liquid courage.

"Come on," he said. "Most of the players are out back where the fire pit is. I need to introduce you to everyone." He laced our fingers together. "You ready for the dog and pony show?"

I smiled. "Only if I can be a big dog—no toy poodles for me."

His lips curled in a half-grin. "Whatever. Just don't called me Maxie-Pooh in front of anyone."

"Doesn't fit with the tough-guy image you got going on?" I asked tartly.

"Call me Maxie-Pooh, and I'll call you Blondie."

I rolled my eyes. "Fine. I'll just smile and wave."

He opened the back door for me and escorted me down the few steps to the center of the crowd that huddled around a roaring fire on the stone patio.

"Yo! It's my man," Ryn said, coming over to us and slapping Max on the back. "And you brought a plus one. Good to see you, Sunny. Welcome to my house." He grinned down at me, and I felt myself relaxing. He'd been sweet to me during our class together.

"I've got something to say, everyone," Max called out a bit later, his gaze encompassing the group. Murmurs came from the crowd of bulky football players and girls. They stopped what they were doing and leaned in to hear him. Someone even turned down the music. It was obvious he was their leader.

He indicated me with a nudge of his head. "Some of you have met her, but most of you haven't. So, I'd like to formally introduce you to my girlfriend, Sunny Blaine. She's beautiful, sweet, and I've never been happier." His aqua eyes gleamed down at me, heartfelt emotion on his face. *Like he loved me.*

I swallowed. He was good.

He waggled his eyebrows at the crowd. "Be nice to her, and don't forget to tell her how awesome I am. Tell her anything different, and I'll kick your ass." He lifted his beer to everyone. "Cheers!"

A few chuckles came from the crowd.

" . . . hi . . ."

" . . . nice to meet you . . ."

" . . . glad it's not Bianca . . ."

The murmurs came and went, and I smiled and waved at everyone—as promised.

"Alright. Let's get this party started," Max said, twirling me around in his arms as the music kicked back up with "She Will Be Loved" from Maroon 5. My stomach fluttered as he wrapped his arms around my waist and held me close. We swayed to the beat, our hips brushing against each other.

"They love you already," he whispered in my ear, his breath caressing my neck. Goosebumps rose over my body.

I lifted my face up at him in what I hoped was fake adoration. He pushed a strand of hair out of my eyes and kissed me on the forehead. I sighed, admitting what had bothered me the most about showing up tonight. It wasn't about the pretending. I could be a fake girlfriend. It was my body that was the problem. I wanted Max Kent.

chapter
ELEVEN

Max

THE NEXT WEEKEND I was trying to hunt down my fake girlfriend. Without luck.

I parked my black 750 Harley in the detached garage next to my house. An over-the-top gift from my dad, the bike had been a reward for the prep school football state championship I'd won my senior year. Of course, we'd been to state three years in a row, but that last year had been *mine*. I'm not being cocky when I say that sportscasters and colleges had been talking about me being great since I was fourteen and how I had an arm like a bullet. I inherited it from the jerk who'd provided sperm for me, but I'd also honed my skill with drills and training. And the Heisman, that gnawing need that drove me? I wanted it because it was the one thing my father hadn't been able to get when he was a college quarterback. Yeah, take that, dickhead.

My dislike for my father started the day my mom delivered me during the ice storm of '95. A bleak day in December, Atlanta had woken to thousands of branches and power lines covered with ice. The city came to a virtual standstill, and my mom's water broke right in the middle of it. Somehow she got herself in her car to drive to the hospital, but then skidded on a patch of ice and hit a tree.

Where was my dad? Screwing a groupie.

A stranger helped my mom give birth in the front seat of her Mercedes. From that day on, she said I was a fighter.

When she finally got ahold of my dad, a woman answered his phone. She told me that had been the beginning of the end for her, yet she never could bring herself to divorce the bastard.

When I was a kid, he'd show up periodically at our house, get back with my mom, then a month later she'd read about him having an affair with some country singer or model. He was a narcissistic bastard who only cared about himself, and I hated him most days.

I pushed the past out of my mind as I planted my ass on the stoop. I'd been cruising the streets looking for Sunny for an hour but hadn't found her. And her house was still dark. She said she had to work at the library this evening, but it closed at nine. It was after ten.

How was she getting home?

Fuck. I should have taken care of this already. She was my responsibility.

I'd given her rides to class on the days we had class together, and she was catching a ride with a friend on the other days—with whom, I had no idea. Which reminded me that we really needed to sit down and go over each other's history just in case we got asked any hard questions.

I'd sent her a text a couple of hours ago to see if she needed a ride, but she hadn't responded. Calls had gone straight to voicemail.

Why was I worried? She was an adult. She could take care of herself. But . . .

But today was weird. I'd wanted her to be home when the bus had rolled in from our away victory against number fifteen Florida. It had been a Saturday night ESPN game, and dammit, I'd wanted to tell her about it. I'd thrown for three hundred and ten and rushed for one twenty, shredding their over-ranked defense. Stellar game. When I woke up in the hotel this morning, the sportscasters were talking about me and the *H* word.

I'd barely seen her this past week. School and practice had both been intense, and my bed had been my best friend. Our little agreement was working well for me. Bianca was ignoring me, and groupies hadn't shown up at the house to hound me. I was golden.

Yet a chill went down my spine—something was about to change. Somehow.

Tate popped his head out the door. "Dude. You want a beer?"

I nodded.

He came out a few minutes later, sat next to me on the stoop, and handed me a Newcastle. "Waiting on your *girlfriend?*"

I flipped him off.

One of the only people I trusted in this world, he knew the low-down on the agreement between me and Sunny. He'd laughed his ass off when I told him.

See. He didn't get it. My determination. My grit. My willingness to do whatever it took.

I took the beer, twisted off the top, and took a swig. "I don't think she likes me very much."

Tate's eyes squinted like they did when he was thinking. "I hope this plan doesn't blow up in your face, mate. There's a lot of shite that can go wrong. If the media finds out you're just doing it for the hype . . ."

I ignored that. No one was going to find out.

Sunny was good at keeping her distance from me, even though I'd catch her in class sending me these weird little glances, an expression on her face as if I was a puzzle she couldn't figure out. But those walls . . . man, she had built them high and tight. She'd been dead serious about not getting involved with me. *Which was fine.* That's what I wanted too.

My cock didn't agree. I was in a dry spell. It had been several weeks since I'd hooked up with anyone. I hoped I'd be able to last . . .

Tate turned his beer up and took a drink. "You don't really know her, though. She could be a nutcase or after your money—"

"I do know her."

"You just met. How can you be so sure?"

I couldn't explain how achingly familiar she was. Sometimes, you just knew when someone was good, and my gut sensed we had affinity. I *liked* her. She didn't care who I was and she sure as hell didn't want to jump in my bed and get pregnant for a paycheck.

Just then the glare of a car's headlights swung into her driveway—a Jeep. The vehicle came to a halt and Sunny exited the passenger side. Bart got out of the driver's side to walk her to the front door. He helped her with her backpack when it slipped down her shoulder.

My teeth snapped. *She was with her ex.*

Tate whistled. "Cheating already? Bloody hell. That's got to be a record."

I sucked down my beer.

Tate shrugged. "Her car's in the shop. Perhaps he just gave her a ride—no pun intended."

I sent him a death-glare and he snorted.

I stared at Bart, my body wired as I set my bottle on the concrete edging of the porch. I stood and paced, weaving around the bushes, my eyes detailing every muscle twitch from the two people across the street caught in the spotlight of headlamps. I studied them, trying to get a read on how they reacted to one another.

He eased her bag back onto her shoulder, and then they stood there staring at each other.

Had something happened between them while I was out of town?

She said something to him and then went inside, shutting the door gently. GENTLY. What did *that* mean? In class, since our run-in, they'd never even spoken to each other again.

Ah, but what happens when you aren't around, Max?

Why did I care?

I was way overanalyzing this.

Bart just stood there, staring at her closed door. My fists tightened.

Scrubbing my face, I got to my feet and stepped out on the grass, being sure to stay in the shadow of our porch roof so he couldn't see me. It helped that our porch light was out too.

"Before you lose your temper and go over there half-cocked, remember she's your *fake* girlfriend," Tate murmured, his tone slightly sardonic.

"My head's on straight," I said. "And mind your own business."

"Bugger, you *are* my business. My mission is to keep you out of trouble. I'm your checker. You asked me to do that shit freshman year, and I take it seriously. I will not let you screw up."

"I'm not in trouble, and this isn't a football game," I said curtly. "I'm just watching how she deals with her ex. That's it."

"Uh-huh."

As I watched, Bart seemed to come to a decision. His shoulders slumped as he turned from Sunny's door, stalked to his car, and drove off.

Good riddance.

I grunted. I should cool off and deal with her tomorrow. I should go inside and watch game tapes. I should take a hot shower . . .

Screw that.

I gave her five minutes as I paced. Giving her time to get settled . . . maybe turn on the television. It also let me chill out.

Tate made an exasperated sound as I headed her way.

I ignored him.

I stood at her door for a few minutes, debating. Again. It was late. We had class in the morning. I could talk to her then. I should wait.

Fuck it. I knocked.

"Who is it?" she asked, her voice quiet in the silence of the night.

I let out a deep exhale. "Max."

"Hang on," she called. I heard lots of flapping and scurrying around.

A few minutes later, she flung the door open, and whatever I'd been going to say got clogged in my throat.

I hadn't seen her since Friday morning in class, and the effect of her took me by surprise.

She'd changed into a skimpy white tank top (no bra) and a pair of tiny flannel shorts. Her wavy hair was up in a messy bun with long strands curling around her face. And was that a nipple piercing poking through her shirt? *Hell, yes.*

My body hummed. I tucked my hands in my pockets—just needing something to do with them because part of me wanted to . . .

"What were you doing with Bart?" I said, keeping my voice cool.

I held it together well considering we'd made a deal for five thousand dollars and the check was in my back pocket.

Her hand went to her hip. "What happened to *hello* and *may I come in?*"

My lips flattened. "Guess I'm not up for pleasantries."

She paused, a little wrinkle on her brow, and shook her head as if to clear it. "Wait. Are you *jealous?*"

"No." My arms crossed. "He was a complete dick in class on Monday and now you're in a car with him. I'm annoyed as fuck. Plus you're dating *me*. If people see you with him, I look ridiculous. Been there already with Bianca. If you wanted to screw your ex on the side, you should have been upfront with me."

Her eyes flashed. "You don't understand. I can explain—"

"No lies."

Her head tilted. "Bianca really did a number on you, didn't she?"

"I don't want your pity."

"It's called empathy." She propped herself against the doorjamb just enough to show me a little bit more thigh. I tore my eyes away. "You never told me why you broke up. I mean I know you had a crazy relationship and—"

My jaw tightened. Just thinking about her reminded me that I didn't need to get involved with anyone. "We broke up because she wanted me to propose after we'd been together for eight months. She told me she was pregnant—but when I asked her to go to a doctor and she refused—I knew something was up. She finally admitted she'd lied to me, and when I broke it off, she reacted by trying to make me jealous. She screwed some of the players who weren't really my friends. She wanted to hurt me or maybe she thought I'd come running back—but I didn't. Maybe she cared about me; maybe she didn't. Either way, it left a bad taste in my mouth."

Her expression softened. "She's not the one for you."

"Are you?"

She straightened. "What do you mean?"

"Are *you* the one for me?"

A few ticks of silence passed. Her chest rose as she sucked in a breath.

"I'm kidding. Jesus, did you believe me?"

She swallowed, looking away from my eyes. "No, of course not."

What the fuck was wrong with me? I raked both hands through my hair. I was completely off. And being an asshole. "Back to Bart—explain it to me."

She nodded stiffly. "Fine. Since you asked so nicely. I called an Uber to get me home from the library and the driver never showed. Then my phone died, so if the driver called, I missed it. Everyone at work had already left, so I was stuck and decided to walk home. Some of those streets close to campus are iffy—there was a mugging there last month. Bart happened to drive by, saw me, and stopped. At first, I told him to go on, but he—he begged me. I was desperate to get home and just crash. It was just a ride home."

He'd begged her.

What a piece of shit manipulator. Had he been following her from work? I honestly didn't put much past him if he wanted her back. There was only one thing to do, and I should have done it earlier.

I dug around in my pockets, pulled out my keychain, removed my Land Cruiser key, and pressed it in her hand. "Here, this is yours to keep. I have an extra at the house. You drive my car until we get this straightened out."

She stared at the key with wonder. "But, but what will you drive?"

"My Harley—or I'll catch a ride with Tate. Whatever. I can't have you walking home in the dark, and I don't want you riding in the same car as Bart—or with some Uber driver."

"Oh."

"Did he try to get you back?" I wanted to know every single word he'd said to her—which was crazy.

"Not really your business," she said.

I propped my arm up on the door and leaned in until our faces were close. She smelled like heaven. "I have a check for you in my back pocket that makes it my business," I said softly, my eyes landing on those heart-shaped lips.

She smirked. "Your macho slash sexy stance doesn't faze me, Quarterback, but if you must know, he was just worried about me being out alone. Yes, he wanted to bring up the past, but I didn't."

"You said I was sexy." My lids lowered.

She blinked, nibbled on her bottom lip—and changed the topic. "Do you want to come in? It's not the Ritz, but it's definitely different. I'll introduce you to Charlie?"

I perked up. I needed anything to distract me from how much I wanted to screw my fake girlfriend. "You have a dog or a cat?"

"Pet unicorn in the bathroom."

And there it was. Any earlier tension that had been lingering evaporated. I let out a relieved laugh. "Nice. Does he crap glitter and rainbows?"

She laughed and the door opened further. "He's just a sticker on the wall, but he's something to see. Well, you coming or going?"

I should go home and rest. "I'll come in."

"You'll have to be gone soon, though. I have to go over those stupid A&P notes before I go to sleep." She rolled her eyes.

"I'll help you. I would have even if we hadn't made a deal."

She gave me a spontaneous hug, the lemon scent of her hair lingering, her body warm as she pressed against me.

"What's this for?" I asked, my hands not knowing where to go. On her tight ass? No, that was wrong. I curled my arms around her waist and inhaled. She just—*fuck*—felt so good. And it wasn't about sex—no, it was more, as if we shared a human connection that meant something I couldn't wrap my head around.

She squeezed my shoulder. "This is for giving me your car key, silly. And I'm glad you won your game this weekend."

I eased away from her hug with reluctance, feeling off balance, wanting to touch her again.

We stepped down into a seventies style darkened room with wood paneling on the bottom and an upper wall that had been stripped of wallpaper. It was small but clean. Bright, colorful pillows and velvet throws were spread across an old pink Victorian-looking couch with a curved wooden back. Live plants sat under the front window and framed pictures lined the old mantle above the fireplace. I walked over to them for a closer look. Most were of her and an older woman with blond hair.

One caught my eye—

What was that? My heart flip-flopped in my chest.

I felt her gaze on me from behind. Yeah, she knew exactly what I was seeing.

I turned around and held out the frame. "Not a football fan, huh? *You'd rather play chess*, you said. Looks to me like you're having a pretty good time at the bowl game last year—in Phoenix. Long way to go for a non-fan." I pointed down at the pic. "This is you, right, with your face painted like a tiger and wearing our team colors? And is this a huge number one foam finger you're holding up? Why, yes. I think it is." I held it up high to the light, inspecting it as if it were a diamond. I burst out laughing. "This is classic. Tate is going to freak when I tell him."

She grimaced, her face flushing. "That trip was for Mimi."

I nodded. She'd mentioned her a few times in passing.

"Anyway," she continued. "I scored the tickets from someone who couldn't go at the last minute. It wasn't a big deal."

"Really?" I said, my voice dripping in disbelief. I walked closer to her, my lids low. "You can't shit a shitter, Sunny."

She fiddled with her shirt, not meeting my eyes.

I smirked. "Your face gives too much away. You love football. I bet you know my stats. I bet you've been following me my entire career—"

"Fine. Just shut up already," she snapped, bopping me on the arm with a sharp knuckle. "I like watching you play, okay, fine. I know you should have run a screen in the second half of yesterday's game when that lineman came after you. I know that in the first quarter you tended to throw too soon, but by the third quarter you had the kinks worked out . . . but it's not like I'm some crazy groupie. I don't stalk you or wear your jersey or pick your locks or even care if I see you on campus. I like the *game*. I always have. I like the crunch of bodies and the rush I get when the quarterback throws the ball or runs it in for a touchdown. What's the big deal? Can't I be a regular fan?"

Deep satisfaction settled in my bones. "You can be whatever you want." Yeah, I wanted to push her against the wall and kiss her.

"Do you like all sports or just football?" I arched a brow.

She sent me an annoyed look and mumbled something.

"I'm sorry. Did you say something?"

She huffed at me, her chest rising. "You're not going to ever let this go are you?"

"Nope."

A defeated sigh came from her. "Football . . . football is my favorite."

"Am I your favorite player at Leland?" God, I was enjoying this.

Her fingers toyed with the neckline around her tank.

"Well?"

"Hmmm, Tate's fun to watch and rarely drops a pass . . ."

"Watch it."

She shrugged. "He's definitely going to be a top five draft pick—but yes, you're my favorite player. Don't get a big head over it either."

I sat down and leaned my head back on the couch and a chuckle came out. My fake girlfriend loved football—and she wasn't a psycho!

"What?" she snapped, still fuming, probably from my smug expression.

I patted the seat next to me and grinned. "Come on, get your notes, darlin'. I'm gonna help you study."

chapter
TWELVE

Sunny

T HE NEXT DAY that I didn't have class with Max, I came outside and took in the Land Cruiser he'd parked on my side of the street the night before.

The carpooling plan was for us to ride together on the days we had A&P, and on the days we didn't I got the car and Max rode his Harley. When he needed to get to and from the field house, he'd catch a ride with Tate. The arrangement seemed easy—but underneath the surface lingered the feeling that nothing is ever what it seems.

I crawled in the luxury vehicle and basked in the smell of spicy alpha male and leather. I popped the glove compartment open and nosed around, but all I found were documents, rural road maps of North Carolina, and a bottle of Bleu De Chanel. Yes. I cracked it open and inhaled, seductive images of Max front and center in my head: him at his door wearing a cocky smile . . . his piercing eyes and sexy hair that made me want to put on some Marvin Gaye and get it on—*okay, stop already.* I ran my hands over the supple seats. Is it bad that I wanted to roll around and sniff everywhere he'd been?

Get to class.

I cranked the car, shouting in glee when I felt the power under my feet.

Ten minutes later, I carefully parked his vehicle in student parking and arrived at the Coleman Arts Building for Lit class.

I took the stairwell to the second floor, and when I came out the door, I ran straight into Bart. We collided, and he dropped the backpack he'd been holding to put a hand out to steady me. "Whoa, Sunny. You good?"

"Yeah. Thanks for the save." I stepped away from his hands as inconspicuously as possible. A laugh came out but it sounded off.

Tuesdays and Thursdays were my Russian Lit class with Bart. For the past two weeks I'd done my best to avoid him, and now here I was practically mowing him down. Nice.

The ride home the other night had been uncomfortable, with me just listening while he vomited out everything he'd obviously wanted to say to me since we'd broken up this summer, mostly *I'm sorry I fucked up, you're the only girl I wanted,* and *it will never happen again.* I told him it didn't change things. Perhaps it had been good for us to let it all out. Now we had closure and maybe we'd be able to move on and be civil to one another.

I fidgeted in the hallway.

He did a half-smile and ran a hand through his auburn hair. "So . . . you and Max, huh?" His eyes clung to mine. Gold with flecks of brown, they were hard to look away from.

"Yeah."

He mulled that over then sent me a curt nod. "I hope he's good to you."

"He is. Thank you again for the ride Sunday." I chewed on my bottom lip. "You and I . . . it's weird being in a class together, huh?"

He nodded and sighed, his eyes roving over me and then coming back to my face. "You look gorgeous today."

I swallowed. *I didn't.* I looked crazy—mostly because I'd barely slept. Max had ended up coming over again to go over my A&P notes.

"Nice shirt, too," he added with a little chuckle, breaking the tension between us. "You sure that's not a sign I have another shot with you?"

I glanced down. Crap. I'd slipped on a tight, V-neck baseball shirt he'd given me. I'd loved the softness of the material and one day when I'd been experimenting, I'd cut out the neck and added a thick blue lace collar with hand-sewn pearl buttons. It was sexy with a dash of tomboy—one of my favorites.

"Funny. I just grabbed the first thing in my closet."

He smiled, albeit a little sadly. "Well, there's no crime against wearing a winning shirt. Come on. Let's find our seats."

We turned to walk in the Lit class, but I stopped when I felt eyes on me and turned back. There was Bianca. Watching us. She swept her gaze over Bart, curled her lip, and shot me a *go to hell* glare. I could feel the disdain dripping from her as she raked her eyes over me, sniffed, and turned her back.

She was trouble. Big time.

Ugh.

After classes, I drove to the local Wal-Mart and picked up a few things that Mimi needed for her pantry. She didn't have a license, so if she had any errands I typically ran them for her. I drove to her apartment, unpacked her groceries, and made sure she was set for the week. I left her out by the pool flirting with Mr. Sully and some of her friends. She'd told all the residents I was dating Max Kent, and since most of them knew who he was, they'd grilled me about what it was like to date a famous football star. I'd lied to all of them, and it was getting easier.

I arrived home around five in the afternoon, and my eyes went straight to Max's place. It looked empty. They'd never put blinds up on the big front bay window, and I could see straight to the television—which was off. I sighed. He had long days at practice, and it wasn't hard to see that football was everything to him.

I found myself wanting to tell him about seeing Bart. About how my heart didn't hurt nearly as much as I thought it would the night he'd driven me home.

Maybe it was better if I didn't confide in him, though.

I settled down at my small desk in the den, opened my computer and scrolled, finding the article I'd bookmarked a long time ago. It was an online piece from the Asheville Gazette about a girl who'd wrecked her car on the bridge overlooking Casey Lake right outside of Asheville, North Carolina. Posted three years ago, it described how a passing motorist had phoned in the accident. It didn't give the motorist's name or any identifying information. The paramedics and police had responded, but it wasn't until the next day they'd got the equipment out to drag the lake. Once they found evidence of the car, divers had gone in to search for survivors. The article concluded with the statement that the search was on-going and the person driving was considered missing. There was no report of a young man on the shore, no report of someone pulling a girl from the water.

I closed out the tab and clicked my laptop shut.

I'd been absolutely terrified that night, but I ran through the woods until I came to a nearly deserted truck stop on the highway, where I begged some young college kids to give me a ride to Knoxville. They had. Once there, I'd bought a bus ticket to Atlanta with the cash I still had in the back pocket of my denim shorts.

The rest is history. Here I was, living and breathing and not doing bad. If I'd stayed on that mountain—I stopped.

Don't, Sunny.

Then Max's face popped in my head.

But he wasn't good to think about either.

I exhaled and went to the kitchen to make sugar cookies. That's just what I needed—something sweet to forget all the bad.

chapter THIRTEEN

Max

TONIGHT WAS OUR *let's get to know each other better* date. I'd been to her house a couple of evenings to study and we'd touched on personal things, but now I wanted to dig into her, get under her skin. There were resistant layers I'd yet to peel away. She'd told me about being from North Carolina and growing up as a preacher's kid in a strict household. I knew her father was sick with cancer and their relationship was strained. Her mom had died years ago in a car accident with a man she'd been having an affair with.

I'd been thinking a lot about Sunny lately. Her lips, those long legs, and the way she looked at me when she didn't think I noticed.

I had a proposition for her—one that had been clawing at me since the moment she'd stood on my front porch. I wanted her in my bed.

"What's your favorite color?" I asked, gazing at her from across the table inside the Orion Coffee Shoppe—the place we'd supposedly met. A hipster place near campus, it held poetry readings and band night for amateurs. I liked it immediately, mostly because it was low-key and no one paid me any attention.

She sent me a side-eye over a bite of her club sandwich. "Blue. Who cares?"

"I do. I want to know everything about you."

"Why?" she said with a noncommittal shrug, completely unconcerned that the great Max Kent was interested in her. I liked that about her. She made me work for it.

"Well, in case you were wondering, my favorite color is blue too."

"Nice," she said. "If a reporter asks me, I'll be sure to let him know. What else you got for me?"

"When's the last time you had sex?" I took a sip of my latte, playing it cool, acting like I wasn't dying to know the answer. I did my best to keep my eyes off her assets. I'd been trying for the past hour, ever since she'd waltzed through the door wearing ankle boots, a pair of skinny jeans, and an *I Let the Dogs Out* shoulder-baring top. Simple. No makeup but lipstick. Hot as fuck.

"It's none of your business," she said around chews.

"Tell you what. Answer my question, and I'll tell you whatever you want to know about the mysterious Max Kent."

She scrunched her nose up. "You're no mystery. You're practically an open book. All I have to do is visit your Facebook or Instagram page."

"Not true. People see what they want. There's more to me than just a talented, intelligent, charming, easy to talk to guy—"

"Okay, fine," she said, cutting me off. An elegant finger swirled around her soda glass. "I haven't had sex since Bart—so since last spring." Smoky gray eyes peeked at me through dark lashes. "He was my first."

I hid my surprise by plucking a piece of bread off her plate and popping it in my mouth. *Holy mother of all things.* She was so damn innocent. My cock ached.

Why did it make me want her even more?

"You were a virgin?"

"I didn't stutter."

"Don't be defensive."

"I'm not," she snapped.

I laughed. "God, I think I love you."

She coughed and the drink she'd had in her mouth flew everywhere.

"Good grief. Don't take everything I say so seriously. And dude, it hurts a little that you looked so terrified." I gave her a wad of napkins from the dispenser. "Here, let's clean this up." Before I realized what I was doing, I inadvertently patted her chest, my hand lingering on the curve of her breast.

She inhaled sharply at the contact, and I immediately pulled back. The best quarterback in the country, and I couldn't even hand a girl a few napkins without fumbling all over myself.

What was wrong with me?

"I have a proposition for you," I said, clearing my throat. "There's obviously some heat between us."

Her eyebrow quirked. "Yeah?"

"What if we had sex—without getting involved, of course?"

Her mouth opened.

I held a hand up. "I mean, it would be a shame to spend all this time together and not enjoy each other . . ." my voice stopped, listening to how the words came out.

It had sounded better in my head on the drive over here.

"I guarantee we'd detonate like a bomb if you'd give us a shot," I added, my voice husky.

"Bombs have been known to implode—and I'd be the one getting hurt. In fact, you've already warned me. Remember? You don't do relationships anymore, and I don't do random sex."

"Someday I want something serious again—just not while I'm in college, ya know?"

"I get it." Her voice was soft. "It's all about the timing."

A few ticks of silence went by.

I was deeply disappointed in her answer—yet part of me was glad she'd said no. Sunny didn't deserve to just be a fuck buddy. She was a girl who only deserved the best. Once again, I resolved to keep it platonic.

Yeah. How long will that last?

"You have any questions for me?"

She mulled it over, her finger tapping on her chin. "Actually, I do have several questions. Let's start with . . . have you ever cheated on a girl?"

"No."

"Have you ever asked for directions?"

I scoffed. "Please."

She grunted.

"What's that supposed to mean?" I said.

"That you're too proud to admit when you're wrong."

"I'm never wrong, Cookie."

She set her sandwich down, a small smile on her face. "That's the best nickname you could come up with? Why *Cookie*?"

I leaned back in the metal chair that was entirely too small for my frame. "Because you're sweet enough to eat." The words fell softly between us.

Time to move on, Max. She isn't interested in sex with you.

"Next question?" I asked.

She nodded, thinking. "Hmmm, if I had to pick qualities in a fake boyfriend, I'd want him to be a great spider killer. Are you?"

"They don't scare me."

"Even the big hairy ones? There's one currently residing in my bedroom somewhere."

I grinned. "Let me come over and I'll hunt him down."

"Right," she smirked. "Here's a good one for you: Would you buy me feminine products?"

"I might come home with baby diapers—but yeah, I'd try my damnedest."

She bit back a grin, but a giggle erupted.

I smiled. "Are you trying to make me uncomfortable, Cookie?"

"Maybe . . . anyway . . . how many times a day do you masturbate?"

"As many as possible." *And I thought about you every single time this week.*

"Why do you want to put *it* in our butts?"

My hands flew up in the air. *"Who said I did?"*

She turned fire-engine red. "Fine. It was just a question—I've always wondered."

Now it was my turn to laugh. "You should see the color of your face right now. For the record, there are plenty of other places I'd like to put *it*."

She waved that comment off. "Do you believe in soul mates or love at first sight?"

I tensed. "Yes."

Her eyes zeroed in on mine. "Seriously? Come on—this is your fake girlfriend. You can tell me the truth."

"If the universe wants us with one person, I dig it. I believe in fate," I said.

"Don't you just think it's more about who is standing in front of you when the time is right? What if you met your one true love at a party when you were sixteen, but because you went your separate ways for one reason or another, you never see her again? Or maybe the next time you see her, she's already committed to someone else."

"I believe that whatever's meant to be will be." I toyed with my water glass, feeling self-conscious. "Maybe it's because I lost my mom early, but I believe a lot of stuff that can't be explained.

"When she died, I—I was lost. I can barely recall anything I did or said that night. But I feel her with me sometimes. She loved my hair because it was the same color as hers . . ." I laughed. "I'd always been a short hair kind of guy, but now that she's gone, I wear it long. I dream about her too. I imagine she's some kind of cool angel in heaven explaining football to all the other angels. They're all sitting around eating chicken wings and pizza and watching me play on a big screen." It wasn't like me to open up about my mom. "I didn't mean to get so serious. Ask me something funny."

"I like you when you talk about her. Your face gets all soft." She sighed. "Anyway, have you met her yet?"

"Who?"

"The girl fate has given you?"

"I plead the fifth."

"Oh."

I swept my gaze over her, taking in the V-neck of her gray shirt. It seemed simple enough with its funny logo, but the shoulders had been cut out and some kind of lacey material had been sewn onto the sleeves and hem.

"Did you make your shirt?"

She looked surprised. "How did you know?"

"Honestly, it was just a guess. It doesn't look like anything I've seen. I like it."

Another nonchalant shrug with a whole lot of *meh*.

She didn't even care that I was impressed with her.

I wanted to push her. "It's obvious you're a talented girl—but can you kiss me without getting all hot and bothered? Right now." I had no idea what I was doing or saying. I was acting on pure instinct.

She glanced at the tables next to us and then came back to me. No one paid us any attention. "You want to do another 'elevator scene'? I thought we agreed on no more kissing."

I shook my head. "Agreements are made to be broken."

What the hell was I doing?

"Here?"

"I dare you."

A hint of steel grew on her face. She'd taken the bait. She stood up, brushed her palms down her tight jeans, and covered the distance between our chairs with two steps.

I stood up to meet her. Her palms touched my chest, those eyes of hers burning a hole through me—or maybe it was the other way around.

Her lips met mine with a soft press and then immediately retreated, but no way was I letting her get out of this. My hand curled around her waist and squeezed. A soft nip, the slide of my hand in her hair . . . and her lips clung to mine.

Yes.

"I guess we should, um, sit down now. People are probably staring," I murmured as we eased back to take a breath. Honestly, I didn't give a fuck who was watching. I just didn't know what to say.

She swallowed, her hands sliding down from where she'd curled them around my neck. She played with a strand of my hair, a soft look on her face. "Yeah."

But neither of us moved to separate.

In the background someone got up to the microphone to read a poem, bringing us back.

We sat down as the waitress approached our table. Her name was Cyndi, and she'd been flirting with me unabashedly since the moment she'd shown us our seats and taken our order. I also noticed she'd undone a few of the buttons on her white shirt since the last time she'd made a pass by us. "How was the food?" She directed her attention to me.

"Great," I replied, indicating our empty plates. I glanced back at Sunny. "You want anything else?"

She shook her head.

"We'll just take the check," I murmured to Cyndi.

Her red lips slid into a knowing smile. "Are you sure there's *nothing* else I can get you?" She giggled.

Okay. This was weird. I focused back on Sunny. "Dessert?"

"No," she said, her face tight as she took in the waitress.

Cyndi sashayed off.

"You've slept with her, haven't you?" she muttered as soon as Cyndi was out of earshot.

My brows knitted. *Where was the sweet girl I'd kissed?* "It's not like I've screwed every girl on campus."

"But she was one of them. There's probably more than just her in here that you've slept with . . ."

My lips flattened. "I *did* fuck her. Once. But I was single and so was she. Not every guy is like Bart. When I care about someone, it's all about them—because there's only a handful of people I've ever cared about to begin with. I don't throw away and squander relationships. My mom taught me to treat women with respect because she never got that from my dad. I don't lie. If it's just to get off, they understand what I want. Got it?"

She rubbed her forehead. "I'm sorry. I—I overreacted. It doesn't matter if you slept with her." She paused. "You never said what happened to your mom."

My heart dropped at the memory. "She died of a brain aneurysm the summer before I started college. We were on vacation—in North Carolina actually."

Her face paled. "You must have been devastated."

Yeah. It had been a wonder I'd been able to throw a complete pass my freshman year, but somehow I'd channeled all that emotion and feeling into football.

She reached across the table and grasped my hand. My thumb brushed hers, lingering.

Cyndi chose that moment to return with our check, giving me a clear view of her cleavage as she leaned down to give it to me. I ignored her, but Sunny still pulled back. I noticed Cyndi had slipped a piece of paper under the check with her phone number on it, but I pretended like I didn't see it when I placed cash on top and handed it back. Her eyes darted to Sunny, a spiteful look there.

We gathered our things and headed out the door into the fall evening. We started walking to the parking lot a couple of blocks over, and without even knowing how it happened, we were holding hands again.

"What are you doing tomorrow night?"

Her face split into a grin. "Pulling down swan wallpaper in my bedroom. The former owners of the house had a thing for birds."

"Nice," I said. "I'm coming over to help you."

"Don't you have practice?"

"I'll come after and bring dinner. You like sushi?"

"I love it," she murmured, "but that sounds like too much trouble for you. You don't get finished until late, and you'll be exhausted. I can cook something if you want. Everyone says my lasagna—"

"No. Don't go to any trouble for me. You have enough going on with work. I'm bringing dinner. It's a date."

She blinked up at me. "Okay."

Wait.

Was I dating my fake girlfriend?

Nah. I pushed that thought away. We were just friends.

chapter FOURTEEN

Sunny

"HE HAS MORE muscles in his back than I have in my whole body," I told Isabella as we had lunch Wednesday at the hotdog place in the Student Center.

"Let me get this straight: you had Max Kent half-naked in your bedroom and didn't try to nail him?"

"He was helping me pull down wallpaper. It wasn't exactly romantic."

She waved her hands around. "He's the hottest quarterback in the history of Georgia. It's imperative you go to pound town. You can tell your grandchildren someday . . . you can write your memoirs. More importantly, you can tell *me* about it." She dunked a French fry in her ketchup and popped it in her mouth. Tall with long raven hair, a snub nose, and sparkling blue eyes, she was a striking combination of pretty and sass. "I don't get it. You're fake-dating the hottest guy on campus, and you're not having sex. You are crazy."

"We're friends. It's nice."

"What's nice is the way he fills out his uniform."

"Can't disagree with you, but there's more to him than just being a jock."

"What?" she sputtered. "Are you actually admitting that you might *like* him?"

Before I could answer, a tall guy with a slightly graduated Mohawk sauntered to our booth and looked pointedly at Isabella. "Hey," he said with one of those male chin nods.

She started. "Why, hey . . . there . . . you. I didn't expect to see you so soon." She sent me a pleading glance. "Um, this is the guy I was telling you about. *From the frat party.*"

Oh. Her one-night stand from a few weeks ago. I smiled up at him, noticing his blush. He *liked* her.

I stuck my hand out, knowing full well Isabella was in a quiet tizzy over there while cramming in her hot dog. She didn't do repeat performances or speak to her one-night stands again.

"I'm Sunny." I shook his hand and checked him out. With the buzzed hair and gauges in his ears, he wasn't her usual. I recalled her explanation earlier of exactly *where* he was pierced and did my best to keep my eyes off his crotch.

He sent me a warm smile, his teeth white and straight. Tall with plenty of muscle, he looked athletic—of course I would notice. He was hot, especially with his square-cut face and whiskey-colored eyes.

"I'm Ash."

"You having lunch?" I was filling in the gaps because Isabella was not helping. She was too busy staring a hole through her half-eaten hotdog.

"I was just on my way out actually and wanted to say hi." He shifted his backpack on his shoulder, his eyes roving back to Isabella.

Hmm. Did I know him? Leland was small, and he was definitely memorable enough that I wouldn't forget him.

"Are you new here?"

He nodded. "Just transferred in from North Carolina. I don't know a lot of people yet, but I met Nicole here at the frat party a few weeks back."

Nicole? I glared at Isabella, but she just chewed faster, cramming fries in and then sucking down her Coke. That little liar.

I glanced back at Ash. "Well, it's nice to meet you. And I'm from North Carolina too—so yeah."

He continued to stand there.

And my goodness, my heart couldn't take it. He didn't know anyone and here he was being ignored by his one hookup.

I went with my gut, based on the openness of his face and the easy way he smiled. "Um, this is kinda random, but I'm in charge of a study group that meets at the library sometimes. Tonight's the first meeting of the semester. Would you like to come?"

"Sure, that would be great." He smiled broadly, a pleased expression on his face.

Isabella muttered under her breath.

"Did you say something, Isa—*Nicole*?" I asked.

"Nothing but *yay*." She shook her hands like she was holding pom-poms.

I smirked. Inviting him was a bit reckless considering she obviously didn't want anything to do with him. Maybe it was because I knew how hard it was to make friends when you hadn't started here as a freshman. I knew exactly how it felt to feel alone. Mimi and Isabella were all I had.

We exchanged numbers, and he left saying he had to get to class.

As soon as he was out of earshot, Isabella flew at me. "I am going to kill you." She yanked out her purse and began to reapply her lipstick.

I smiled. "You'll actually have to have a conversation with someone who's had their appendage in you."

She pointed at me. "You, my dear, have no right talking to me about pushing guys away. We both have relationship issues so don't be trying to fix me."

Ugh. She was right. Whatever.

A few minutes later, Bianca walked into the restaurant with Felix by her side.

Stuck like glue, Felix's hand was tucked in her back pocket to keep her close. She laughed up at him when he said something, and I had to admit, they looked good together, her dark to his light. A bulky guy with clipped dark hair and scruff on his jawline, he was attractive—but sweaty. "Why does he look so shiny? He practically glows with sheen."

Isabella followed my eyes and shrugged. "Word is he works out all the time. Trying to be better than Max, I suppose." She sent me a considering glance. "FYI: beware of Bianca. Felix is just her latest. Word is she still wants the number one quarterback. I don't want you to get hurt, Sugartits."

Yeah. Neither did I.

My eyes went to Bianca's leopard-print miniskirt and frilly black shirt. She looked more like a model than a student. I gazed down at my denim shorts. I really needed to ramp up my sexiness—especially before the home game this weekend. I hadn't been able to attend the first one this past weekend because of work, and it was making Max antsy that I wasn't in the stands watching him play—like a good girlfriend should.

As if she knew what I was thinking, Isabella chimed in with her opinion. "You need to wear something slutty to the next game."

"You offering to let me in your closet?" I grinned.

"I am the best."

I laughed and tossed a French fry at her. She tried to catch it with her mouth, making me giggle harder.

Bianca swept her eyes over at us, as if our shenanigans annoyed her. A sneer curled on her face as she went from me to Isabella.

Isabella flipped her off, and I laughed.

But underneath the table, my hands tightened. Yeah. I was feeling possessive of Max, and no way was I going to let her outdo me at the game. I definitely needed to go shopping . . .

chapter
FIFTEEN

Max

"**G**REAT GAME LAST weekend." The pretty, twenty-something assistant smiled up at me as she led me into the Athletic Director's office Wednesday afternoon.

She indicated I sit in a roomy leather armchair, her eyes brushing appreciatively over my frame as I settled in. "Dr. Carmen will see you in just a minute."

"Great." As usual, I hid my nervousness behind a cool smile.

As soon as Coach Williams had called me this morning and asked me to meet him here, I'd gotten clammy, my nerves itching at me and making me antsy. For the life of me, I couldn't figure out what the hell I'd done wrong. No one got called to the AD unless it was bad news.

I rolled my neck to relax, my gaze checking out the heavy wood furniture, dark blue velvet drapes, and expensive gold medallion wallpaper. I took in framed photos of Dr. Carmen with past players, NFL players, MLB players, and even President Obama. I grew tenser. The place reeked of money and power. It had nothing to do with football, yet it was the place where big decisions were made. This is the office that hired Coach.

The door opened and three people entered. One was Coach Williams, who sent me a stern eye—pretty much his standard *I see you there, player,* which he gave us at any given moment. A tough and burly fellow from Alabama, he'd been at Leland for ten years and hadn't had a bad season—although he hadn't had a National Championship either. In his fifties, he was completely bald and wore it like he didn't give a shit. I respected him a lot.

In contrast, Dr. Carmen was a slim guy in a pricey suit and a pretty tie. Like most of the administrators here, he carried himself with poise and a ready smile. A politician. He reminded me of my father.

The one person I didn't recognize was a middle-aged lady in a beige pantsuit. "Ah, there he is," said Dr. Carmen as I rose up to greet them. I mumbled something about how it was nice to see him again, although I couldn't remember the last time I'd actually laid eyes on him unless it had been the spring athletic banquet. He didn't mingle with the regular folk.

We shook hands and he turned to the woman. "I'd like to introduce you to Millicent Walton. She's going to be your PR person for the next few weeks."

My brow wrinkled. "Oh?"

He slapped me on the back and laughed. "Hey, don't look so surprised. Everyone's tapping you as a finalist for the Heisman—especially after that game against Whitman this past weekend—damn, son, you're racking up the stats."

We'd won all three games of the season so far. I nodded and said something about it being a team effort.

Millicent shook my hand with a firm grip. She was a petite thing with short blond hair, and when she spoke her voice was smooth as silk, her smile direct, and eyes warm.

"I'm honored to be working with you, Max. I'm an LU alumni myself."

"Have a sit, have a sit," Dr. Carmen said, waving his hands around, seeming anxious to get started.

"Okay." I sat back down after making sure Millicent had found a seat.

Carmen reclined back in his fancy leather chair, steepled his hands on his desk, and considered us. "First of all, let me say that Leland is thrilled to have this kind of attention on the university. We've never had a Heisman winner, and it's an incredible honor to even have it whispered. Of course, last year there was some brief talk of the award, but it never panned out." He inhaled sharply. "But *this year* the hype is bigger, and Millicent is here to facilitate a smooth football season for you. She'll be helping you with your image issues."

"I don't need a babysitter, sir."

"I agree," Coach said curtly. "He needs to focus on the game—not the reward. It's a team sport—not just a Max Kent game."

Dr. Carmen shrugged and grimaced. "This isn't an option, gentlemen. This is coming from Dean Wood."

Oh. The head honcho of the university.

He turned to Coach and tapped his finger on the desk, the hollow sound echoing in the room. "I know you want a championship. I do too. This—*Kent*—will get us there. I promise." His eyes narrowed. "And it goes without saying that every play is crucial. Kent needs to rack up his stats. We'll need your help with that."

Coach's jaw tightened and his face flushed.

I tensed. Shit. Dr. Carmen was mucking with his team.

"I need your support," Dr. Carmen said again, his voice light as a feather, yet I sensed the tension in the room. "Do I have it, Coach?"

"You're the boss," Coach said, his eyes flat.

There was an entire undercurrent of politics going on here, and I was right in the middle of it.

"What exactly do you have in mind?" I asked, leaning forward. I didn't like the hold he had over Coach, but I kept my face calm. I was in. The Heisman *was* my fucking dream.

Dr. Carmen smiled tightly. "First and foremost, don't screw up. It's no secret you're a bit of a hothead on the field, but the key is keeping it where it belongs and not in the locker room or in public," he added.

He meant Felix.

He acted like I got in tussles all the time—it was *one* incident.

"To get to the top, you need to be exceptional in every way," he said.

I lifted my hands. "I am." I wasn't bragging.

"Right, right. I know you have the 3.7 GPA and you're pre-med; you respect your teachers and do your work. But you need more." He nudged his head at Millicent, who'd been listening intently, her head slightly cocked as she watched me like a hawk. Assessing me like I was a science experiment.

"That's where I come in," she said with a confident little bob of her head. "If you agree to my services, I'd like to get started now." She gave me an expectant look.

I nodded and settled back as she pulled out a pad of paper from her bag. "Our main focus is your image. Today, let's talk about your personal relationships, your family, and of course I'd love to set you up with some volunteering opportunities such as St. Jude Hospital or a shelter of some sort. Is there a particular charity you're interested in?"

I answered back with a couple that my mom had been involved in, and she jotted down everything at a furious pace. In the meantime, Coach mumbled something about needing to get back to the office. He wasn't happy.

Dr. Carmen said goodbye to me and followed him out.

"What about your father?" Millicent asked after we'd covered the fact that I had little to no family around me.

I stiffened. "We don't talk much."

Her face softened. "I understand strained relationships, but for the sake of the award, perhaps we could arrange a photo opportunity for the fans and media after one of the home games? I suggest an easy game—homecoming?"

I shrugged and gritted my teeth. "Sure."

She smiled. "Great. And according to your social media—which is very clean by the way, nice job—you now have a girlfriend . . ." she shuffled through her notes and then glanced up at me. "Sunny Blaine?"

I nodded, getting anxious. "Yes. You're not, like, investigating her, right?"

"Girlfriends are good as long as the relationship isn't volatile. Don't forget there are pesky little camera phones everywhere—so no public altercations, please. Careers have been ruined with video footage of players abusing their significant others."

I cringed. Fuck. I'd never hit Sunny. I'd never hit Bianca no matter how many times she'd egged me on.

She continued. "I've quite enjoyed the pics you've posted of you and her. She looks good next to you—a tall blonde. Nice choice," she said in a matter-of-fact tone as if I'd picked her out at the Girlfriend Store.

Which wasn't too far off from the truth.

I wondered what I would have done if she'd said Sunny was bad for my image.

She ran through a list of things I shouldn't do, which in college-boy terms pretty much meant not drinking, using drugs, or getting in fights. In other words, don't be a shithead. I agreed. Easily.

She also suggested I get a haircut, and I refused. After I explained why I'd let it grow out, she smiled and scribbled it down. "Great material," she said.

Her attention to my personal life was enough to make me jumpy. Hell, I was no saint. Obviously. But they sure expected me to be.

After exchanging times and dates for another meeting in a week, the session was adjourned.

I let out a sigh of relief and turned to open the door for her but stopped at her next words.

"Of course, it's hardly my business what your future plans are, but if you have an *inkling* that Sunny is going to be in your future, perhaps this might be the perfect opportunity to take it a step further. Like an engagement?" Her voice was hopeful.

I had suggested the very same thing way back in the beginning when I'd first met Sunny, but when she nixed it I let it go.

Millicent bit back a smile. "You should see your face. You went white—which means, I guess, that a wedding is off the table."

"Uh, yeah."

Disappointment showed on her face and her shoulders slumped. "Oh well, it was worth a shot. People love a good romance, and you two are beautiful together." She made a *pffft* noise. "Ignore me. Wishful thinking on my part."

But I couldn't ignore her.

Her words lingered long after I'd left that office. They'd replayed in my head a thousand times before I'd even driven home.

A wedding . . . people love it.

My gut had been telling me the same thing since I'd first met Sunny and suggested the fiancée thing. I headed home, changed into some athletic shorts and a tank, and went for a run. I ran all the way to the football field and just stood there on the fifty-yard line looking up at the stadium.

I was on a precipice and everything I'd ever wanted dangled right under my nose.

What was I willing to do to get it?

chapter SIXTEEN

Sunny

I WAS FEELING dead on my feet as I stood at the sink doing dishes after I got home from the library study group. It was past ten and I still had homework to do, but my mood was good despite being tired. Mimi was feeling well after a check-up at the doctor for her flu shot, and I'd aced a quiz in A&P that morning. Studying with Max had helped—which was surprising considering how distracting he was. I washed another glass and set it on a towel to drain.

We'd gone to the Student Center yesterday—just to be seen. He'd paraded me around, right through throngs of girls ogling him and even some guys. We shopped in the Tiger Bookstore, and when the checkout girl had flirted with him, he'd completely ignored her. He'd only had eyes for me.

But it wasn't real.

Maybe he was already sleeping with someone on the side.

He *was* a virile guy. And gorgeous. I couldn't imagine him not getting laid left and right.

A creaking noise came from the small back porch adjacent to the kitchen. I stopped washing and turned my gaze there, peering through the small window over the sink. It normally had a clear view of the porch, but it was dark and I didn't have a light out there.

There had been a cat out there one night in the neighbor's yard eating from their dog's dish. Maybe it had ventured to my back porch.

I headed over to the table to go through my backpack and work on my notes.

The sound came again, a scratching sound. Chills ran down my spine. Immediately my eyes went to the door to make sure it was locked. It was.

But was the front?

I dashed through the house in my socks, nearly slipping in the hallway when I collided with the entry table that had come with the house.

It wasn't.

Crap.

I flipped the deadbolt and went back to the kitchen, heart thundering. There'd been some recent muggings close to campus, but that was several blocks from here, yet unease lingered. What if someone had been watching me at the window the entire time? What if they knew I lived alone?

I turned off the inside light, and with my phone in hand I peeked out the window again, this time squinting and taking in every single detail I might have missed before. I saw my blue garbage can, sitting where it normally does until pick-up day on Friday. There was an old washing machine out there that the landlord had yet to carry off. It wasn't worth much judging by the rust. Neither were the dead houseplants I'd set out when I moved in. A white cat was next door, eating out of the neighbor's dog dish. And there you go. That was the culprit . . .

My eyes went further out, and that's when I saw it—something white hanging on one of the porch posts. A note? Probably something the landlord left. I had sent him an email earlier that I was going to repaint the kitchen next. He'd mentioned something about giving me a check for paint.

I really should go get the check.

The noise had more than likely been the cat next door.

Okay, go get it then, smarty-pants.

I grabbed a heavy-duty flashlight—just in case I needed to whack someone over the head—and eased out onto the rickety porch.

I raced to the post, snatched the white thing, ran back inside, and locked the door.

It was a long white envelope with my name scrawled across the front.

I tore it open, but there was no note—just a long-stemmed daisy. With a frown, I twirled it around in my fingers. Soft and delicate with white petals and a spongy yellow center, it was pretty and delicate . . . and my professor landlord had definitely *not* sent it.

Was it Bart? He'd sent me several bouquets last spring after we'd broken up, but I'd either turned them away or given them to friends. I paused, recalling my conversation at lunch with Isabella.

Wasn't she going to a hump-day party tonight at the Tau house, Bart's frat?

I called her. "Hey. Can you tell me if Bart's there?"

A pause. "Uh . . . have you lost your mind? He cheated on you."

I waved her off even though she couldn't see me on the phone. "Someone left a daisy on my back porch just now. I want to make sure it wasn't him."

"Okayyyy, let me find the bastard." I heard her walking around the frat house, opening doors. Someone yelled at her in the background and she giggled. "Oops. Sorry. Go back to fornicating." A door shut.

And so I waited.

A few minutes later, she ventured out to the dance floor, and I heard her pushing and shoving her way through couples dancing to an Adele song. "Bart the Asshole! Where are you?"

I giggled.

Sure enough, she found him wrapped up with a girl on the dance floor. She covered the phone, muffling the sound, but I heard his disgruntled voice telling her to fuck off.

She got back with me. "He's been with her all night, Sunny. I saw them together on campus today too. Maybe Bart has finally moved on."

So it wasn't Bart, unless he'd gotten someone to do it, and that just seemed scary and way out of character. *It wasn't him.* He'd own it. He'd want me to know he was trying to get me back.

Isabella offered to come over and sit with me if I was scared, but she sounded a bit loaded; plus she'd ridden with her roommate.

"Are you okay?" she asked.

"It's just weird."

I told her goodbye, sat on my bed, and looked out the window at Max's house. His bedroom light was on, so I texted him.

Thank you for my gift.

No response.

Hello? I typed. *Are you there?*

I didn't get you a gift. Sorry. What did you get?

Dammit. I really wished it had been from him. I typed, *Someone left a daisy on my back porch inside an envelope with my name on it. It's strange.*

Are you scared?

Maybe, I texted.

Want me to come over? Warning: I sleep in the nude.

I giggled, already feeling lighter. *What makes you think you are spending the night?*

Someone left you a creepy flower. I'm staying the night there or you're staying here.

He was right. I didn't want to be alone.

I can sleep on the couch, he offered. *But I know you want me in your bed, Cookie. Don't lie.*

I pictured his long and muscular frame draped over my small apartment sofa. Guilt flew over me.

Hello?

Just shut up and come over, I said.

chapter
SEVENTEEN

Max

I'D BEEN GOING over notes in bed when I got her text. I jumped up and threw on some shorts and a shirt.

"Where ya going?" Tate asked from the couch where he was sitting with Kiki, a girl from one of his classes. They were watching a horror flick.

"Someone left something weird—a daisy—at Sunny's. Going to check it out."

He arched a brow. "Want me to tag along?"

I looked at his arm around Kiki and the way her fingers had drifted to his thigh. Yeah. They'd be in his bedroom soon.

"Nah. If you hear me scream though, come on over."

I ran across the street, but before knocking on her door I jogged around back to check things out using my phone as a flashlight. Everything seemed fine. I stalked back to the front and checked the Land Cruiser, making sure she'd locked it. I exhaled, sweeping the dark street. Nothing moved. Whoever had left the gift was long gone.

I knocked and she opened the door wearing a pair of Minion pajama shorts and holding a hammer.

I laughed.

"I know," she said sheepishly. "I never should have texted you. It's silly. I hope I didn't wake you up."

I was tired. Football and then training had kicked my ass—but it was worth seeing her in those pajamas.

"Nope. I was up."

She smiled and opened the door wider, letting me pass and get a whiff of her fresh scent.

I plopped down on the couch and she sat next to me. She walked me through hearing the noise and then finding the flower, explaining how Bart was at his frat party tonight.

"Maybe it was the kid next door," she said, yawning. "I see her out playing outside all the time. She knows my name, too."

Maybe. I made a mental note to keep a sharper eye out for her house.

We settled into the couch further, and I lifted my hand and trailed it through her hair. Her head drifted closer until it rested in the crook of my arm. I caressed her head, massaging her scalp as she told me about her day. Little stuff. She'd dreamed up a name for a future boutique—Bend the Trend—and she'd been reading for her Lit class. I didn't ask about Bart. I refused to think about him being in a class with her where I wasn't around. I refused to acknowledge why it made me jealous.

I told her about Felix and how he got on my nerves because he was constantly watching me when I trained—as if trying to suss out how to beat me or how to play me somehow.

Half an hour later, her breathing grew deeper and her head lolled around on my shoulder. She'd fallen asleep. I grinned. We hadn't even turned the television on.

I scooped her up and carried her to her room where I checked out the queen-sized bed. Sweet baby Jesus, I'd take up the whole damn thing.

She didn't ask you to stay the night, I reminded myself.

Right.

This wasn't a booty call; this was *me* being a *friend*.

I pulled back the soft white duvet, laid her inside, and pulled the covers over her. She snuggled down into her pillow. I sat there, watching her. Long strands of white-blond hair were spread everywhere.

I should go.

She grabbed my hand as I got up to leave. "Stay."

"Why?"

"I don't know . . . because I want you to. And I trust you."

Those words hammered at my heart. Trust. She trusted me. My heart raced because I knew it hadn't come easy.

"I have to sleep naked," I murmured, already pulling my shirt off by reaching behind my neck and slipping my head through. I pushed my shorts down, kicked them to the side, and stood there in my black athletic boxers. "But I'll keep my underwear on . . . just so you don't have a heart attack at the enormity of my package."

She snorted, her gaze flitting over my crotch. "Whatever. It looks rather small to me."

"You're lying, and I will pay you back." I jumped in the bed, my size and weight dislodging her and making her flop around. I stuck my cold feet to her backside and she yelped and scuttled to the other side.

"Hey! Not fair. Just when I had it all warm," she protested, her body hanging on the edge of the bed trying to escape.

"Come back and I'll keep you toasty." I reached over, wrapped an arm around her, and tugged her until her back was aligned with my chest.

"Mmm," she said, her bottom wiggling into my crotch, making me bite my bottom lip. *Fucccccccck.*

"You feel perfect. My little heater." She sighed.

"Uh-huh." I sucked in a sobering breath. My balls ached. I closed my eyes and swallowed down the growl in my throat. One good hard squeeze from her soft hand and I'd come all over the place.

"You sure this is okay?" she asked. "You seem tense."

"Yeah, I'm golden, Cookie," I croaked. She no doubt felt my erection, but being the sweet girl she was, she was going to ignore it and not comment.

She yawned. "I'm glad you came. Now I can sleep."

Perfect. I put her to sleep.

" . . . long night at work. I had to put books in the basement . . . place gives me the creeps. I hate closed off spaces . . . and spiders, as you well know. There's one living in this room somewhere, by the way. I haven't found him yet . . ." she yawned again.

"So you told me earlier. I'm here to keep you safe," I murmured, brushing at the hair on her shoulders. I sighed, feeling oddly content. My fingers twisted some of her hair and pulled it off her neck to see more of her skin. The tattoo I saw was surprising, although I don't know why. Maybe it was because it didn't exactly fit with the quiet image she portrayed.

I studied it. Small blue feathery angel wings framed the back of her nape, from where her hairline started to where her neck met her shoulders. Written in delicately scripted letters were the words, *She wore her scars like wings.*

Tightness gripped my chest.

Protectiveness rushed through me. I tucked her in closer and pressed a kiss to her neck. As long as she was with me, they'd be no more scars.

chapter
EIGHTEEN

Max

I EASED OFF the bike seat, football on my mind. Tonight was a home game against number one ranked Louisiana Lafayette. We had to win.

"Nervous?" Tate asked as I came in the house through the back door. He noticed every twitch of my hand and shift in my mood, which is what made us such a good duo on the field.

I nodded. "Stupid, right? I've played a hundred times, but—it always gets to me."

He handed me his Newcastle. "We're going to win."

"I like your confidence, man." I took the bottle. "Here's to taking down number one."

They'd beat us last year—mostly because of me. I'd thrown two interceptions during the last quarter and our offense had never recovered.

We wandered around the house to the front porch, and I checked out Sunny's place. Sure enough, the Land Cruiser wasn't there, which meant she was still at work. The body shop had ordered a new front end for her and it was taking longer than normal to fix. I couldn't say that it bothered me. I liked her depending on me.

Tonight, for the first time, Sunny would be at a game, and I had a kick-ass plan ready to get me over the top with the Heisman.

My stomach flopped around, anxiousness rumbling.

She was going to be angry. I could feel it . . . taste it. Hell, it permeated the air around me.

I shook it off.

Focus on you. *What you want.*

Sometimes you have to play dirty to get what you want.

An hour later I came out of my room dressed in brown slacks, a pale blue button-down, and a navy blazer. My long hair was everywhere. I wouldn't put it up until the game. It was typical for the players to dress up before and after game, especially since Sports Center was hosting game day.

Tate checked me out with a critical eye, raking his gaze up and down.

"Irresistible enough for you, Mr. Fashion Critic?" I said and held my hands out.

"It's missing something . . ." He snapped his finger. "I've got it. One word: bowtie."

"Dude. It's fine," I called after him as he jogged to his room.

He came back in the kitchen with a myriad of bowties, most in crazy colors and patterns.

I sent him a look. "Seriously?"

He waved that thought away. "I think this one. Very Renaissance man."

"Do you think she'll say no tonight?" I asked, looking down at the one he held up for me. Navy with white checks, it was the least offensive one to my more manly tastes. I took it from him.

He grinned. "No clue, man, but you're crazy if you don't hit that—"

My hackles rose. "Ease off."

"Whatever. I could have her if I wanted. Girls can't resist me when I pour on the *bloody* accent."

"Shut up." I dug my finger into his shoulder and pushed him against the wall. A picture of the team that a groupie had hung when we moved in fell to the floor and shattered.

He pulled away, brows drawn together. "What the fuck-all? It was a joke."

I ran both hands through my hair. "Sorry. Just don't talk that way about her."

"You've been off for a while, mate. Since you met Sunny." He grabbed a broom and dustpan to clean up the mess. "You're into this girl."

My lips tightened, and I pivoted and stalked away from him, landing in the hall in front of the mirror. I popped my collar and adjusted the tie. Tate was wrong, and tonight would prove it. The only thing I was into was football.

chapter
NINETEEN

Sunny

THE DAY OF the game arrived.

I picked up Mimi in the Land Cruiser and then stopped to grab Isabella before we headed to the stadium. Since Isabella's ticket was for the student section, she went off to hang out there while Mimi and I took primo seats on the first row near the forty-yard line.

Mimi got settled, crossing her jean-clad legs, and fussed with her lipstick. She glowed with excitement. "Did you get your hair done this week?" I asked, noticing she'd covered the gray that she sometimes got in the part of her hair.

She preened. "It's not every day you get such great seats. Of course I got my hair did."

I rolled my eyes.

"Things must be going well between you and Max," she commented.

"He's . . . amazing." He'd given me his car, he's paid me up front for being his fake girlfriend, and he'd kept his hands to himself. And he'd spent the night with me. It had been incredible.

So why was I feeling anxious?

She sent me a mischievous grin. "Remember, if you want to keep a man, you gotta keep him focused on your assets."

"Which is?"

"Your brain, dear, your brain. Get your mind out of the gutter." She gazed around at the crowd with a satisfied grin. "Now point me to where I can get something to wet my whistle. Back in my day, they didn't sell alcohol at a football game."

While she waved down the drink vendor, I did a quick outfit check.

The dark blue dress (a Leland color) I'd borrowed was a bit over the top for a game, but I wanted to look good for Max. Isabella had plucked it from her closet, dangled it under my nose, and declared it was the *one*. Short and tight, it was made from one hundred percent silk and had peek-a-boo cut-outs near the bust and waist that hinted at my pale skin underneath. I finished the look with leopard-print stiletto slingbacks. Isabella's as well since there never seemed to be time to go shopping.

One thing about having an eye for art is I knew how to apply makeup even though I rarely wore it. Today I'd used a heavy hand. My foundation had perfect contouring, with emphasis on my high cheekbones and straight nose. I'd been told my best feature was my gray eyes, so I'd played them up with hues of blue. Eyeliner created a tasteful wing effect, and I'd filled in dramatic eyebrows. A nude lip-gloss finished it. My long hair had been straightened until it hung in a shiny waterfall down my back, contrasting vividly with the dress. This was my first big public appearance, and I hoped I looked like the kind of girlfriend Max Kent would have. I'd been relieved to see several eyes watching us as we walked down the stadium steps to our section.

Of course they're probably just wondering who got those fantastic seats.

Dressed in their gray and blue uniforms, our team jogged from the inner part of the stadium, and the home crowd went nuts. Mimi and I jostled to our feet to do the wave along with everyone else.

I watched Max's number seventeen jersey as he stood on the sideline going over plays with the quarterback coach.

The game got off to a rocky start with Louisiana scoring before we had points on the board. I chewed on my thumbnail, caught up in the action, hoping Max came up with a big play soon. When the other team scored again, I watched him pace on the sidelines, his posture wired.

At halftime Mimi elbowed me in the ribs and nudged her head at the Jumbotron. I planted a smile on my face and waved. The camera swung away but not before I saw Bianca sitting a few rows back with her sorority sisters, glaring at me.

"Who's the girl giving you the evil eye? She looks meaner than a striped snake," Mimi murmured around the rim of her draft beer.

"Max's ex. This was probably her seat last year." I shot a look over my shoulder at her, a glittery pendant around her neck catching my eye. It was a star-studded number seventeen hanging from a gold chain. My teeth ground together.

Who did she think she was still wearing Max's number? What about Felix?

The players headed back out from the locker rooms, and I grew nervous. My hands clenched around my Diet Coke as I tipped it up to take another sip. I chomped on the ice.

Mimi patted my knee that had been vibrating up and down. "Stop your worrying."

I paused. I mean, yeah, I got into a game as much any true fan, but it was more than that. I was emotionally invested in Max.

Max jogged down to the field, heading for his coach. They talked heatedly for a few moments until Coach Williams threw his hands up as if he was done and Max stalked off.

My brow wrinkled. He'd been rather distant the past couple of days leading up to the home game, and I'd assumed it was stress—but this looked different.

Max ran over to a cameraman a few paces away. I took in his face, trying to get a read on him, but he looked almost serene, which was weird during a game.

He stalked over to the barrier that divided the stands from the field and jumped it. The fans went nuts as he brushed past them, some not even realizing it until he was down the aisle. The Jumbotron followed him.

"Good Lordy, what's he doing?" Mimi asked, clutching at her chest.

"I don't know," I said rather weakly, taking the chance to study him the closer he came. He was beautiful, his shoulders impossibly broad. To add to the distraction, his helmet was off and all that dark brown hair was flowing around his chiseled features as if he had a fan in his face.

"He's coming over here," Mimi commented.

He was. But why?

I stopped breathing . . . right when he came to a halt in front of me and knelt down on one knee.

Eyes the color of a wild ocean gazed at me.

He took my left hand in his right one.

"Max," I breathed, my heart fluttering.

He gazed up at me. "Sunny Blaine, will you marry me?"

The stadium went wild. In a daze, I looked up at the Jumbotron and felt like I was watching this happen to someone else. Camera phones flashed all around us.

My first clear thought was *I'll kill him.*

Aloud, nothing came out but a faint wheeze. Clearly someone had stuffed a giant wad of cotton in my mouth. Clearly I needed something a lot stiffer to drink than this Diet Coke. Clearly my fake boyfriend was *a freaking raving lunatic.*

He sent Mimi a grin—as if to say *I really got her, didn't I,* and she handed him a black box. My eyes flared as I looked from her to him. *Had he . . . had she?* Good God, they were in cahoots. Which explained why she'd been jittery when I picked her up earlier. She kept patting the big purse she always carried, and even on the way over to the stadium I caught her poking through it a few times. I'd just figured she was nervous about meeting Max. Apparently they'd already met.

Mimi squeezed my hand. "He called me last night and asked to come over. He asked for my approval . . . can you believe it? What a gentleman. Of course, I said yes. He's a keeper, Sunny." Her eyes glowed. Freaking GLOWED.

The box opened, and my stomach churned at the sight of the large round solitaire diamond ring that was nestled on the black silk. I blinked repeatedly to clear my vision.

With deft fingers, Max eased it out of the lining and slipped it on my left hand.

I stared down at it. Then back at him.

Kiss her, Kiss her, the crowd chanted.

We were the focal point of the entire world.

Max stood and tugged me up with him until we were standing. He slid his hand around my neck and pulled his face to mine. The sky was blotted out as he kissed me.

But I hadn't said *yes*! I wouldn't say *yes*. Not to a fake engagement.

The applause of the stadium was deafening. And his kiss—it was deadly. Despite my rage, my body craved him. His lips were hot, so hot, and my tongue met his with a vengeance. We kissed hard, and I nipped at him, my teeth scraping across his lips. But the only one who'd end up bleeding in this scenario was me.

He eased back to take me in, and with a final look at my face he gave a thumbs-up sign to the entire stadium. They went nuts, chanting his name.

"I'm sorry," he whispered in my ear, letting his hand trail down my arm as he stepped back from me. He walked away backward, eyes on me the entire time. The announcers for the game told everyone who might have missed it that Max Kent had just asked his girlfriend to marry him, and she'd said yes. More cheers came as they replayed him on his knee in front of me with a giant YES written across the top.

I plopped back down in my seat. Frozen.

" . . . did you see her face? Shocked . . ."

" . . . most romantic thing in football . . ."

" . . . luckiest girl in the world . . ."

My face went hot. Even my ears burned. I wanted to crawl under a seat. I felt like such a liar.

"You're gonna be okay, hon. Just take a breath," Mimi whispered as the Jumbotron finally moved away from me. "Don't be embarrassed. It's sweet the way he proposed . . . he wanted everyone to know he'd found the girl of his dreams."

"Is that what he said?" My voice was barely a whisper.

Mimi beamed. "He said the moment he saw you, it was meant to be." She sighed and looked over to him, his back to us as he watched the kick-off on the field. "I've worried so much about you since that Bart fellow, but Max is going to make you happy, Sunny. He's the calm in your chaos."

The calm in my chaos . . .

God.

What a lie.

If I'd thought I was angry before, I was wrong. He'd end up hurting Mimi when the charade ended. She'd be disappointed in me, in him, and her love of football would probably be tarnished.

Didn't he ever think about anyone but himself?

I exhaled. "Mimi, there's something I should tell you . . ."

My phone pinged with a text. Isabella.

OMG. WTH just happened?

Max Kent asked me to marry him, I replied.

DUH. The whole world saw that. I just picked my jaw up off the ground.

I'm going to kill him, I added.

Why?

One word . . . Heisman. I typed out furiously, my fingers flying.

I admit it. I swooned a little. I'll be his fiancée if you won't.

Max threw to Tate in a twenty-five-yard touchdown, but I barely noticed. I seethed.

Come sit with Mimi and take her home after the game. I have to go, I sent her.

Won't it look weird if you leave the game?

His problem, I texted. *I can't stay here.* I was going to cry. Tears pricked at my eyes at his deception, itching to fall, and I knew that once that dam burst, I'd have a hard time explaining why I was so upset.

You're like super popular now. Maybe you can hook me up with one of those hottie football players. Just kidding. Not kidding. Sorry. Not Sorry.

Mimi gasped when our defense caught an interception from the Louisiana quarterback. Our offense came out to the field, snapped the ball, and Max threw it straight to Tate who ran it in for another touchdown. My chest constricted. I didn't care who won. I hated football right now.

A few minutes later, Isabella was sitting in my seat. I told Mimi someone hadn't shown up for their shift at the library, and my boss Pam had texted and asked if I'd come in. It sounded ridiculous, especially since I'd just gotten engaged on national television, but there was no getting around the fact that I had to disengage before I fell apart. Mimi kept asking if I was okay and if she'd done the right thing by not telling me, but I hugged her and assured her my exit had nothing to do with Max and everything to do with picking up extra money, especially if I wanted to plan for a wedding.

I cringed as I told her. Lies made more lies.

Plus, there'd be questions:

When's the big day?

Who are your bridesmaids?

What kind of dress will you get?

An invisible dress because there'd be no wedding!

I walked past the crowd, who eyed me with intense curiosity, and kept my head down. Just as I slipped into the breezeway, I glanced back one more time to see Max on the field again calling a play. Even though hundreds of people stood between us, I felt his intensity.

"That was a pretty little show," came a silky voice in front of me.

I spun around. Bianca.

She did a slow clap and then fluffed her brown hair over her shoulder with blood-red fingernails. Up close, her gray halter top was the perfect complement to her dark complexion, and her matching skirt dripped with blue lace, the same blue as the players' uniforms. My eyes went back to that necklace, and my fingers itched to yank it off her neck.

She sucked her bottom lip through her teeth. "You must have been practicing that look of shock all week. I suspected something from the very beginning, you know . . . especially when I heard him say in class that you guys met at the toga party last year. Max wasn't even at that party. I know because I was."

I stiffened and pivoted around to leave, but her nails dug into my arm.

"Oh no, you're not running off,' she said, her eyes narrowed. "I bet he's paying you. You seem like the type who'd need money. Not that I'd blame you. He's a maniac in the sack, and who can blame you for wanting *someone* to notice you."

"You're babbling," I said quietly. "Can't you just congratulate me, Bianca?"

She scoffed. "I'm not stupid. I *know* Max. All he cares about is football, honey. And if he's asking you to marry him at a game—it isn't because he wants to live happily ever after. It's because he wants the attention. He has to have it all, so much that there isn't room for anything else."

My hand tightened on my purse. "You don't know the Max I know." Why was I defending him?

"I know what he likes, and it isn't sweet little girls like you. He likes his sex hard and his girls harder. You"—her brittle eyes raked over me and found me lacking—"are way too nice for him, and if you're smart, you'll leave before it hurts too much."

"Isn't Felix enough for you?"

"Max is the best, and he only wants the best. Which is me. Here's some info: he'll never be over me. I'll be the one he comes running back to once he gets through with whatever he's got going on with you. You're nothing."

Nothing? I'd pulled myself from hell to be where I was today. I'd lived through a mother leaving me for a man she was having an affair with. I'd lived through my father lashing my back with a belt. She didn't know anything about me.

"You don't know who you're screwing with," I said softly. "I'm not always a nice person. You just have to push me far enough."

Her carefully manicured eyebrow arched. "Then prove me wrong."

chapter TWENTY

Max

I'D FUCKED UP. Big time. My gut screamed the words at me.

" . . . beating the number one team in the country. How does it feel?" The reporter jabbed a microphone in my face, and I refocused. He went on to talk about the rest of the season and the teams we faced.

Sweat still dripped down my face from the last play, and I wiped it with the back of my hand. We'd won the game thirty-five to seventeen. Louisiana had never come back after the half, and we'd crushed them in the last quarter. It was our biggest win so far—but all I could think about was Sunny.

I chatted about the game, my eyes trying to stay on the reporters huddled around me, but my eyes kept darting to the stadium. *Where was she?*

Another journalist eased in front of me, halting my way to the locker rooms. "What can you tell us about your new fiancée? Do you have a date set for the big day? How long have you known each other? Do you think we can get a quick interview with her?"

"She's a sweetheart. For the rest, it's between us. Thank you." I gave her a nod and a cool smile.

Why did I feel sick after winning one of the biggest games of the year?

My stomach churned as I marched down the line of reporters, flash-bulbs and pats of congratulations coming from everywhere.

I searched the stands again. I'd forced myself to keep my attention off her for the rest of the game, but as soon as the game had ended, I'd glanced up and found Mimi sitting next to a sullen girl with black hair. The dark-haired girl had flipped me off and mouthed something that looked like *fuck you*.

Felix's bulky frame stepped in my way as I walked in the doors of the locker room.

"What?" I snapped.

Everyone around us froze, eyes darting as we faced off.

He had these weird eyes—almost navy colored—with a line of white around the pupil. "Just wanted to congratulate you, man. Fans are gonna love that. Smart."

My hands clenched, itching. I didn't trust him. I moved past him to my locker.

"I can't wait to meet her at your party tonight."

I turned around slowly. "Party?"

He worked on getting his pads off. "Dude. Your girl is already planning your life for you and you don't even know it. Your engagement party. Sunny invited the team and whoever else. It's all over Instagram."

Several of the other players agreed, and I nodded, pretending to go along. *Sure. Yeah. Party at my house.*

Not a good idea.

Not when I knew damn well she was angry.

I showered, changed back into my dress clothes, and went with Coach and some of the other first string to hold a small press conference, something we did after each home game.

Coach grabbed my elbow right before we walked out to take our seats. "Be in my office Monday morning, Kent. We have some harsh topics to discuss."

"Yes, sir." I nodded. I'd never in my entire life disobeyed an order from the coach, and he expressly said no when I'd told him I wanted to propose to Sunny at the game.

We took our seats at the table, the school mascot and banner behind us as a backdrop. Lights flashed, reporters popped off questions, and Coach went through them, calling on myself, Tate, and a couple of other first string players to chime in.

An hour later, it was over and Tate and I headed home in his Tundra. Because of all the cars, we were forced to park on a street several houses away from ours. I clenched my teeth and prayed no one called the cops on us.

Sunny had parked my Land Cruiser in the middle of our yard at a crazy angle, the tires mired up in grass and dirt.

We entered the house, and people congratulated us for the win and me for the engagement. Across the staircase, someone had made a hastily scrawled banner with *Congrats on Your Engagement, Max and Sunny.*

I looked around everywhere inside, but no Sunny.

I headed out the back door and made my way through back slaps and fist bumps. Keeping my face cool, my eyes scoured the groups of people congregated around the pool.

I saw Bart—*what the hell was he doing here?* He sent me a dirty look as he talked to a couple of the players. I sized him up, trying to see what she'd seen in him. He was handsome in a poster boy kind of way. Clean-cut. Well dressed. Focused on his goals.

But . . .

All I could see in my head was him being Sunny's first, and then breaking her heart.

He strode toward me, carrying a beer. A petite brunette trailed behind him and he said something to her, causing her to stop following him.

It hadn't taken him long to find someone else, but no way did she measure up to Sunny.

He came to a stop in front of me. His eyes swept over me and his lips compressed. "I don't see what Sunny sees in you. You're an arrogant sonofabitch who thinks he's better than anyone else."

I stiffened, my fists tightening, adrenaline still high from the game. "What do you want?"

He sucked down a drink and glared at me. "Sunny." And then he walked away.

I swallowed, itching to chase after him and hash it out—but why? She wasn't mine. And I couldn't get into any fights. It would ruin everything. I shook myself off, willing myself to cool down and let go of the adrenaline coursing through my veins.

My eyes landed on long blond hair. *Finally.*

She sat with Ryn and the dark-haired girl from the stadium at a patio table near the fence. Thank fuck. I was beginning to think the entire party was payback and she wasn't even going to show.

I made my way over to them, weaving in and out of the crowd.

I halted as she tossed back amber liquid from a shot glass. *Tequila?* Great.

I barreled and elbowed my way through the thick crowd, done being nice to everyone.

"Hey. I found you. You having a good time?" My hand caressed her bare shoulder, but when she stiffened, I let it fall.

She held another shot up in my general direction and tossed it back. Her eyes said, *Bite me.*

"Do you mind if I sit by my fiancée?" I said to Ryn, my face tight.

Ryn held his hands up like *sorry to be in your way* and stood. "Got no clue what's going on. I just sat down to help pour the drinks." He slapped me on the back and leaned down to whisper. "She's had quite a few, friend. Just so you know."

I took his seat, my slack-clad leg brushing her bare one, and she flinched.

I sighed. "Who's your friend?" I indicated the girl next to her.

Sunny shrugged. "She doesn't like you very much right now."

"Go fuck yourself," the girl said sweetly, then came over to my seat and gave me a quick hug, the type you'd give your best friend's fiancé. "That's for them," she said, her gaze encompassing the entire back yard and several who'd been sending us curious glances. Bianca's group was one of those. And Bart who lingered by the fence. Watching.

The dark-haired girl waved at them all and then flipped them off.

Sunny stood up, swaying on her feet until I righted her with my arm.

"We should talk," I said in a low voice so only she could hear.

Her arms crossed. "Fine. Talk."

I felt eyes on us from everywhere. "Not here. Follow me."

She let me lead her to a secluded corner of the yard where fewer people wandered. I turned to her, taking in the hardness around her eyes.

Fuck. I'd put that look there.

She took a deep breath as if gathering her thoughts, and then pointed at the diamond on her finger. "This is a giant lie. Mimi believes it. The whole freaking world believes it—except for Bianca! I never agreed to this. Never." Her lips trembled. "I was just starting to think you were different." She broke eye contact with me, her eyes blinking rapidly. "You aren't the person I thought you were."

Heaviness settled on my chest. "I can explain about tonight—"

She cut me off. "You did it for the Heisman."

I nodded.

"Football will always be first with you."

"Yes," I said softly. "It trumps everything."

With clenched fists, she bit her bottom lip, struggling to compose herself. Her eyes speared me, a look of determination in them. "I'm not going to cry. You aren't worth it. It's just—for a while there—I thought you were different, Max. I was wrong."

Fuck.

"Sunny. I'm . . . I'm sorry you're upset." I took a tentative step closer to her, my hand splayed out. "Tonight could have been the deciding factor for me—"

She shook her head, waving me off as she backed away from me. "Stop talking about yourself and everything you'll gain. *You deceived me.* How far will you go, Max?"

Silence ticked, the tension ramping higher as we stared at each other.

"You're just like Bart," she bit the words out.

The words tore through me. I raked a hand through my hair. "*I am not him."*

Someone cranked up a Rhianna song and she turned further away from me, giving me a view of her stiff back as she searched the yard. She was obviously looking for an excuse to get away from me. I watched as her eyes landed on Bart, lingered for a moment, and then moved on.

God. I swallowed and shoved my hands in my pants. What a total fuck-up this night was. I'd taken her trust and thrown it back in her face, and worst of all, I'd *known* this would be her reaction.

Had it all been for the glory of the Heisman—or was part of me pushing her away, afraid of getting too close? Fuck. I couldn't think straight.

"Tate," she called in a strained voice, waving at him from across the yard. "You're up for the next dance, buddy."

"You're walking away?" I asked and reached out for her, but she stepped back, nearly stumbling. I caught her arm before she fell, straightening her, but she pushed me off, anxious to get away from me. I sighed. "We need to figure this out, Sunny."

"I—I just can't."

She sent me a final look and marched off.

I fumed, watching them go to the pool area someone had obviously designated as a dance floor. A makeshift bar was across from it and someone had even brought a keg. My own house and I had no clue what was going on . . .

The dark-haired girl approached me. "Yeah," she mused. "You screwed up with Sunny, Quarterback."

"Who *are* you?" I snapped.

Critical eyes raked over me. "This is what you need to know, okay? When her dad hit her one too many times, she left. When Bart cheated, she ended them. And now you—trying to pull a sly one *when Mimi is there.* Mimi is all she has left in the freaking world, and you tampered with that. You're going down."

I closed my eyes. She was telling me what I already knew—but now, now it was sinking in.

"And by the way, Isabella's the name. I'm the one looking out for her—which is damn funny since I'd told her to snap you up because she's been lonely. But now I can see your true colors. You don't deserve her."

I scrubbed my face. "You're right," I said. "I didn't think it through—"

She reared back, disgust on every line of her face. "Oh, don't be sorry now. Prepare yourself to be broken up with—oh, probably right after this song."

chapter
TWENTY-ONE

Sunny

TATE AND I danced. He had some crazy kind of hip-hop flair that should have looked ridiculous on his big frame, but it was funny. I found myself laughing more than dancing. It was probably the tequila, but I didn't care at that point. Ash and Isabella joined Tate and I in our circle as we moved to the music. He'd shown up for a couple of library study sessions, and Isabella had immediately apologized about lying to him the night they hooked up. They'd set up a tentative little friendship.

Tate fell on the ground and did a hilarious rendition of the worm.

Yeah, my fake boyfriend had trampled the shit out of my trust, but it was fine 'cause I couldn't feel my face.

A slower country song came on, and Tate and I went with the flow. I stepped into his arms, and he wrapped his forearm around my waist but kept his grip light.

"Love, maybe it's a good idea if we don't dance together." His gruff voice resonated in my ear.

"Why?" I looked up at him. He had a strong jawline, gentle brown eyes, and a killer smile. I got why girls went nuts over him.

"Max's looking a bit wonky." He nudged his head toward a sullen Max, who stood near the pool. A couple of players talked around him, but he watched us.

Tingles of awareness zipped up my spine at his gaze.

He's fine was about to come out of my mouth when I saw Bianca and some of her girlfriends sashay up to him, blocking my view.

My grip on Tate tightened. "He seems to have found some company."

"Maybe, but it's you he wants."

"How do you know?" I said rather sullenly.

He shrugged. "He told me he talked to you about his mum, and he never does that. You might find this hard to believe, but he's a very private person."

"He went behind my back."

Tate thought about it. "All I can say is he isn't thinking straight. He's insane during the season. Football is his world."

"What about Bianca? Does he still care about her?" Might as well pump the best friend for info while I had the chance.

He shook his head, his blond hair waving around like a lion's mane. "Bianca was more of a pride thing because she screwed other players, but with you . . . it's *you*."

I slid my eyes in Max's direction. His jaw flexed as he watched us dance. There was a possessive streak in him, even if we were pretend. I recognized it because I was the same.

Bianca wore a wounded expression on her face as she talked to Max. She held a red Solo Cup, her free hand gesturing around wildly at the party—and over at me. She gazed up at him like a distressed kitten. My lips tightened. *Poor little Bianca, my ass.*

"He could have asked any girl to be his fake fiancée. But he asked you—a random girl he'd never met before." He arched a brow at me. "I adore dancing with you, but perhaps you need to deal with him, love. He isn't going to stop being jealous, and I do have to live with him. Plus, do you really want to let Bianca win this round? She's over there all over your bloke."

I was angry with Max, yet my heart ached for him. Stupid, stupid heart. It didn't know what to do.

But Bianca was an entirely different animal. I despised her.

Was it horrible that even though I couldn't have him, I sure as hell didn't want her to have him?

Making a decision, I said a quick goodbye to Tate and left the dance floor. I edged around the girls as they talked about the game until I faced Max, giving them my back and cutting off whatever Bianca had been saying to him.

He glanced up at me in surprise, and the air thickened with electricity. Relief flickered on his face. "Sunny—"

"*Finally,*" Bianca interrupted. "Here's the happy couple together." She glided closer, her sorority sisters' huddle following as if they were attached at the hip. "Now that you're here, I must congratulate you on the entertainment during the game." Her once distressed look had morphed into something hateful. "You have to know it's very difficult for us to believe, especially since you just started dating."

"Sometimes you just know when you've met the one. I knew the moment I saw him." Truth rang in my voice, but I shoved that away. *Hard.* This was my game now. I came in close to Max and kissed him, pulling back before he could deepen it.

I slanted my eyes at her when I eased back, watching her face flame and enjoying the satisfaction of it. "He's a maniac in the sack, by the way," I added softly. I focused back on my *fiancé.* "This party's crowded. You wanna be alone?"

His arm came around me, his words husky. "I know you hate to leave our own party, but yeah."

Bianca watched us with her hands on her hips. "I don't think so," she snapped, her body stiffening as she tossed her shoulders back. "Don't think you can snub me—"

"He will never be yours, Bianca," I reminded her. "You had your chance and you screwed it up."

Her eyes flashed as her hands clenched at her side, and before I could duck, she splashed the contents of her cup in my face. Beer ran down my nose and to my lips. I wiped at my eyes. My tongue came out to taste the bitterness. I'd never cared for beer.

A hushed pause came over the crowd.

"I think it's time you left *my* party," I gritted.

She scoffed. "You should leave. You don't belong here."

"Enough, ladies, let's keep this civil . . ." Max started, but I held my hand up at him. My eyes told him everything. *You've done enough. Step back, mister.*

He got my message and nodded tightly.

I focused on Bianca. "You're done messing with me and the people I care about."

Max started at my words, but I didn't dare look at him.

She curled her lip. "You barely know him."

I faked a rush, taking two steps toward her and stopping when we were nose to nose. Her eyes flared, and she hobbled backward. Seeing an opportunity, I helped her along with a little shove—just a tiny one. She lost her balance in her ridiculous shoes. With her arms waving like windmills, she toppled straight into the shallow end of the pool.

She came up sputtering, shock on her face as mascara trickled down her cheeks. I watched her flounder, hoping I looked a whole heck of a lot more confident than I really was. I hadn't meant for her to land in the pool, but I'd take it.

"You bitch," she shrieked, her wet hair stringy as it clung to her scalp. "You'll regret this, I swear."

Isabella rushed to my side, Ash and Tate behind her. Isabella's eyes went from Max to me to Bianca. A wide grin split her face and she did a little dance. "Sunny Blaine, you rock." Then she popped her phone out and snapped pics of Bianca.

Someone whooped, and several people jumped in the pool. Within minutes, the water was full of people swimming in their clothes.

Max was looking at me, his face incredulous.

Tate chuckled. "You bloody shocked him into silence."

I tore my eyes off Max's face, my gaze wanting to linger there.

But I couldn't let it.

I leaned against Isabella, my knees week. I was crashing. "I want to go home."

"I'll take you," he murmured, moving to come around to my side.

"No," I said quickly, holding my hand up to stop him from getting too close. Just being near him made me feel sick. Maybe that was the tequila, but either way, I needed space. "I can't."

His lips tightened, looking at the faces of my friends. "Fine."

Isabella crooked her arm in mine, breaking the tension. "I'll make sure she gets home okay and gets cleaned up. Why don't you start throwing out the trash?" Her eyes darted to the pool where a wet Bianca struggled to get out on the ladder. Her sorority sisters had gathered around to pull her up.

"I'll go with them and make sure they get there okay," Ash offered.

I nodded, sent a final look to Max, and walked away.

EVEN THOUGH I'D had the tequila to dull my pain, I was restless that night when I finally crashed. My dreams were filled with images of Max on his knees in front of me.

And my body?

I ached for him.

I got up at eight, feeling off-kilter and exhausted. After two cups of coffee and a Pop-Tart, I was alive enough to shower. After I got out, I glanced out the window, wondering if he was up.

I forced myself to forget about him as I dressed in yoga pants and a T-shirt. I put my hair up in a messy bun and headed out to the Land Cruiser. Max said it was mine for the weekend, and I wasn't going to turn it down, even if I was still angry with him.

There was a note tucked under the windshield wiper blade.

My heart raced at his scrawling handwriting, and I pictured him sitting at his kitchen table late last night, penning it.

Dear Sunny,

I'm a goddam arrogant asshole for assuming you'd be all-in for the fiancée thing.

You hit the nail on the head, buddy.

You've been such a good friend to me, and I ruined it. I got caught up in wanting a big bang, and when the PR person suggested it, I ran with it. I thought about asking you first, but then figured not telling you would make the moment seem more spontaneous. I also thought it would be easier to ask for forgiveness than permission. I was wrong. It was calculated and the only person I was thinking about was myself. If you want to end things now, I get it. I will go to Mimi's and explain everything. You can keep the money, and I will still pay to get your car fixed. Hell, you can still drive my car. I don't want you to be unhappy, and I don't want you to hate me.

I could never hate him.

I don't want to destroy our friendship over this.

Friendship? I wanted to stab that word with a knife.

You're probably asking yourself why we are even friends, and I wonder too why you'd ever want to have anything to do with me again, but the truth is, you make me into the person I've always wanted to be. You don't expect anything from me. I've never met anyone like you, and the thought of losing you makes me feel . . . desperate.

Will you forgive me for asking you to marry me?

When he put it like that, it was hard to stay mad . . .

With Love,

Max, AKA Mr. Quarterback

Ugh. I tucked the letter in my jean pocket.

My phone pinged and I saw it was him.

Hey.

I stared at it. Should I respond or pretend I hadn't seen it?

I see you.

I glanced across the street. There he was on his porch, standing bare-chested and staring a hole through me.

I see you too, I texted.

Can we talk?

I shifted from one foot to the next, staring at him. His hair was a halo of dark around his face, his shoulders slumped and his usual grin absent. He looked a mess.

I don't know. I have a lot to do today. Some of us have to work.

Whatever you're doing, I want to help, was his reply.

I ignored that. *Is the engagement all over the local news?*

Even made Sports Center.

Nice.

FYI, pics of Bianca raging in my pool are all over social media.

Are you mad? I asked.

Hell no.

Good. Because I don't regret it, I typed out.

Can we talk?

There was no use in ignoring him or refusing. I got the feeling Max wasn't the type to give up. But I could make it hard for him. *If you want to spend the day with me, you have to help me paint the trim in my kitchen.*

Done.

And I promised Mimi I'd clean her house today.

Done.

You get toilet duty, I texted.

I peeked up to see his fingers hovering over his phone with a weird expression on his face.

I've never cleaned a toilet in my life, he replied.

I assumed.

But what you don't know is how good I look in rubber gloves, he replied.

I snorted.

Show off your muscles today, was my text back. *Mimi will need the pretty to help her cope when you explain to her how we aren't really engaged. I've been thinking and I want you to tell her everything—from the day Sierra hit my car to where we are now. I want you to be sweet to her and kiss her butt. You need to make it up to her. I suggest you bring a signed football, a jersey with your number on it, and a maybe a bouquet of flowers. Tickets for the rest of the home games wouldn't hurt either. Deal?*

I watched his head came up to take me in. Even though several yards separated us, I felt the intensity of his gaze. He sent me a nod and typed out, *I'll do anything as long as you aren't mad at me anymore. I didn't sleep at all. I've been up since four this morning. I. Am. So. Sorry. Please forgive me.*

Goosebumps flew over my skin. Why was it so hard to stay upset at him? God, I was weak when it came to him.

You know why, Sunny . . .

Put some clothes on, Quarterback. We got chores to do.

I heard his chuckle.

Give me five to mess with my hair. Don't want to disappoint Mimi.

chapter
TWENTY-TWO

Max

"**Y**OU'RE BEING BENCHED for the next game," Coach Williams said when I met with him in his office Monday afternoon after practice. He sat behind a heavy oak desk, framed photos and banners of Leland's winning seasons behind him. I'd put two of those banners up there.

I sat in the hard chair across from him. My lips tightened—but I nodded. "Yes, sir."

Getting engaged hadn't exactly turned out like I'd planned. Yes, the media had eaten up the story, putting me all over the sports news—even the mainstream shows. *Good Morning America* and *The Today Show* had both played the footage this morning. We were the new *it* couple in the media—at least for now. It was good. It kept my name out there, floating around and reminding the voters that not only was I a great player, but I was in love with a sweet girl.

The problem was Coach was angry and Sunny was still weird around me even though we'd mended fences.

Mimi had forgiven me. She'd just watched us as we cleaned her house, those eagle eyes dissecting me until I felt like a bug under a microscope. She'd clapped and laughed like a loon when I cleaned her toilet. Heck, she videotaped it and claimed she was going to post it on Facebook—although I wasn't so sure she knew how to post a video.

And now I was being benched.

"Felix will start when we play Georgia Saturday," he went on to say.

"I understand," I said with gritted teeth. I'd known the possible consequences of my actions and I'd done them anyway.

An expression of sympathy crossed his face. "Son, you're the best player this school's ever had. Don't fuck it up over a girl. The players and the fans will blame you."

Fuck it up? I was trying to have the best year of my life. He didn't know what he was talking about. My PR was eating this shit up, but I didn't remind him of that. It made him angry to think that I was only thinking about myself. "Yes, sir."

After chewing on me for a few more minutes, reminding me of the way last year had veered off course when I'd let Felix and Bianca get to me, he finally ordered me to run miles. I left his office and headed back to the gym where I jumped on the treadmill and hammered out ten miles. Sweat dripped from me as I pushed. And pushed. I had to keep my focus and not get involved with Sunny. There had to be a line between us and I couldn't cross it because once I did, I'd be all-in with her. And I wasn't ready for that. Not yet.

We'd driven to class together this morning. I kept things cool. So did she. Sure, she'd agreed to continue the fiancée charade, but the closeness we'd had was gone. She was back to building a wall between us. I wanted to pull her out of class, take her to an empty classroom, and just . . . talk.

But I didn't.

That week there were no more visits to the Student Center. No more late night study sessions. I did text her each day to make sure there hadn't been any flowers left on her back porch. There hadn't.

I stopped by Mimi's house on Tuesday and Thursday when I was done with practice and knew that Sunny was at work. After texting her to see what her favorite foods were, I brought Italian take-out one night and Chinese the next. I didn't say anything to Sunny about our visits because it wasn't about brownie points. I felt like a heel for involving Mimi in my scheme, and truthfully, hanging out with Mimi wasn't hard work. Hell, she was a sharp lady who liked beer and football.

On game day when Coach announced in the locker room that I wasn't starting because I'd disobeyed him, the entire team glared at me. Felix wasn't me and they knew it. Which is why at the half when we trailed by fourteen, I was dying to get on the field. I needed it. Surely, he hadn't meant for me to sit out the *entire* game? Hell, that was meant for players who'd been arrested . . .

But he'd been angry.

After his pep talk at the halftime break, I went to him, helmet in hand. "Coach, let me fix this. I don't want the entire team to suffer. You're completely right about me, and I humbly apologize. I haven't been focused enough, and I continue to put my own needs before the team."

He studied me with a scowl on his face.

And he walked off.

Fuck.

I gritted my teeth in frustration and walked to the back of the locker room where Felix was getting a shoulder rub from one of the trainers. I sat down next to him on the bench. If I couldn't play, I'd help him.

He glared at me, his lip curling in derision. "Having a bad day, Kent?"

Ignore what an asshole he is. Think about the game. "Dude. You need to snap faster. The defense is eating you up—and keep your eyes on twenty-one. As soon as the ball's snapped, he's reading you like a book—"

"Not your game. It's mine, so back off," he said curtly.

I swallowed my pride, refusing to walk away even when it was clear he wasn't going to listen.

"Whatever issues we have, you need to let it go. Take my advice . . . please. I have the experience, and I know where you're screwing up."

"It's not your game," he bit the words out like bullets.

I clenched my fists. "I don't care *whose* game it is. What I *do* care about is this team, and if you want to win, then you need to listen. It takes all of us, Felix."

I felt a slap on my shoulder and flipped around. It was Coach, and by the look in his tired eyes, he'd heard me. "That's the kind of attitude you need to have, Max." A brief flash of a grin. "Now head out and start warming up."

"I'm playing?" My heart jumped.

"Yeah." He narrowed his eyes at me. "But no more fucking around."

I nodded. "Yes, sir."

BY THE END of the game, we'd beat Georgia twenty-eight to twenty-one. I'd thrown three touchdown passes and had rushed for eighty-two yards. Badass game.

Ryn was having a party at his place—just beer and maybe a card game. Nothing crazy. I'd halfway invited Sunny, but she'd said no. *It was okay,* I told myself. I'd decided that the less time I spent with her, the easier it was to forget how much I wanted her.

I'd been outside by the fire pit for about an hour when Tate walked over to me and leaned down so only I could hear him. "Mate, Sierra's inside."

"No shit." I jerked up. "Where?"

"I came out of the upstairs loo, and there she was in line waiting to take a piss. You going to say anything?"

"Hell, yes," I called to him as I stalked to the back door. As I made my way through the kitchen and up the staircase I garnered a few slaps on the back and comments about the game and my engagement, and I nodded absently.

There was a line of about five people outside the bathroom. The door opened and out she stumbled. She took one look at me, rushed over, and tossed her arms around her neck, smelling like beer and stale cigarettes.

"Max! Oh, how I've missed you!" She pressed a kiss to my chest, burying her nose in my shirt. "Did you miss me?"

No. I pulled back. "Sierra. We need to talk."

She crooked her arm in mine and smiled up at me. "Anything for you, Max baby. You want me to go down on you? Come on, let's find an empty room." She laced her hand in mine, tugging me toward one of the bedrooms.

"No."

She pouted. "Meanie."

I pulled her off to a corner at the end of the hall as far as I could get from people. "You hit my fiancée's car a few weeks ago when you left my house."

She scrunched up her face as she swayed on her feet. "I—I don't really remember. Did I? I don't think so. That doesn't sound like me . . ." her voice trailed off.

"You did. She saw it. You can't be drinking and driving."

Why did I have to explain this to a grown woman?

She wrapped her arms around my waist, her hands landing on my ass. "God, you're so sweet to be looking out for me. That's why you're my favorite. I want you so bad right now . . ."

I set her away from me and stared down at her, trying to make her eyes meet mine, but they kept bouncing around. "Sierra. Listen to me. I'll cover your little accident this time, because I don't want to explain it, but if you come to my house again, I'll call the cops. Don't even think about picking my lock. Don't let Felix talk you into shit. Do you understand?" I bit the words out.

She blinked up at me. "This Sunny girl . . . she's got you all tied up, huh?"

"None of your damn business. But stay away from her too." A muscle twitched near my eye as a theory formed. "You didn't leave a daisy at her place, did you?"

Confusion flitted across her face. "What do you mean? That's ridiculous."

"Whatever. Just stay away from her or I'll make sure all your football players know how you like to wreck cars when you leave their place. Got it?"

She straightened her shoulders and slurred, "I don't like you anymore."

"Good."

Her face fell. "I'm sorry. I do like you. *I want you.*" She leaned in and kissed me on the mouth, her tongue all over my face, licking and trying to get past my compressed lips.

I pushed her off, but not before she responded with her own laugh and flounced away, weaving from side to side as she made her way back down the hall.

I glanced over and Bart stared at me.

"What are you looking at?" I barked.

He said something to the girl he was with then came up to me, a hardness to his face that I'd come to recognize whenever we faced off.

He was tall—but not as tall as I was. I glared down at him. "You got something to say?"

"I heard what you said to the groupie."

"Yeah, so what?" I shrugged, leaning against the wall, but make no mistake, I wasn't relaxed. Nope. I'd be glad to ram my fist into his face and work out some of this frustration eating me up.

"I'm impressed . . . turning her down when Sunny's nowhere around?"

I gritted my teeth.

He stuck his hands in his pockets, a thoughtful expression on his face. "I really thought you didn't care about anyone but yourself."

"You don't know me—so don't assume I'd dick around like you did."

He stewed on that, his mouth flattening. He stared back at the girl he'd left near the banister, then he focused back on me and raked a hand through his auburn hair. "Just . . . be good to her, okay? Because I was a shit, and I didn't realize it until it was too late. I'm trying to be better now."

"You wish."

"She deserves someone good. You better be it."

I crossed my arms. "You still love her?"

He swallowed, looking away from my eyes.

And wasn't that my answer?

"Fuck off," I said and brushed past him, needing to distance myself from Bart and his *feelings*. It reminded me that someone had once been crazy in love with Sunny . . . and it hadn't been me.

She'd had someone before me.

Someone real.

An hour later I was sick of the party and back home. I sat on my porch with my phone in my hand thinking about Sunny.

Drunk texting was never a good idea—so why was I contemplating it?

I glanced at my watch. Midnight. I checked her house from my seat on the steps of the porch. Yep. All the lights were out.

Are you awake? I sent her.

She didn't reply.

I texted her again. *Hello. Are you there?*

This better be a freaking emergency. I was sound asleep until my phone buzzed.

I need you.

I pictured her sitting up in bed and staring at the phone with sleepy eyes.

Why?

I want to see you. Now, I sent.

You're demanding.

I know.

And an asshole, she added.

I know.

But I like you.

A sigh of relief came from me. God. I'd needed to hear those words since the fake proposal. I closed my eyes, imagining her in her tank top and flannel shorts, her breasts straining against the fabric, her nipple piercing begging for my tongue. I groaned, shifting in my jeans. Down, boy.

I'm sorry, I said.

For texting me?

For everything. You can give the ring back if you want. I deserve it.

We've moved past that now.

You can keep it when it's all over.

Is it real?

Yes.

Did you pick it out?

I paused. *Tate did. One of the groupies works at the jewelry store.*
A few ticks went by.
I asked her, *Does that bother you?*

Would you pick out your real fiancée's ring?

Yes.

We're fake, so it's fine. Right?
It didn't feel fine. It felt off and weird and I wished I'd picked it out.
Right. Can I see you?

What are you really saying? Spit it out, Quarterback.
I wanted her so fucking bad . . .
I'm drunk and I want to have sex with you . . .

Not going to happen.

I won't stick it in your butt. Promise.

Ha.

Will you send me a naked pic of you?

No.

Will you open your window and flash me?

No.

I was just kidding anyway.

Really?

Yes, really. I was hiding behind my humor, not wanting her to see that I'd been scared as shit these past few days. Part of me had been worried about football, but another side of me could only think about her.

Hello? Are you still there, she texted.

Just . . . can we start all over and try this thing again?

What thing?

I sighed and let my fingers fly. *I want to laugh and go to class together, drink coffee with you, talk about how much better the Falcons are this year. I want to study with you. Just . . . I need you to tell me that I have another chance . . . because I'm not Bart. I will never hurt you like that.*

A full minute went by.
I'd just spilled a ton of guts here . . . and she had nothing?

Fuck. Can I just hold you in my arms and watch you sleep?

I'll unlock the door, she replied.

chapter
TWENTY-THREE

Sunny

H E SAUNTERED INTO my bedroom wearing low-slung jeans and a tight black shirt, his wavy hair a mess as if he'd raked his hand through it a million times. Dark scruff covered his chiseled jawline, and his full lips tilted up in a half-smile. With an effortless, almost feline grace, he rested one bulky shoulder against the doorjamb and considered me with intense eyes.

Looking away was unthinkable.

"You look gorgeous," he murmured.

At the growly sound in his tone, my stomach grew heavy, and my heart kicked up.

Time and time again, I was taken aback by his off-the-charts hotness. But it wasn't his looks that tugged at my heart. Not really. It was *him*—his innate charm that made me want to strangle him one second and then hug him the next.

And I knew why. We'd never been strangers. Not even from the beginning.

I propped my head up with my arm as I lay on my side facing him. I patted "his side" of the bed. "I've been keeping it warm for you."

He grinned, his top teeth tugging on his bottom lip. *Was there anything he did that wasn't sexy as hell?*

"I'm pretty hot already," he said, eyes at half-mast.

"Mmm."

I bit my lip as he pulled at the back of his shirt, pulling it from his neck and over his head. It landed in a pool of black on my floor. His jeans were next. He popped the snap and shoved them down and off his legs. I swallowed. Holy football miracles. I was glad I'd left the lamp on. His package strained against his tight black briefs, and my hand itched to cup him, tug down his underwear and wrap my mouth around his . . .

I sat up in the bed and scooted over to him.

His eyes went straight to my breasts. I wore a thin pink camisole, a pair of lace panties and nothing else. He took it all in, his throat moving convulsively, hands clenching at his sides.

"Just don't move . . . okay?"

He nodded, his blue-green gaze glittering as I got up on my knees and pressed my palm to his chest—right over his heart.

The touch of his skin sent a jolt of heat through me. My eyes met his. "It's beating so fast."

"Yes," he said huskily, his velvety voice caressing my skin, making me breathless.

"I'm glad you're here." I rested my head on his shoulder, inhaling his woodsy scent.

"Sunny . . ." His voice was strained, and I raised my head to look at him. His face was bewildered, as if he didn't know how he'd come to be where he was. "I was being real on the phone. I didn't come over here to fuck you. I don't want it to be like that between us. This is something . . . I don't know what's going on . . . but I've missed you this week, and I don't want to mess it up tonight by doing something neither of us is ready for."

His words tore at my heart. I put my hand over his lips. "I know. I feel the same way. But I want to kiss you. Without anyone watching. No audience. Just me and you."

He nodded and cradled my face, staring at me like he was terrified he was going to fuck it up. He gazed into my eyes until the very air buzzed. Soft and slow, he pressed his lips to mine, inhaling me as if I was the finest Belgian chocolate he'd ever tasted and he'd never get another piece. A nip of his teeth, his hand at my waist, and I was gone. Butterflies went crazy. Our kiss was pure, unadulterated magic, making me powerless in his arms. He was gut-twistingly perfect, and I wanted to drown in him. I didn't need air. All I needed was Max Kent and his lips and tongue.

We sank down onto the bed together. His tongue traced mine, and my body yearned to give him everything.

We kissed. Over and over, learning each other, sighing, our breaths mingling.

In between kisses, we talked about our dreams. He wanted to live in New York someday and have a wife and a whole house full of kids. He told me about growing up alone without relatives or siblings. I told him how I'd run away at seventeen and had let my father believe I was dead until I was eighteen. I told him how I wanted a love I could call my own.

Our dreams weren't that different.

And after we talked, our lips found each other again. Deep kisses. Hard kisses. Soft ones. We explored and tasted, yet our hands never went past our shoulders. This wasn't about sex or getting off. It was about us being real—and as for me, well, fate was ripping apart my rule of not falling for him, tearing at the very fabric of my resolve. I was falling in love with the guy I'd tried my best to guard my heart against.

chapter
TWENTY-FOUR

Sunny

ASH WALKED UP to the circulation desk where I sat with my A&P notes spread out across the counter. "Hey, Sunny."

"Hi," I replied as I pushed my notebook to the side and straightened up so I could lean over the counter and chat. He came in almost every night I was working and we usually ended up talking about everything. He was two years younger than me at nineteen, but because his IQ was off the charts, they'd let him start college at sixteen. His eyes were the warmest brown I'd ever seen with streaks of gray feathering out from the pupil. I felt relaxed around him, like I'd known him my whole life. I secretly hoped he and Isabella would become a couple.

He indicated the protein wrapper on my desk. "Nice dinner there. You sure it's enough?" he commented.

"Didn't have time for anything else." My schedule had been nuts between classes and work.

He propped himself against the counter. Clad in skinny jeans, Vans, and a black waffle Henley, he caught the attention of several girls who walked by.

"I can run to the Student Center and grab you something if you want?"

"Nah, that's okay, but thank you." I smiled. "You're one of the sweetest guys, which is kinda funny with the Mohawk and piercings . . ." I blushed remembering exactly what was pierced according to Isabella. "Not that I judge people by appearance, but you know what I mean. You kinda look like a—"

"Thug?"

I laughed.

"I'd do anything for you, Sunny. You introduced me to everyone you knew right off the bat. That was cool. You're a nice person—like deep down I see you're always looking out for others."

"Oh?"

He nodded. "You'd do anything for the people you care about."

Bianca and Felix waltzed through the door. She wore a pair of dark sunglasses on her face—even though the sun had set—and as far as I could tell, she didn't even glance over at me as they headed to the study carrels in the back.

Fine by me.

Ash's eyes bounced from her to me. "She's leaving you alone now?"

I nodded. "Won't even look me in the face."

In class, she avoided me at all costs I'd noticed too, her face remote and cold, waiting until Max and I had left the room before she even picked up her books.

"Good. If she starts anything, let me know."

"You gonna fight her for me?" I ruffled his hair.

"You bet."

He left to go upstairs and I got busy scanning the books in the drop box and doing the usual tasks before closing up. Pam, my manager, popped out of her office and reminded me I needed to head downstairs to the basement to take a cart of discarded books the library had removed from the shelves.

I cringed at having to go down to The Dungeon, as we called it.

I checked my phone.

Max had texted me. It had been over a week since our sleepover, and things were different between us. Softer. We hadn't gone beyond kissing, but every brush of his fingers, every heated glance he sent my way, made me weak.

The Walking Dead premiers tonight, he'd written.

Why can't you watch normal TV? I replied.

Like The Bachelor? Please. All those guys are bastards.

Keep your shirt on, I texted. *You're just jealous.*

Whatever. Pick you up soon. Meet me outside the library?

K

Knowing I was going to see him gave me the motivation I needed to head down with the book cart. One of the first buildings on campus, the library's employee elevator was ancient and hadn't been renovated when the upstairs had been constructed. I got in the small space, pushed the button for the basement floor, and whistled on the way down. The motor made a grinding sound, like the wires holding the thing were rusted. The place was the perfect setting for Max's zombie show.

The door slid open and I stepped out gingerly, my hand immediately going to the light switch on the right of the cold concrete wall. One of the florescent bulbs blinked annoyingly, like it usually did, and made a metallic clanking noise that sent chills straight up my spine. I glared at it. One of these days, I was going to come down here and this place was going to be pitch black. I made a note to tell Pam that maintenance really needed to check the wiring in this place.

I wheeled the cart past dusty discarded desks and study carrels to a hallway that led to a series of locked doors on either side. All were storage for various items. I unlocked and entered room 105, the biggest storage area and the room where everything went to die. I felt sad for every single book there that would never be read again. During the day, when I didn't work, I imagined it might be a pretty cool place as sunlight poured in from the ground-level windows near the ceiling. But at night, it was dark and musty, chocked full of metal shelving, rickety chairs, and an eerie padding sound which I took to be the vibrations from the heating and air system. Or maybe it was the footsteps of the patrons above me. Either way, the place gave me the heebie-jeebies.

I shoved a doorstopper in place with my foot and flipped the light switch. And just like last week, this one didn't work at all. The maintenance person was slacking. Luckily I was prepared. I clicked on the mini LED flashlight I'd bought at Wal-Mart when I started this job and stuck it in my mouth as I used both hands to push the cart to the back of the room.

Using my flashlight, I walked down the dusty aisles, shelving the non-fiction books in the correct Dewey Decimal order. It was taking longer than I thought it would. The library closed in ten minutes. Getting worried she might forget I was here, I tugged out my phone and typed a quick text to Pam, then shoved the phone back in my pocket.

I'd just shelved a book about Egypt when I heard the creak of a distant door. My stomach jumped to my throat. There wasn't supposed to be anyone down here but me.

A soft shuffling sound echoed from the main part of the basement, and I stilled.

An image of a giant rat flashed through my head.

Then a gnarly-looking spider with fangs. Ugh.

The door to my room slammed shut, and I screamed, the shrillness shattering the eerie quiet of the room. My hands clenched the cart, shoving it out of my way as I ran for the front of the room. The flashlight fell to the floor in my haste.

A laugh pierced the quiet after my scream, the sound muffled by the door between us.

I twisted the knob but it wouldn't open. A rattling sound came each time I shook it, and with a sinking feeling, I suspected what the flashlight confirmed when I looked through the rectangular window on the metal door. A chair had been pushed up under the handle, locking me inside.

Fear rose in my stomach.

I took a step back.

"Who's out there?" My voice was thin and reedy, bouncing off the concrete walls.

Nothing but silence greeted me.

I slapped my fists against the metal door. "Let me out!"

The laugh came again—a girl's.

"This isn't funny!"

And then I heard movement and a tapping noise, fading. Someone was running.

I put the light back up to the window, trying to illuminate more of the hallway. It didn't show me much, but the window in the door across from me caught a reflection of light as the stairwell door down the hall opened and someone slipped inside. Whoever the culprit was, she was leaving by the stairwell that led back upstairs.

Every scary movie I'd ever watched flashed through my head. I fumbled for my phone, but when I tried to call out I realized I was so deep in concrete that I didn't have any service. Which meant Pam had never gotten my text.

With hands that trembled from adrenaline, I jerked my phone into the air as if that might improve the service. *Nothing.*

I swallowed down the helpless feeling eating at me, trying to keep it together. My brain scattered in a million directions as I paced a small patch of floor lit by the streetlight coming in from the ground-level window high up the wall.

The room sat directly underneath the circulation desk. Maybe I could make a big racket by pushing down the shelves, but I didn't think that would be enough noise even if I could manage it. My eyes went up to the ceiling. If I had something tall, maybe I could poke it at the ceiling to get their attention upstairs.

The library was closing in five minutes. I wanted to hurl. Most of the patrons were on their way out, and Pam was probably right in the middle of calling maintenance to start the lock-up process. She always got so flustered around closing time, and she never checked the basement.

I'd clocked out early once or twice last week to study. What if she assumed I'd done it again? I sent up a prayer that she'd check my clock-in ticket in the mail room.

I ran back to the door and took up pounding again, this time using a heavy tome from one of the shelves.

It got me nowhere.

I panted and rested against the metal. For good measure, I kicked at it and yelled obscenities. Not only was I scared shitless, but I had an A&P quiz the next day and I needed to study for it. Randomly I wondered if this qualified as an excused absence. Probably not with Whitt.

Headlights skimmed past the window above me, and I ran to the back wall and pointed the flashlight up to check out the ancient-looking window. It was plenty big enough for me to fit through, but how was I going to get up there?

I pushed the cart over to the wall and climbed to the bottom rung, only a few feet off the floor. It wobbled on its wheels, and I teetered before falling off and hitting my elbow on the floor. Shit.

I sucked in a deep breath and concentrated on calming down. I was okay. This wasn't the lake. I wasn't in a car. I had air—albeit a little moldy.

I pulled myself off the floor to try again. I had an idea. When I used to take walks in the mountains and would find myself without phone service, sometimes climbing a tree or just getting a few feet off the ground would do the trick. So, I nixed the more dangerous idea of actually climbing out the window and focused on just getting phone service.

I wrestled with the metal cart again. Moving slow and steady, I stepped up to the first shelf, gained my balance, and then tried for the second shelf. The metal cart vibrated from my ungainly movements, but didn't tip over. *Baby steps, Sunny.* Holding my balance precariously, I pulled out my phone and held it up as high as I could.

One, two, three seconds passed and nothing.

Then it pinged!

A text from Max came through. *Hey. I'm here.*

Then came another one. *You okay? I'm here and walking around. Everyone is gone. I'm worried. Call me.*

Victory soared, and I typed out a reply.

Stuck in basement room with a window on west side next to parking lot. Come get me!

In my excitement, the flashlight that I'd tucked in my jean pocket crashed to the floor. The cart tilted when I reached to catch it, and I fell straight to the floor.

Everything went black.

chapter
TWNETY-FIVE

Max

I RAN AROUND the side of building to the area where she'd indicated. Rummaging through the landscaping, I found a ground-level window that looked down into the basement. The weak streetlight made it tough to see detail, but I made out white-blond hair and the barest shadow of her figure on the floor.

Urgency hit me, and I beat on the window while yelling her name. There wasn't a soul in the parking lot to yell to for help.

I whipped my shirt off, wrapped it around my hand, and slammed it against the glass I got nothing but bruises. I stopped. *What if I knocked the glass on her?* Bad idea. Shit. I slipped my shirt back on, my brain racing.

The seal on the window was old and faded, a window that had probably been here since the university first opened in 1963. I took out my pocketknife, pried it between the metal sections on the old lock, and tugged until it popped off. Success. I slid the window up and maneuvered myself until I was sitting on the sill. I aimed to miss what appeared to be a cart and jumped to the left. Pain ricocheted up my right leg when I made impact with the floor. Thank God it was carpeted.

A flashlight lay on the ground. I grabbed it and focused on her.

"Max." Her eyes fluttered open, landing on the window. "Did you hurt yourself?"

I shook my head, my eyes already checking her for bruises. My hands followed, running over her arms and legs. "Don't worry about me. What happened to you?"

"I fell off the cart trying to get service. My arm hurts—near the elbow."

Maneuvering her up to sit between my legs and face me, I took her sweater off to get a better look. It had a wide neck and slipped easily over her head, revealing her black lace bra.

Mentally groaning and trying to ignore the swell of her breasts, I used the flashlight to inspect the purple bruise on her arm. "You took a bump, but it's not broken." I pushed a strand of hair out of her face. "What else?"

"My head," she said with a wince. "I hit the edge of the cart on my way down."

There was a small bump on the right side of her temple, but it didn't seem too serious. "Let me see your eyes." Her face turned back toward me, the paleness of her skin striking me deep in the gut. "Your pupils are good. How many fingers do I have up?"

"Two. People always hold up two."

I gave her a squeeze, relief washing over me at her teasing tone. She was okay. "Good news is I don't think you have a concussion. Bad news is I completely freaked out when I saw you and didn't call the campus police." I'd been reacting on instinct, and my instinct had been yelling, *Get to her!*

I glanced around the room, my eyes getting used to the darkness, taking in the details. I landed on the metal shelves. "I can get us out of here with those." I glanced back at her. "Are you in pain anywhere else?"

"Just my leg, but I think it's okay."

"Let me look," I said. "Take your pants off so we don't miss anything."

She paused for a moment, then nodded. She slipped her booties off and unbuttoned her jeans. I helped her slide them down her legs, sending up a *thank you* they weren't her usual skinny jeans.

A huge bruise, about the size of my hand, was purpling on her outer right thigh.

Even in the obviousness of her injury, my mouth dried at how hard my dick was for her.

Be a freaking gentleman.

Right.

"It looks like your leg took most of the hit. You're lucky." I pressed my forehead to hers and kissed her lightly. "You scared the shit out of me." I caressed her cheek. "How did you end up stuck down here?"

"Someone locked me in. I—I was putting away books, and someone shut the door and wedged a chair under it. I think they ran away, because I saw a shadow in the stairwell."

I inhaled sharply. "Who?"

"I don't know . . . but they . . . *she* . . . laughed at me. I mean, the sound was feminine but I guess I can't be sure." Her face paled as she looked back at the door. "They just left me here. I—I hate places I can't get out of." Her hands squeezed mine.

Cradling her in my lap, I ran my hand through her hair and palmed her scalp. She leaned tightly into my chest, her nose pressing against me and inhaling my scent. I comforted her, while trying to contain my anger.

Whoever did this—was going to fucking pay.

chapter
TWENTY-SIX

Sunny

H E'D RESCUED ME. Again.

I'd realized exactly who he was the moment he'd opened that door weeks ago. He was older, his hair was longer and muscles bulkier, but I'd never forget *him*. The angel with the lush lips, broad shoulders, and perfectly chiseled face; a man brave enough to swim out into a dark lake to save me.

Then, I'd realized *who* he was—Max Kent, the king of all quarterbacks—exactly the kind of guy I didn't need.

Plus, he hadn't remembered me. Oh, he'd mentioned a connection, but that was *nothing* in comparison to me. He hadn't had that profound moment where the universe realigned itself when we met.

That knowledge had ripped into me, and from that moment on, I'd done my damnedest to ignore fate—but then perhaps this was the way things were supposed to play out for us. Perhaps this was a lesson for me, and I should see it through until the end whether it ended happily or not.

Either way, I *was* meant to meet him again. I *was* meant to get another chance. Right?

I sat up in his lap, curled my hand around his neck and touched the dark strands of hair next to his face, pushing them out of the way. God, he was beautiful, and he'd come down a twenty-foot drop to get to me.

Fate always knew exactly what I needed.

Clarity happens to all of us when we need it most. Sometimes it takes a knock to the head when you fall off a cart to get it through to you. Screw the fact that he might never remember the epic moment we'd had. He was mine. My heart knew it. My body knew it.

My hand cupped his cheek and my eyes searched his, yearning for him to wake up and remember me. "I've wanted you for so long, Max." Need colored my voice. My nose ran up his neck, and I licked and kissed the pulse throbbing at his throat.

"What are you doing?" he ground out, his lids lowered to half-mast.

I lifted up his shirt and slipped it over his neck. "What I've wanted to do since the day I saw you." I kissed each eye, the tickle of his long lashes reminding me how amazed I'd been at the way water had clung to them the night we'd first met.

His breathing was ragged. "Sunny . . ."

"I want to taste every part of you." I moved to kiss his bicep, my tongue outlining his tattoo. "Every. Single. Inch." My hand palmed the rock hard bulge in his jeans, making him toss his head back and groan.

I tugged down the right cup of my bra, showing him the bar piercing there. Made of sterling silver, it was flanked by delicate hearts. "I've seen you looking at this, and I think about you when my shirt rubs against my nipple. Touch me."

A dark growl came from his throat, an animal sound, as he fused our lips together. His fingers plucked at my piercing while his other hand slipped to the back and unsnapped my bra, letting it trail excruciatingly slow down my stomach. His knuckles brushed my peaks, and I shuddered as desire speared me.

God. I wanted him desperately. I had for so long.

"You're so perfect." He bent his head, his lips latching on to my piercing and tugging. Heat exploded inside me, and I yelled out, clutching his head to my breast. His mouth flicked at my nipples and sucked. His fingers, roughened from years of football, cupped my breast as he inhaled me, going from one to the other, his scruff scratching against my skin. I groaned. I was going to come before he even had his pants off.

My hand dipped inside the waistband of his jeans until I found the velvet skin of his length.

"Oh, fuccccck . . ." he called out, the words dipped in need.

His hand slipped under my panties. "You're so damn wet," he grunted, satisfaction pouring off him as his fingers flitted across my slit. I arched into his touch, yearning for more.

"Sunny, you're driving me crazy," he growled and stood up, tugging me with him. I nearly cried out at the loss of his touch. He kicked his shoes off and shoved down his jeans, revealing his long, thick cock. My heart thundered. He was huge.

His eyes locked with mine. "You sure?"

My hand reached out and lightly stroked him, caressing him. He jerked into my hands as my fingers slipped over his head and then coasted back down. I melted even more as I watched the myriad of emotions flitting across his face. Need. Lust. *Love?*

In this moment, I'd take whatever I could get.

He parted my legs and slid a finger over my sex, sliding in to tease me. Whimpering, I wrapped a leg around his waist, giving him more access. He growled and gave me more, burrowing two inside me, sliding in and out, curling his fingers and rubbing against a sensitive place inside me.

He worked me fast and then slow, murmuring my name, as I writhed against his hand, sensation honed in on that one place.

Yes.

"Max, more." My hips moved with his touch, watching him as he bit his lower lip.

"You're on fire." Bending down, he bunched up my panties in his hand, tore them down my leg and tossed them in a corner of the room.

With desire in his gaze, he laid out his shirt like a small blanket and said, "Lay back down."

My insides quaked, and I couldn't get there fast enough, lying back on the floor and watching as he knelt at my feet. He kissed me reverently, his mouth drifting over my chest and stomach. He lifted my leg and adored my inner thigh, the curve of my calf, the arch of my foot. My hands were busy too. I ran them through his hair and down his chest, my fingers learning the sculpted muscles of his body. Exploring. Touching him in all the places I'd only dreamed of. He spread my legs and eased between them, his gaze electric. He bent over me, parted me and found the heart of me with his tongue. I screamed out his name. It was an assault of the senses, watching him dip his head and devour me, his fingers drawing circles on my nub. His teeth toyed with my clit and I lost my mind, my climax echoing off the walls. My body clenched around his fingers, pulsating, while he watched with a heavy look in his eyes.

"I've ached for this moment," he said softly. "Forever."

Something vulnerable flitted across his face, but quickly disappeared. He studied me intently, his hand cupping my face, and for a second, I thought he might say something else—but he didn't.

He kissed me hard then, the erotic taste of my skin mingling in our mouths.

"I want you inside me," I said when we pulled back to take a breath.

He reached for his nearby jeans, pulled out a silver foil from his wallet, and slid on the condom. With his athletic grace, he eased between my legs, careful of my injured side. Positioning himself, he inched inside slowly, letting me adjust to the fullness, checking to see if I needed more time.

All I needed was *him*. Every nerve in my channel lit up, grasping for more.

I reached up and pulled his head down to mine. "More," I whispered.

He went further inside, easing in and then sliding out excruciatingly slow.

"Max . . ." I begged. "Give it to me."

He came right back, his hand tugging my face to kiss me deeply as he stroked into me, building up to a fast-paced rhythm. I writhed and clutched his shoulders, sensation building at the base of my spine. My nails dug into his hipbones as I arched into the sleek slide of his cock. He went harder, faster, bending his head to my chest.

"Sunshine . . . this . . . you . . . so much . . ." his voice was gravelly and full of need. Desperate.

Yes. Yes. I rotated my hips against him, swiveling.

He adjusted for a new angle with his hips, going deeper, and I took it all, trying to give back as good as he gave. "You're mine," he breathed against my neck.

My heart jumped at those words. Palming his scalp with my hands, I pulled his face to mine and stared at him, willing him to know *me*. "I'm yours."

His finger slipped between our connected bodies and found my center again and strummed, spreading the wetness. Gasping, I lost myself completely, my fingers digging into his back, tearing at him as I shattered into a million pieces. I didn't know where he ended and I began. The sheer enormity of *us* made me gasp as I gripped his shoulders and rode out my orgasm.

I'd never had this with Bart.

He roared his release, his neck muscles in stark relief as his cock tightened and expanded inside me. Panting, he rested on top of me for a few heartbeats and then flipped us over until I was lying on him. Neither of us spoke for a few seconds, just our heavy breaths filling up the silence in the room.

I cleared my throat, my heart still pounding. "Was that . . . was that normal?"

He knew what I meant.

That hadn't been hook-up sex.

That had been out-of-this-fucking-world-mind-blowing-when-can-we-do-it-again sex.

"Max?" I asked after he'd been silent for too long.

His long lashes dropped against his cheek, as if he didn't want me to see what he was thinking. He swallowed. "Not normal."

Yeah. That. *That* was just the answer I needed. "Thank you," I whispered.

chapter
TWENTY-SEVEN

Max

WHEN I CAME to about an hour later, she was still draped across me, her right leg between mine. The floor was cool but not cold. I barely noticed. It could have been an iceberg in here and I wouldn't have moved from this spot.

Her eyes peeked open, and my greedy gaze ate her up, taking in the way her body fit neatly into mine. Since the moment we'd met, she'd checked all my boxes for what I'd never realized I wanted in a girl—and it was more than just looks. Sure, she was beautiful, but it had been her willingness to stand up to me that first day that had gotten my attention. I'd seen the vulnerability in her that day too—the careful way she kept her distance from me, holding back. God, I didn't want her to do that anymore.

I rose up and kissed her. "I want you slow," I said against her lips, my hips already arching into her.

"Yes . . ." She grasped my cock and stroked with the heel of her hand, rubbing over the head.

I kissed her harder, my hand on her ass, pushing her into me. She spread her legs just enough for me to glide across her velvet center.

"Fuck . . . Sunny . . ." I teased her with pulses of my hips, my cock weeping at the thought of riding her raw. But I didn't do that. Condoms were a must.

I scrambled over to my jeans, pilfered through my wallet until I found one. I kissed it and sent her a grin. "Last one." I walked back to her and came to a complete stop, noticing what was in the back corner past the shelving. "I'll be damned."

"What?"

I bent down and swept her up in my arms. "There's a chaise lounge back there."

A wide smile broke out when she followed my gaze. "Lead on, Quarterback."

My lids went low. Because my mind was dirty as hell. "You're gonna ride me."

She shuddered, her eyelids squeezing together.

We made it to the pillowy chair, just barely, because my hands were too busy cupping her creamy breasts. I fell down on my ass and brought her with me.

"It's probably been here a hundred years," she said, a flush on her cheeks.

"Do you care?" My hand roamed the curve of her hip. I squeezed.

She shook her head, a curtain of hair hiding her face. That shyness again. I loved it.

After sliding on the condom, I gripped my cock and slid inside her. She moved over me and I played with her piercing, sucking. My touch was tender as I cupped her face and watched her move.

Everything but us faded away.

Crazy. Intense. And so damn good. It scared me a little—but I pushed it away.

Tingles of pleasure washed over me, and I grunted, my pumps faster. "I want behind you," I whispered. She nodded, and I flipped her over, held her waist, and glided inside. She was dripping wet, and I groaned as I took her, her feet planted on the floor to keep us steady. My fingers went to her clit and stroked in little circles. I bent over her and whispered how hot she was and how much I wanted her.

Tossing her head back, she met my eyes, the heat I saw sending me higher. Something else passed between us—a breathless moment wrapped in such need and intensity that I couldn't fathom it. I didn't understand it, and it was forgotten as she came apart in front of me.

"Max!" she called.

My hand dug into her hips. It felt like we'd done this a million times. I could do it a million more. "So fucking good with you . . ." I breathed as I pounded into her and came hard. My back arched, basking in the sharp pleasure, and I continued to pump, my cock barely softening, still aching to feel encased inside her.

A few more spine-tingling strokes, and I pulled out, my breathing out of control. My hand caressed down the base of her spine. The moon had risen higher, the light showing tiny scars on her back around her shoulder blades and the center of her back. I counted ten or so. I inhaled sharply, battling, aching to ask her, but she turned over to face me, her face soft. *She* was beautiful . . . the *moment* was beautiful. I didn't want to ruin it with a bad memory. Those marks would be a conversation for another time. I kissed her and eased down next to her, our limbs entangling as she snuggled into my side. Time passed but we hardly noticed, our hands clinging to each other.

I held her tight and thanked the stars I'd found her.

AN HOUR PASSED. Maybe another one. Honestly, I lost track while holding her. With as much care as I could, I eased out of her arms and padded over to my jeans where I pulled out my phone. Two in the morning. I rubbed my head.

I headed back over to her and kissed her awake. She blinked up at me and I grinned. "Morning, Cookie. We gotta get out of here."

She nodded and dressed. We pushed the shelves to the window, bracing them with other shelves. It was sturdy enough that I had no qualms about climbing it. Sure, I could have tried to just get service to call the campus police to come unlock the door, but this was easy stuff.

I got to the top of the shelving, put my hand down for her to grasp, and heaved her up step-by-step. Once she made it to the top, I shimmied through the window and then helped her come through with as much care as I could.

Watching her get to her feet, I saw the ugly bruise on the side of her head again. My mouth tightened.

I put an arm around her, and we walked toward my car in the parking lot.

"You're angry," she said as she rubbed her arms in the October air.

I nodded. "I just keep wondering who would do this to you. What if they'd tried to hurt you or even set the place on fire? It's fucking insane." I pulled out my phone. "I'm going to call campus police. You okay with talking to them?"

She nodded.

The police dispatcher answered, and I gave them the rundown of what had happened. I told them we didn't need an ambulance but would need to file a report. They told me a unit was en route to take our statements.

Her eyebrows knitted as we waited for them to arrive. "Do you think it was Bianca?"

I thought about it. "She's got a mouth on her, but to actually do something so full of malice? I can't see it."

Her lips tightened. "She'll do whatever she has to get you back."

I didn't buy it. Unless Felix had been behind it. "Maybe it was Bart and he got some girl to do it."

She shook her head. "He might be a liar, but he'd never do this. I always felt safe with Bart—even when he was angry in class that first day. He wouldn't hurt me."

Because he still fucking loved her, I thought. I pushed away how insecure that made me feel.

I sighed. "Then we're back to square one. Maybe the police can check the cameras and figure it out."

She nodded, and I tried to play it cool, but worry pricked at me. First the daisy thing and now this—what was next? The thought of anyone trying to mess with her drove me nuts. "Maybe you should resign from your library job." I tapped my hand against my thigh, thinking. "Once football is over, I can keep my eye on you more, but right now . . ." I stopped. Feeling frustrated. Shit. I was hardly ever home. How was I going to watch over her?

"I appreciate you being worried for me, but I can't quit my job. I can take care of myself . . . *alone*. I've been doing it for a long time."

We stared at each other in the cool parking lot as a range of emotions flitted across her face. I couldn't read them.

"What are you thinking about?" I asked, grasping her hands in mine. Since the moment we'd come out of the basement, I sensed that somehow I'd disappointed her.

Sadness flickered in her eyes. "The past."

"Don't judge me by Bart, Sunny. It isn't fair."

She sighed, her shoulders slumping. "I'm not judging you by him anymore. It's not that. It's just you have this big future. You're *you* and—" she cut her words off and swallowed, shaking her head. "I'm scared. I can't handle my heart being broken again, Max. *I just can't.*"

"You're the only girl on my mind right now. *You.*" I eased over to her, tilted her face up, and pressed my lips to her still swollen ones.

She nodded still looking uncertain, but I let it go. I had other things I wanted to talk about. I leaned against my SUV and laced our fingers together. "Will you tell me about the scars on your back? Was it your dad? It's just . . . Isabella said something once, and last night . . . they didn't bother me," I assured her softly. "They're beautiful. They're you."

She bit her lip and nodded, staring at the ground. "My father . . . he changed after my mom died. He . . . he wanted to control me and make sure I didn't turn out like her. He lashed me with a belt and the buckle left scars. It only happened a few times—but the last time, I knew I couldn't stay anymore. I came to live with Mimi." She paused, her hands twisting. "He didn't ruin me—I want you to know that. I don't even hate him . . . I think. He was so in love with my mom, and when she left us and then died—it ripped his whole world apart."

I couldn't relate to the abuse, but I got that love could be a powerful thing and that it could change people.

"Anyway, there's a core of strength inside me . . . this need to just live and be happy. And I know that fate has a big life ahead of me, and whatever happened to me back then isn't going to screw it up. And maybe . . . just maybe, awful things had to happen to me before I ended up in the right place."

Her gray gaze connected with mine, and I read hope there.

I held my rage for her father in and focused on her. *I'm sorry* might come across as pity, so I didn't say it. Instead, I kissed her lightly and hugged her, wrapping my forearms around her small waist and pulling her tight against me. "I've got you," I whispered. "And you are in the right place."

chapter
TWENTY-EIGHT

Sunny

O N A SATURDAY afternoon nearly two weeks after the library incident I stood outside one of the premier wedding shops in the Atlanta area, a chic little place called Boutique Celeste. I was fake dress shopping.

It was rather cold for the first week of November. I shifted closer to the store, anxious to get inside and get this task over with.

Isabella and Mimi flanked me on either side, my bodyguards. I say that because they'd both been sending me concerned looks for the past week. Just this morning Mimi had commented on the hollows in my cheeks. Isabella had chimed in about the shadows under my eyes.

I just missed Max.

Since the library, I'd seen less of him. We'd had lunch together several times, but for the most part we hadn't been alone. I had my car back, so we weren't driving to class together. Of course, he'd check in with me, texting late at night after practice. He always sounded exhausted. Most times he wanted to come over, often insisting, but I brushed him off with excuses that I was in bed or studying. He was in the thick of football season, or he probably would have pressed me more.

We'd had our magical night in the basement, and it had been everything, but since then I'd decided to give him some space until he figured out exactly what we were. *Shit.* I didn't know what we were. Perhaps sex only complicated us. I didn't know. What I did know was that he had a ton of pressure on him, and I didn't want to mess with his head like Bianca had.

Thankfully there hadn't been any more crazy incidents or flowers left on my stoop. We still didn't know who the culprit was though. There was no video footage from the stairwell, just views of the library entrances and exits. Campus police had pored through them, along with my manager Pam, but there was nothing suspicious. It was frustrating—and scary. If the culprit had planned it, it meant they'd been waiting for me to finally make a trip down to the basement. My hope was that it was a harmless prank decided on a whim by someone who didn't even know me.

A pretty young girl in her mid-twenties with long brown hair rushed toward us from across the street. "So sorry I'm late," she gushed with a sheepish grin. She stuck her hand out. "I'm Carrie Longmire with WBBG Channel 7, and I also freelance with the *Atlanta Gazette* for their Lifestyle section. Millicent asked me to write the article about your engagement."

"Of course." I shook her hand and introduced Mimi and Isabella. Max had informed me of this a week ago, and I'd agreed. I was seeing this darn thing through to the end for him.

We went inside the mirrored double doors and one of the shopkeepers met us immediately, a huge smile on her face. Of course, Millicent had prepped the owner of the boutique of our arrival.

After air kisses and introductions, we made our way through the store to a small posh sitting area surrounded by a wall of mirrors. Mimi and Isabella both took a glass of champagne that was offered by the sales girl. Carrie declined.

"Miss Blaine, would you like a drink?"

I shook my head, my gaze bouncing off the heavy crown molding of the ceiling, the beautiful gold filigree wallpaper, and the wraparound leather seating. This place was insanely beautiful. And the dresses were a sea of billowy soft whites and creams that glittered under the sparkly lights of the diamond-drop chandeliers.

It wasn't real, I reminded myself. I gnawed on my lower lip, fighting back tears—God, it was so entirely stupid to get emotional, but since the night we'd been together, I was walking a tightrope with emotions, and at any moment I was going to fall and break into a million pieces.

The saleslady brought me back with a clearing of her throat, making me start. "If you don't want champagne, I'd be happy to run to the back and grab you a water or a soda?"

"I'm fine, but thank you."

She nodded and ushered for us to sit down.

"Based on the phone interview we had, Miss Blaine, we've put together a few styles we thought you might enjoy." With a clap of her hands, a myriad of tall and stately models emerged from doors inset inside the mirrored walls.

I sucked in a sharp breath at the visions in white. Elegant dresses with sweetheart necklines, strapless ones with pearls and beads, and a couple of quirky styles with lace and chiffon bell sleeves. One of them, a timeless body-hugging fishtail design, caught most of my attention. Sparkling crystals had been sewn into the material, dripping in a V design to the floor. I imagined pairing it with a purple and pink bouquet and bridesmaids dressed in slinky silver dresses. "They're beautiful," I whispered.

Each model did a pirouette in front of us and then walked back to stand in a line.

"Gorgeous," Mimi gushed. "I always wanted a big wedding for your mom but she eloped."

"Is there a particular one you like?" the saleslady asked me.

"No, Bette, but thank you." I softened the next part with a smile. "Do you mind if we go ahead with the interview now? The girls can change if they want, and we can browse your store afterwards." I hated the thought of them just standing there while we talked.

Bette looked horrified at my words. Ugh. I was failing at this horribly. I wasn't acting like a typical bride.

"Yes, that's fine, but the girls will remain," she said. "They are here for *you*. Please let me know if you'd like to see any of the girls in another design." She marched off, her back straight.

"Damn," Isabella whispered to me under her breath as she peered at me over the rim of her champagne glass. "Rich people really know how to shop, snooty saleslady and all."

Carrie, who'd been quiet during the entire viewing of the dresses, beamed when I turned my attention to her.

"You ready?" I asked.

She nodded and pulled out a voice recorder and a pad and pen. She started in with her questions, first beginning with how Max and I met. We'd worked on our "meet-cute" story since that first day in A&P and had decided to stick as close to it as we could. In other words, we'd met at a frat party briefly and had reconnected over the summer when we bumped into each other at the coffee shop.

"What's Max Kent really like?" Carrie asked, twirling her pen. "We're all dying to know." Her face flushed. "I'm a big fan of his too."

"Oh, you like football?" Mimi asked eagerly. She'd talk to a fencepost about sports.

Carrie shrugged. "No. He's just hot."

"Oh." Mimi settled back down.

So much for that.

I rambled off some answer about how smart Max was. Other answers came to mind—soulmate, incredible lover, brave, tender—but I pushed those aside.

"So is the date set yet?" Carrie asked.

A snort came from Isabella, and I sent her a glare. *Don't mess this up for him*, I conveyed. She stuck her tongue out at me, and Mimi popped her on the leg. Isabella flinched and ended up spilling a bit of champagne on the front of her shirt. I giggled. I'd woken up in a bad mood, knowing I was coming here, but I loved my little family.

I focused back on Carrie and smiled as I lied through my teeth. "We're planning on late next year, but no venue has been chosen. The draft is in January, so as soon as we know what team he'll play for, we'll be moving . . ." my voice trailed off.

Max would be leaving Atlanta—and me—soon.

"I'm the maid of honor," Isabella told her with a smug smile, reaching over to the tray on the ottoman style coffee table. She grabbed the champagne bottle and poured herself another glass.

"Yes," I said.

"Be sure you spell my name right too, Isabella Monroe. I-S-A-B-E-L-L-A and M-O-N-R-O-E."

I quirked an eyebrow at her. She hadn't exactly warmed up to Max since he'd sprung the proposal, but she was trying because I asked her to. I was committed to the fake fiancée stuff because I wanted Max to have everything he wanted. Mimi, on the other hand, continued to sing his praises.

Carrie made a note and moved on with her pre-approved questions, and I answered as best I could. My traitorous eyes kept drifting over to the fishtail dress. The model was a statuesque blonde and her hair had been swept up in a disheveled but utterly appealing style. A simple chiffon veil was attached somewhere in her hair. It trailed to the floor in a pool of white.

"You like that one?" Carrie asked softly, and I blinked, realizing that she'd put most of her stuff away and we were just having a regular conversation.

"I do."

Mimi reached over and squeezed my hand. "Try it on, hon. It won't hurt."

"Oh, you've found one you like?" Bette exclaimed coming up behind us. She clapped her hands excitedly making me jump. I imagined she'd been hovering somewhere watching us the entire time. "Which one?"

I nudged my head at the blond model.

She sighed, her hand over her heart. She really was the perfect shop lady. "Ah, yes, Blythe Couture. Very elegant—and not everyone can wear that style, but you certainly could, Miss Blaine."

"Oh, please try it on," Carrie said in awe. "Just to say that I saw Max Kent's fiancée try on a dress . . . it would make for a great line in my article . . . even if it's not the one you end up wearing." She blushed.

I twisted at the ring on my finger, thinking. Reaching over to the ottoman, I poured myself a full glass of champagne and gulped it down.

"I'll do it," I announced, much to the pleasure of Bette who beamed. I sent Isabella a pointed look as I stood and followed Bette to a dressing room. "Pour me another glass of champagne, girl. I'm gonna need it after this."

chapter
TWENTY-NINE

Max

O N THE WAY home from our game, I texted Sunny after her
interview to check in on her.

Can I see you tonight?

I need to study.

I exhaled, my fingers typing. *We lost tonight. I need someone to talk to.*
I need you.

I settled for watching the passing trees out the bus window when she
didn't respond right away. I imagined her staring at her phone, debating.
It was apparent she was pushing me away since we'd had sex in the basement—and there was nothing I could do about it, not while I was right
in the middle of football.

I'll bring sushi, I added, my hands gripping the phone tightly.
Okay.
I sat back, relieved I'd get to be alone with her, yet part of me still

fumed at our first loss of the season—all my fault. I'd thrown two interceptions—freshman year shit. I scratched my gruff and leaned my head back on the vinyl of the bus seat.

I'd like to blame it on my twitchy ankle I'd gotten from the library a few weeks ago, but the athletic coaches had checked me out that day, put some ice on it, and it had been good. They told me to keep it easy for the rest of the week, so Coach had me sit out a few hard practices. The result had me feeling rusty, and today it had showed.

"Mate. Chill. We lost. We still have Appalachian State next week. Easy peasy," Tate said from across the aisle.

I raised my head up. "I let us down. That guy came out of nowhere and snatched it . . ." Whatever.

"It was double coverage, dude," Ryn said from the seat in front of me.

"Don't sweat it. Next week. We got this." Tate's eyes went to my leg. "No more injuries, okay—even if you are rescuing a girl."

Yeah, yeah. He was asking the impossible.

When she was around, I couldn't think straight.

"Go ahead and be a hero anytime you want," Felix called from the very back of the bus. Of course the team had heard about the rescue when I'd had to explain my ankle. "I'll play next week."

I flipped him off.

"Easy," Tate said softly. "Don't give the wanker the satisfaction of knowing he makes you mad."

Coach sent us *I have my eyes on you* glares, and I tried to shake off the tension, which was way more than just a loss. I'd been on edge since the library, ready to jump at anyone's throat.

God. I was tired. I leaned my head back against the seat and slipped in my ear buds, putting in some old-school Beastie Boys. Thoughts of Sunny niggled at me, pricking at my memories, and within minutes, I was out.

I dreamed.

My mom was dead, lying on a sterile hospital bed. Her lashes rested lightly on her cheeks and part of me expected her to open them and send me her usual smile.

"You don't have to stay," the doctor murmured. He put a tentative hand on my shoulder, and I shook it off.

I picked her hand up as tears pricked at my eyes.

"The aneurysm was in her brain—there wasn't anything you could do," he murmured as if reading my thoughts. "Her death was instant."

I nodded. Yeah. They'd gone over it with me—again and again. It was just so sudden. I wanted to yell at the doctor—tell him that it wasn't fair—that she was all I had—but I held back, all of seventeen going on ancient.

I tucked her hand under the covers, touched her cheek lightly, and then walked out the door.

I had to get out of there.

I exited the hospital and found my Harley. The bike was new, and she'd insisted I drive it up for our vacation while she followed in her Mercedes. I'd parked it in a fire lane when I'd followed the ambulance. Fuck them. Let them try to tow me. I'd fucking . . .

I stopped, squeezing my eyes shut as I sat down on the concrete curb next to the road, exhausted. She fought to be happy for so long and right when she'd gotten there . . .

Someone walked past me, whispering, and I realized I had to get further away.

I got on my bike and rode out of the parking lot with nothing but my backpack and wallet.

I drove and drove until I had no clue where I was.

Needing to piss, I drove down a rural gravel road to a shoreline that overlooked a huge lake.

I wanted to throw rocks in it, scream at it. So I did. I yelled obscenities and rammed my fist into my palm. I cursed at God for taking her.

Toeing my shoes off, I laid down on the rocks, letting them dig into my backside. I didn't care. At least it was something.

My heart ached.

I wanted my mom back . . .

I wanted Sunday morning waffles.

I wanted her to hug me right before a game.

A sob tore at my throat. Fuck. Not again with the crying shit.

A convertible Mustang sped by on the bridge above me, swerved, and hit the guardrail.

I sat up.

A grinding noise shattered the eerie silence as the rail gave way and the car soared into the lake.

I didn't stop to think. Off came the clothes. I snatched my knife from my backpack, and in seconds I was in the water and swimming to where I could just barely see the top of the car.

Down I swam, putting all my grief into saving a life. If I could do this . . . there was fucking hope left in the world. I cut a hole and grabbed a hand that came through. I tugged the person out.

Once on the shore, I checked for vitals—no breathing but I had a pulse—and did CPR.

Beautiful relief hit me when she came to, her face deathly pale.

Strings of long hair wrapped around her neck and shoulders, and I moved them out of the way, noticing that even wet, her hair was blond. When dry, it must be nearly white. Her face was delicate, with a small nose and full lips. Lying in my arms, she didn't look real.

How old was she?

My fingers brushed her shoulders and she trembled at the touch.

I wanted to ask her name—but I didn't.

I didn't have to.

Luminous gray eyes peered up at me.

"Sunny," I whispered.

My eyes flared open as I awoke with a jump. *Fuck me.* She had been in front of me the entire time—and I'd forgotten *her.* I'd always remembered helping a girl out of a watery grave—hell, I'd even told Tate about it freshman year, but the other details . . .

I raked a hand through my hair. *Did she remember me?*

She did. My gut knew it.

And suddenly my heart was pounding. *Was this why she'd been off with me lately?*

"Bad dream?" Tate asked.

I blinked and rubbed my eyes, still wrapping my head around the knowledge.

"Must have been. Dude. You okay?"

No. I wasn't. I shook my head, pushing his voice out as he continued to talk. So many things clicked into place—the automatic connection, that magnetic pull I felt, how she'd never been a stranger to me.

"You getting off the bus?" Tate asked as he gathered up his gym bag.

What?

I gazed around. We'd pulled up at the field house and parked. "Yeah. I—I need to see Sunny."

Tate had already texted a groupie to pick him up, and he headed to her car as he stepped to the curb. Ryn was riding with me, and we headed to the Land Cruiser parked closer to the field house.

I'd just crawled in the front seat and cranked it when I heard a girl scream.

"What was that?" Ryn said as we both flipped around to look out the rear window. We saw Bianca and Felix arguing a few feet away next to her white Lexus. She'd apparently been here to greet him.

Let it go, Max.

But then he jabbed his finger in her shoulder.

My eyes swept the lot. Of course, all the coaches had bolted, either heading off in their car or they'd gone into the field house to dump equipment. The only people left were the handful who'd been in the back of the bus.

Ryn and I got back out of my car and headed to where they were. Because I had issues with Felix, I let Ryn step in first. I was the captain of this team, but sometimes that came with knowing when not to open your big mouth.

"Nothing to see here," Felix snapped when Ryn asked what was the matter.

Bianca sent me a pleading look, almost as if telling me to go away. She played with her wrists, red marks on them. He'd tugged on her. Maybe she'd been in his face? My hands tightened. Whatever the reason, there was no excuse for manhandling a girl—not when you're as big as Felix.

A flush rode his cheek, showing a definite handprint where she'd slapped him. I'd been on the receiving end of that as well, once, only I'd walked away.

Ryn looked at Bianca. "I'm not leaving until you tell me you're okay."

He pointed to my car. "If you don't feel like driving, we can take you wherever you need to go."

She nodded and seemed to compose herself. "It—it's fine. I'm sorry I startled everyone. Felix—Felix didn't know I was going to be here, and we had an argument."

"Do you need anything?" I said.

"No. I'm going home." Her gaze went to Felix. "Alone."

Felix narrowed sly eyes at her, his lip curling. "Do what you want—but I won't be alone tonight."

As if his words had electrified her, she straightened up from where she'd been leaning against her car. She pointed her finger at him, frustration and hurt mingling on her face. "You think you can do whatever you want just because you wear a jersey and I care about you," she said. "But I'm done letting you get away with treating me like dirt. It's over." Her voice broke and she swiped at a tear that slid down her cheek.

Her eyes landed on me. "Even you," she whispered.

She opened her car door and with a peel of her tires, she flew out of the lot.

For the first time since we'd broken up, two things became very clear.

First of all, I'd never cared for Bianca the way I should have. She was too unstable and flighty for the long term. Had she just been the best fuck I'd had in college at the time? Maybe. Nothing I felt for her even came close to Sunny.

And second, I'd never cheated on her, but I hadn't given her the attention she needed. I hadn't spent the time with her she'd wanted because I hadn't been ready to commit. Not really. Football had always been first. It still was.

At the same time, I wasn't going to let Felix push her around either. She was a human being for fuck's sake, and if he'd been pushing her around . . . my fists clenched.

Felix started to walk away toward his vehicle, and I grabbed his arm and flipped him around. Ryn got between us. "Whoa, guys. We don't need another fight between you two."

I bit my words out slowly, making sure he saw the promise in my eyes. "If you ever hit her, I'll break your arm. You'll never throw another pass again."

An ugly snarl crossed his face. "You're too scared of ruining your career to back that up. Fuck off."

Then he popped away from us and jogged to his car.

We watched him speed off. "Dude, he looked scary," Ryn said. "Should we be worried about her?"

"I don't know." I rubbed my temple.

Ryn exhaled. "Do you mind if we just drive by Bianca's and make sure he doesn't go over there? I know she's not your favorite person, but . . ."

Yeah. I saw where he was coming from. I nodded.

chapter
THIRTY

Sunny

M
AX WAS HALF an hour late, and I assumed the line at Woo's to get our take-out was longer than he'd expected. I'd sent him a text earlier to check, but he hadn't responded.

I poured myself a cup of hot chocolate and hugged it as I took it to the couch in the den. I flipped on the television, curled a furry blanket around my feet, and waited.

And waited.

My stomach growled, reminding me I was starved. I'd zipped home from Mimi's, taken a long hot shower, and then straightened up the house for Max after I'd gotten his text. Now, I was done. Pretending today at the bridal shop had exhausted me. I took another sip of cocoa and rubbed my chest.

A knock came at the door.

I flew up off the couch, ran to the door, and flung it open.

Isabella and Ash stood there. I hid my disappointment by smiling.

"Hi there!"

"Did you even look before opening the door? What if I'd been the Daisy Man!" she exclaimed dramatically. She jiggled a six-pack of Corona while Ash showed me his stack of pizza boxes.

I grinned. "Beer and pizza. Come on in, my friends."

Ash chuckled, his big shoulders gliding effortlessly in a tight black shirt. "Sorry to intrude. I'm not sure who this Daisy Man is, but Isabella insisted you needed company." He shot a glance at her. "We were all set to hang out at my place, and she insisted on coming here."

I sent her a look that said, *Afraid to be alone and get cozy with Ash?*

She glared. *Yes, bitch. Now shut up.*

My eyes said, *Only because you have food and I'm hungry.*

"And who is this Daisy Man you guys are talking about?" Ash asked.

"Some weirdo left her a daisy on the back porch weeks ago. Scared the bejesus out of her," Isabella said, getting down some plates for us.

His eyes focused on me, a worried wrinkle on his brow, and I remembered something I'd been meaning to ask him. With classes, work, and getting over to check on Mimi, I'd missed a few study sessions at the library. This was the first time I'd seen him in a while. "The night I got locked in the library, did you see anyone using the stairwell at the back of the building—the one for maintenance?" My shoulders slumped. "Apparently, the police can't find any evidence."

He shook his head. "No. Isabella's already grilled me on the details of that night. I didn't see anyone near the stairwell."

I grimaced. "Did you see anything odd that night?"

He mulled it over. "Not weird, really, but I saw Felix leaving the library with a girl that wasn't Bianca. I just assumed he was an asshole who cheated on his girlfriend. You think it's important?"

No, but I pressed him. "Who was it?"

He shrugged. "Some redhead. Beats me what her name is. I'm new in town."

"The police aren't really concerned about it and are taking it as more of a joke," I said. "Maybe they're right."

Isabella sent me an expectant look. "Where's Max? We brought plenty for him too." I'd texted her earlier that he was coming over but hadn't mentioned the sushi. "I assumed he'd already be here."

"Yeah. Me, too." I helped myself to a slice of pepperoni, thanking them again for stopping by to have dinner and check on me.

A knock came half an hour later while we were watching *Dirty Dancing*.

Relief mingled with annoyance when I saw it was Max. At the door, I took in his low-waisted jeans and the soft knit of his cobalt blue sweater. "You're late."

His hand rested on the doorjamb as his eyes met mine. "And I didn't pick up dinner. I'm sorry."

My face stayed impassive. "It's good. I ate already."

"Yeah?" His eyes went to the commotion behind me, watching Isabella and Ash in their sock feet, sliding around on the hardwood in my den, attempting to dance like they knew what they were doing. I smiled at their antics. Isabella was convinced Ash looked like Patrick Swayze, hence the movie selection.

"What's going on?"

"They're reenacting a scene from *Dirty Dancing*." At Max's questioning eyebrow, I elaborated. "Ash lost a bet, so she's making him pay."

"Ah." He raked a hand through his dark hair. "Anyway, I'm sorry. I should have texted, but my phone died."

"There's a charger in your car."

"I wasn't paying attention." He grimaced. "I can explain though."

Whatever. I crossed my arms.

"You're beautiful," he said, his gaze soft, lingering on the bare-shoulder blouse I wore. His eyes landed on my lips. "Even when you're ornery."

My body leaned into his as if it had a mind of its own. "Do—do you want to come in?"

He nodded and trailed after me to the kitchen. "I saw Bianca tonight. She and Felix had a blow-up when she met the bus at the field house. I followed her home and found her crying in her car outside her apartment. We talked . . ." his voice stopped. "You okay?"

His words hit me like a sledgehammer. "I'm fine." I held it together by looking sightlessly into the fridge, forgetting why I'd even opened the door.

"Ryn was with me."

So? My lips tightened. Just hearing her name, knowing that she suspected we weren't real, drove me insane. Sometimes, I was even surprised she hadn't gossiped more about us or at least tried to tell the media. Maybe she did care about Max.

"Nothing happened," he said.

I flipped back around and let the fridge slam shut behind me. "I don't care. It's fine. Come on. You can finish the movie with us, but after that I need to study." I started to walk away.

"She broke up with Felix."

I froze, my pounding heart the only thing I could hear for a moment. I turned back to him. "Are—are you getting back with her?"

He reared back. "Fuck no."

"If you want to, I'll understand. We can 'break up' early . . ."

"Stop it. I don't want her . . . haven't in a long time." His voice was gruff.

"Yeah?"

He nodded. "I didn't touch her except to make sure she got in her apartment. We made sure Felix wasn't there and left. End of story."

He followed me into the den and sat next to me on the couch. Isabella and Ash sent us curious glances, and I figured it was easy to see things weren't quite right. Finally the movie ended and they both left. I saw them to the door and made a date to have lunch with them soon.

When I walked back into the den, Max's words hit me in the face.

"I remember you," he said quietly, a tumultuous look in his eyes.

My heart jumped. Trembling, I stumbled to the couch and plopped down next to him before my legs could give out. My world shifted, realigning itself and I cupped my cheeks, feeling, checking to see if this moment was real.

For a moment I couldn't breathe.

This is what it feels like to lose your breath over a guy, I randomly thought. I just looked at him.

He squeezed my hand. "I think my subconscious has been trying to tell me for a long time, and tonight I had a dream about a girl whose car went into a lake." His face filled with wonder. "You're that girl . . . the one who ran away into the woods. You were so beautiful . . ." he stopped, pinching the bridge between his nose, contrition on his face. "You ran away—and I let you. God, I should have gone after you and given you a ride . . . *something.*"

I bit my lip. "I wouldn't have let you. It all happened so fast for me to think really, but I couldn't involve you in my mess."

"It was the night you left your dad, wasn't it?" He focused piercing eyes on me. "You must have been terrified. I mean, now—it all makes sense."

I nodded. "Yes."

He touched my hair, almost gingerly, and let his hand drift down my cheek to my arm. He laced our fingers together. "My mom died the night of your wreck. One second we were getting the keys to our cabin, and the next she was lying on the ground. She'd been complaining of a headache for days . . ." He cleared his throat, emotion working his face. He tugged at his bottom lip.

I slid over closer to him and rested my head on his shoulder. "I'm sorry."

He leaned against me and we supported each other. "It happened the summer before I came to Leland. We were on a last little hurrah vacation together—and then you—it was like I was there, but I wasn't, ya know? In the days after she died, sometimes I couldn't recall what I'd had to eat that morning. All I did was play football, and it saved me. But how could I . . . forget you?"

The saying *maybe he's just not that into you* came to mind, but I didn't say it. I believed the universe had pulled strings for us—but did he?

"Stop."

"Stop what?"

"I see your wheels turning. Look at me." He turned my chin toward him. "I'm sorry I didn't remember you from three years ago. My brain just filed it away—or locked it up—I don't know. Maybe I wasn't ready to see it? Does that make sense?"

I nodded.

"And tonight? I'm sorry I didn't text you. It was an oversight."

I blinked, because it felt like he was changing the subject too fast, as if he was unsure about dissecting the night we met.

But I went with it. "I believe you about Bianca." He wasn't Bart, and he never would be.

Relief crossed his face. "Thank God." His thumb caressed my lips. "Sunny . . . I want you so much that it scares the fuck out of me."

"I'm scared too." Of getting my heart shattered. Of you not having the same feelings for me that I have for you.

He kissed me, his lips soft but then insistent, his tongue demanding.

My anxieties were shoved away, and my overwhelming need for him skyrocketed. We'd been apart so long. I whipped my shirt off and his fingers traced the outline of my breast then dipped in to skate across my nipple, strumming it, making me moan.

We went at each other like crazed animals.

He jerked his shirt off while I unclasped my bra, and within seconds we were skin to skin, brushing against each other. His forearms lifted me up and sat me in his lap while I kissed down his throat to his chest, my teeth nipping at him and then soothing it with kisses.

He tugged down my pants and shoved my underwear to my knees, his fingers finding me like a homing beacon. He strummed me, and I moved with him, arching into his every stroke.

"You're drenched," he growled. "Fucking mine."

Almost frantic, he unsnapped his jeans and pushed them down just enough to pull out his cock. Straddling him, I stroked him up and down as he played with my breasts, sucking on one then the other, his scruff like fire, hurting so good.

"I don't have a condom," he whispered in my ear. "But I'm clean."

I wanted him like that. I rotated my center against his hard length. "I'm on the pill."

"Fuck, yes," he groaned.

He tossed his head back and called out my name as I settled him in deep.

But then he took over. Fast. Furious. Perfect.

Hands held my hips and he thrust into me. He tangled a hand up in my hair and tugged my head back, and once my neck was arched, he sucked me hard. It made me hotter. Desperate. Wetness dripped between us. I screamed his name when I went over the edge.

He came soon after, satisfaction and something else that I couldn't read on his face as he kissed me.

chapter
THIRTY-ONE

Max

HOMECOMING ARRIVED. ALL week I'd been obsessively study-ing the opposing team's defense and perfecting my pass. I was not going to lose another fucking game. Then my dad called and announced he'd be at the game tonight. Encouraged by Millicent and my chance at the Heisman, he was eager to come. I hadn't seen him since last Christmas, and it was screwing with my head.

Ryn pulled me to the side as we waited to take the field. "What the hell is wrong with you today? You're distracted."

He wasn't wrong. Stress was eating at me. Every single thing I did, every play I made was crucial.

I rubbed my head. "I'm fine."

But I played like shit during the first half. We were up by ten when the defense read my play, and I threw the ball right into the beefy hands of one of the Carolina players, who ran it back for a touchdown.

At halftime, my gaze locked with Sunny's and I sent her a two-finger kiss and held it up. It was something she'd come up with early in the season—a public display to make me look good when the news covered me or it was photographed.

Now, it actually meant something to me, but I didn't know how to define it. I didn't allow myself to think about the depth of emotion she created. It was as if I was standing at a crossroads and I couldn't decide which direction I wanted to move.

Coach sat me down in the locker room. "Whatever's been eating at you, work it out of your system."

Right. I resolved once again to push Sunny—and my dad out of my head.

In the fourth quarter, I threw a gorgeous touchdown pass to Tate. We scored again with a field goal in the next series and won us the game.

I met Dad after the game, and we headed to the press conference where I was asked questions and then Dad and I posed for photo ops. Later, we piled up in his Escalade, picked up Sunny at her house, and headed to an exclusive Italian place. Millicent had tipped off a few choice reporters that we'd all be there.

At the restaurant, he talked loudly to everyone we passed who knew him, signed a few autographs, and generally made an ass of himself over Sunny.

He finished chewing a bite of his filet and considered me. In his late forties, he was still a handsome man with sandy brown hair and a trim build. The only hint of age was a slight dusting of gray at his temples and the crow's feet around his eyes.

Sunny kept eyeballing us, probably sensing the tension roiling off me.

I zoned in when I realized he'd been talking for a while.

He finished a long critique about my throwing technique and how it was off. Then he went on to talk about the merits of the freshman quarterback at Ohio who'd been taking up most of the news coverage for the past two weeks.

Sunny set down her knife and fork on her plate. "With all due respect, Mr. Kent. Max is the highest rated quarterback in the country. No freshman at Ohio can hold a candle to him."

A burst of laughter came from him. "Oh honey, call me Byron. I'm way too young to be Mr. to you—and you're my future daughter-in-law. Hopefully, we'll be seeing a lot more of each other in the future."

She smiled politely, but I sensed her reserve. She'd worn a soft blue dress with pleats at the neckline and a flowy skirt and strappy heels—which I fully intended to take off with my teeth later.

Dad set down his napkin and considered her. "Are you pregnant, dear?"

I froze mid-bite. *What a fucking jerk!*

Sunny looked at me and then at Dad. "Ah, no. Perhaps I shouldn't have worn this loose dress." She smiled wryly and shrugged.

She was too damn nice to him.

I set my fork down. "I'd appreciate it if you minded your own damn business."

"You're my son. Am I not allowed to ask questions?" His expression changed, growing pensive. "I know we haven't always seen eye to eye, but you're growing up, getting married, and I'm cutting back on my hours at the station. Maybe we can spend more time together."

My food wanted to crawl up out of my stomach. "Now?"

"I know I wasn't always there for you—"

I scowled. "You were never there. And now you want to show interest when life is going well for me?"

He folded his hands together. "Don't be a little bitch, Max."

Keeping my voice low and making sure my face stayed impassive, I said, "I'm here right now for the photo op, so they can see a father and son together." I waved my hand around at the people in the restaurant. "But it's all a goddam lie."

Seconds ticked by as we stared at each other. His phone on the table pinged, and he flicked his eyes down at it. Mine followed, seeing it was his current girlfriend, some ex-supermodel. And it just hammered it home.

"You can't fix something that you never cared about in the first place." I nudged my head at the phone. "Go on, answer it."

"Can I interest you in any dessert?" the server said as he reached our table, oblivious to the tension.

"Sunny, do you want anything?" I asked.

"No," she said quietly.

I read disappointment on her face before she quickly covered it.

I exhaled heavily, feeling the exhaustion from the day catching up to me.

What did she want from me?

I pushed the thought away. I couldn't let anything get to me right now—not when there was only one regular season game left. Tonight I'd nearly screwed up everything when I'd thrown that interception.

"We'll take the check," my father added, tucking his phone back in his pocket.

Good.

I was ready to get the hell out of here.

chapter
THIRTY-TWO

Sunny

W E WENT BACK to Max's after dinner with his dad. He made love to me as if on autopilot.

This is a photo op. We're a goddam lie.

My heart dipped at the memory of those words he'd uttered to his father.

Doubts crept in. *Did he mean that about us too?*

On Sunday morning, I left his bed while he still slept and went to my place. After showering, I headed to the kitchen to make a chocolate pecan pie to take to Mimi's later for our early Thanksgiving celebration we were having since Ash and Isabella would be out of the state for the holiday.

My phone pinged with a text, and after I'd poured the mixture into a pie shell and popped it in the oven, I picked it up.

The text was from an unknown number.

Watch your back.

I set it down on the counter. *Don't engage.*

Even though I didn't want to worry Max before a game, I forwarded it to him. I couldn't lie to him, and he'd be upset if he found out after the fact.

Someone knocked at my door and I jumped.

This whole thing was making me antsy. I checked the window and saw Isabella's white SUV.

I headed to the den and opened the door. Isabella and Ash stood there, each of them holding a dish to take to Mimi's. "Happy Friendsgiving," they both cried in unison.

I grinned and got them settled while I headed to my bedroom to get dressed.

Max burst through my bedroom door as I was putting on mascara. "I just saw your text. Where's your phone?" he said sharply. "I want to see the number."

I nudged my head at where it sat on the vanity table amid all my makeup. "It's an unknown number, probably a burner."

He picked it up and glared at it as if expecting the phone to speak to him. His finger did a flurry of movements, and I craned my neck to see what he was doing. He'd taken a screenshot of it and then sent it to himself. "I'm going to forward this to the campus police. They need to be aware of what's going on."

"Thanks." I turned my back on him, smoothing out an eyebrow.

He paused, his eyes searching mine in the mirror. "Everything okay? You left without saying anything this morning."

"I'm fine."

He smirked. "*Fine* is never fine when it comes to females." He leaned against the wall, crossing his arms, giving me a nice view of his biceps.

My lips tightened at being reminded of his other conquests.

I applied another coat of lipstick to keep my hands busy. He watched, making me jittery.

"Can you give me some space, please? I can't finish with you staring."

"What's wrong with you?" he asked. "You've been weird lately."

I set down my eye shadow on the vanity top. "Some of the things you said last night—it got me to thinking. I mean, we're having sex, but is that all we are?"

His brows knitted. "No."

"Then what are we? Define it." I hated the insecurity I heard in my voice—but I just needed him to tell me how he felt.

A muscle clenched in his jaw, his face hardening. Distance grew in his gaze. "I can't do this a few days before a game—"

I held my hand up. "Fine. Then let me finish getting dressed."

He stood there as if he wanted to say something, his shoulders tense, but then pivoted and left, neatly shutting the door behind him.

Once at Mimi's, things went well. Her apartment was comfortable and before long, we'd all eaten and the guys had disappeared to do chores for Mimi—which mostly consisted of getting down her Christmas decorations from the small attic she had.

Mimi watched Max drape green garland around the mantel in the living room as Frank Sinatra holiday music filled the air. He pulled a snow globe from one of her boxes and set it on the coffee table. "Such big hands around that globe."

My lips twitched. "Stop having sex fantasies about Max, Mimi. It's weird."

Isabella just snorted.

"Just because I'm old, doesn't mean I'm blind. I still got some life left in me yet." She put away dishes in the cabinet. "You know, I see how he looks at you."

I stopped wiping her table. "The only thing important to him is football. Always will be."

chapter
THIRTY-THREE

Max

MONDAY I WOKE up, showered, and dressed in jeans and a flannel that Sunny had commented she liked once.

My chest ached, and I rubbed it. She needed me to reassure her about us—but my head was all over the place. Pressure was everywhere—from Coach, the players, and myself.

Not to mention, today was my mom's birthday. I pinched the bridge of my nose. I'd give anything to have her here with me when I played my last regular season game this week.

You look like hell, I told myself, staring into the mirror at the dark shadows under my eyes.

Tate was peering into the fridge wearing boxers and nothing else when I came into the kitchen.

"Morning, Gorgeous," I said, setting my backpack on the counter. "You ready for this week?"

"No." He sent me a bleary-eyed look as he opened a carton of OJ and drank it straight from the mouth.

My phone pinged. It was my dad.

I'm coming back to Atlanta this weekend for your last game.

Just great.

I replied, *Do what you want.*

His next text blew me away. *I'll call you later. I know what today is. She's on my mind too.*

He'd remembered it was her birthday?

I was fucking shocked.

Tate gave me a considering glance. "You okay, mate?"

I nodded and leaned against the counter. "Yeah. Just family stuff gets me worked up—and I don't need it before a big game."

Tate took another swig from the OJ. "What do you need?"

Sunny came to mind, but I didn't say it.

I grabbed a Gatorade from the fridge. "Just the game, man."

I stalked off, not wanting to talk anymore. I went outside and immediately checked out Sunny's place, making sure everything was fine. It appeared to be, so I walked to my Land Cruiser.

What the hell? I came to a halt at the knife in my front driver's side tire. I dropped my backpack to the ground and inspected it. Not only had they stabbed the damn thing, but they'd punctured it in several places before leaving the knife for me to find. I yelled for Tate and he came out the door, still clad in boxers.

We checked out the rest of the car, and sure enough the passenger side door had a deep gouge going all the way through the paint to the metal of the frame.

"Bloody hell, someone doesn't like you very much," Tate said, scratching at his jawline. "I know you're thinking Felix, but with the game coming up . . . it seems risky for him to pull this."

I paced around the car again. Someone had been right outside my bedroom window last night screwing with my property. With Sunny just across the street.

Was she okay?

My mind flew in a hundred different directions . . .

I called her but she didn't pick up. I knocked on her door, and when I didn't get an answer, I ran around to the back and knocked. Nothing. I peeked in the windows and had a direct view into her kitchen. Everything looked fine. I jogged back to my house.

Tate was still standing in the yard, hands on his hips like a mother hen. "Everything good?"

"I guess she's in class already." *I hoped so.*

Feeling a sense of urgency, I booked it to the detached garage where I kept my Harley.

"Let me know if she isn't in class," Tate called out to me as I backed my bike out. I adjusted my helmet, Tate handed me my backpack, and I cranked it up. Within seconds, I was on the road and pointed toward the Clark Science Building.

By the time I parked and got inside the building, I was five minutes late. I took the stairs at a run. I got to the third floor landing and almost smacked into a couple kissing when I turned the corner. They split apart and the male spun his head to see me.

Felix.

"Watch it," he muttered, his face flushed and sweaty. His eyes narrowed when he saw it was me.

I was planning on ignoring him—until I caught a look at *who* he was with. It wasn't Bianca, and for that I was glad. After the game when I'd followed her home, she'd told me that he hadn't actually hit her, but he'd pushed her a few times. She'd made excuses for him . . . he was frustrated about the game, etc., but he was trouble waiting to happen.

"Hey, Max," Cyndi, the waitress from the coffee shop, said. She raked fingers through her long red hair as she tried to put it back in place. My eyes went to her shirt, which was halfway unbuttoned, giving a perfect view of her cleavage.

"You see something you like, Kent?" Felix asked, a sneer on his face.

I shook off his irritating tone. *Don't get sucked in.* I forced a nonchalant shrug. "Carry on," I said and kept going up the stairs.

He called up after me. "You seem to be running late this morning,

Kent. Hope everything's okay."

I stopped on the landing above him and glared down. "Yeah. You wouldn't happen to know anything about that, would you?"

His shoulders puffed up. "Just being civil, that's all. Making conversation."

I searched his face, looking for clues that he'd been the one who messed with my car—but all I got was a blank stare. No gleam of amusement or knowing look. Either he'd learned to hide his expressions better and had become more sinister with his pranks, or he didn't have a damn clue what was going on.

I exited the stairwell and rushed into class. There she was in her usual seat and all my anxiety melted. She had her blond hair up in a tight ponytail and wore a gray shirt that said *Nap Queen*.

Mr. Whitt came into class and we got started, but Felix's image loomed in my head again. Something was tugging at me, pricking, and I couldn't nail it down.

Then it dawned on me. The knife in my tire—I recognized it. Coach had given the team pearl-handled knives freshman year after we'd won the Southeastern Conference. He'd also had them engraved with our first initial on the metal end. It was small and barely noticeable, but most decidedly there.

The knife in my tire had a pearl handle.

I waited until Whitt wasn't looking, pulled my phone out, and texted Tate, asking him to check the knife.

He replied right away. *I was just about to text you. I remembered too. Yes, it's the same. I pulled mine out to compare. The initial on the bottom is F.*

Fucker!

"Where are you going?" Sunny asked as I gathered up my things. "Max?"

My chest rose as I shoved my laptop inside my bag. "I'm going to find Felix. He messed with my car this morning."

"Don't," she said softly, careful to keep her voice low so Whitt wouldn't hear us.

I slipped out of class, ignoring the look Whitt sent me.

"Max, wait!"

I flipped around to see Sunny had followed me. I bounded down the steps of the stairwell, stopping at the third floor landing and spinning in a circle. He was gone. I raked my hands through my hair. "He was in the stairwell five minutes ago—with Cyndi," I said once she came to stand next to me.

"He wants you to lose your cool, Max. Don't let him win."

She was right, but what else was he capable of?

I WAITED OUTSIDE the Clark building for an hour, but I didn't see Felix leave when classes got out. I did see Sunny head out for her next class, and I waved at her as she made her way in the opposite direction. As for Felix, I figured he either left through another exit or was in another science class.

I drove to where he lived with a couple of other football players. His Tahoe wasn't there, but I parked and waited.

Tate called.

"What?" I said, answering the phone after taking off my helmet.

"I know you're pissed, but you need to chill," were the first words out of his mouth.

"Why?"

"Because if you go off half-cocked, you're going to hurt yourself, him, and the entire team. Plus, what if it wasn't Felix? Maybe someone is setting him up. Just because it's his knife, doesn't mean it was him."

That sounded farfetched.

"You have to think long and hard about what you do next."

Oh, I was. It was all I could think about. My fists itched to pound him into the ground.

"Think of everything you've done this year for the team—and the whole fake thing with Sunny—are you just going to throw all that away?"

"I don't think I can be around him and not punch him," I bit out.

"I know. Just get through the game. We're so close. Just think about your shiny little trophy. Felix would laugh his ass off if you threw it away on a fight with him. He'd love it if you broke your hand on his face."

I exhaled a deep breath and clenched my hands.

Maybe Tate was right.

Just get through the game.

I blew out a breath, pushing my rage down. "Then, I'll need a work out at the gym."

"Good call."

I clicked the phone off, cracked my neck, and cranked my bike.

chapter
THRITY-FOUR

Max

TUESDAY DAWNED, AND I woke up as soon as the sun peeked in through Sunny's blinds. Only a few words had passed between us last night when I'd shown up at her door, just a silent communication that I needed her.

After my workout at the gym the day before, I'd decided to go see Coach. I'd laid everything out on the line for him, from the daisy to the basement to the knife in my tire. He called Felix into his office and confronted him with my accusations. Felix pushed it off with a nonchalant shrug, convincingly denying any involvement in anything. He said he'd lost his knife over a year ago. He also brought another guy on the team whose name began with an F.

Frank.

Frank was a good defensive player and had no beef with me.

Whatever. It was all bullshit.

In the end, Coach only scolded Felix for perpetuating the tension between us and told him he was watching him. *Watching him?*

Angry and frustrated, I left the office and went straight to Sunny's where I crawled in her warm bed, burying my face in the scent of her in the sheets. She put on a soft gray tank and curled up next to me. We fell asleep holding each other.

Now it was morning, and I was damn grateful to wake up next to her. My hand touched the curve of her cheek, trailing down to the delicate lines of her throat. My thumb hovered over her pulse, seeing the increase of its rhythm. She shifted and moaned, her body arching into me.

I went further, my hand slipping under her tank and splaying across her breasts. My fingers toyed with the jewelry on her nipple, tweaking it until her eyes opened, a heaviness there that I knew was desire.

My hand kept going—painfully slow. It splayed across her ribs, counting them, thanking the heavens she was whole and complete and alive and with me. My fingers drifted over her lace panties, then I changed my mind and went to her nipple and drew little circles around it with my fingers. Her bottom teeth tugged on her lip, a little gasp coming from her parted mouth as she wiggled closer to my hand.

"Do you want me to touch you?" I whispered, leaning down to lightly kiss her on the lips.

Her eyes flared. "Yes. Please."

My fingers slipped under her panties, dancing across her skin with a slowness that wrecked me. I buried my face in her hair and went for her neck, my mouth finding purchase and sucking hard just as my finger delved inside her.

Her entire body shuddered. I stroked her until she gasped my name, then I stopped and went back to her nipple, to those maddening circles.

Her hips rubbed against my thigh, her leg twitching against mine as she tugged me closer to her. "Don't tease me," she said.

"Not yet," I growled, my tongue licking the edges of her ear.

I lifted her tank up and over her head, tossing it to the floor. Gazing down at her, I got lost. She was all creamy skin, long blond hair, and legs for days.

I groaned as her hand pushed inside my briefs and stroked my cock, making me nearly come. I pulled away from her touch. "Tricky girl," I whispered before leaning down and wrapping my lips around her nipple, first one then the other. She grasped my head to her chest, her breaths coming in hurried pants as she arched off the bed to keep my mouth on her.

"I love waking up with you," I said against her skin.

My fingers found her clit and circled, making her cry out. I put one languid finger inside her and then two, working at her gently. I crawled down her body and put my mouth on her, sucking. The air thickened around us, need rolling through both of us—and still I waited.

And just when I didn't think she could be any sexier, she wiggled away from underneath me and scooted up to the head of the bed. Using her thumbs, she slid her underwear down her legs, and my hungry gaze followed. She turned over on her knees and gazed at me from over her shoulder.

Fuck.

She was dripping, all pink and soft skin. She trembled when I spread her apart with my fingers and went back to suckling at her from this new angle until finally her whole body tightened, her internal muscles clenching as she came around my mouth and fingers.

With one fluid motion my cock was inside her, riding out her spasms, barely hanging on to my own sanity as I slammed into her. She held on to the headboard, long hair hanging down on either side of her as I put my hand on her back, adjusting her to an angle where I could fuck her as hard and deep as I could.

And still she wanted more.

I gave it to her.

I kissed her scars, my hands tracing the lines of the tattoo on her nape. Time heals all wounds, but the scars remain, making you who you are. To me, hers were a beautiful mosaic. I admired her more because of them . . . because she'd come out of darkness and learned to fly.

Her muscles clamped around me as she came again, and this time I went with her, calling out her name. I never wanted this sensation to end. I never wanted us to end. Never. Never.

Still inside her, I moved, hard and ready for her again. I wanted her over and over and over until neither of us could move, until she begged me to stop.

My right hand stroked the lines of her spine, and she shuddered, her hair still hanging down on either side of her face. I leaned over her and moved it out of the way. Our eyes locked. One, two, three breaths—and the world tilted, everything sliding around until it fell gently into place.

I loved her. I loved her.

But I was terrified to say it.

THANKSGIVING CAME AND I spent it with the team for a special meal while Sunny went to Mimi's. They had plans to go shopping on Friday—something about special flip-flops being on sale. I had intense practices anyway and didn't need any distractions. Our big game was Saturday, and all my focus was there.

I missed her.

It was the knocking at my door that woke me on game day.

I checked my phone. It was six in the morning, and too damn early for a normal person.

I lumbered out of bed, pulled on a pair of jeans, and opened the front door where a teary Bianca practically fell in my arms. I caught her to keep her from hitting the floor.

What now?

"Bianca?" I asked, as I set her back on her feet. "Wanna tell me why you're crying?"

"It's Felix."

My chest rose. For the sake of the game, I'd let the knife thing go, but I didn't want to be reminded of the asshole. I spent my time avoiding him this week as much as possible.

"He hasn't hurt you, has he?"

She wiped at her face with her hands. "No. I almost wish he had."

Okay.

I exhaled and opened the door wider. "You best come inside."

She tugged her sweater around her shoulders and sat on the couch.

Tate came out of his room in his boxers and took in the scene. He squinted at me. "What's she doing here?"

He'd never liked her.

I shrugged. His guess was as good as mine.

She fluttered her eyes. "I came because of something I found out last night. I'm sick of keeping secrets, and as much as it hurts me to say this, I think Felix is out of control."

"Go on," I said.

She bit her lip, an apologetic gleam in her eyes as she took me in. "I know Felix has pulled pranks on you—like the snake freshman year. What you don't know is he also left a daisy at Sunny's door just to screw with her. He wants what you have . . ." a small sobbing sound came from her as fresh tears flowed. "And he probably only dated me because he knew it would bother you. But what people don't realize is that I really care about him. I wanted him to have everything too. I wanted him to have your spot, and I pushed him and urged him on when he'd do things. I tried to make him jealous by talking about you—but I'd never condone what he's done lately."

My senses sharpened. "Like what?"

"I went to his place last night to see him—I don't know—just because I still care even though he's seeing Cyndi. He let me in. He—he bragged about messing with your car and getting away with it."

I slapped my fist into my palm.

Tate came over to us, his hand on my shoulder. "Dude. It isn't like we didn't figure it out already."

She closed her eyes. "He's also responsible for Sunny being locked in the library."

Cold fury ran over me. My teeth snapped and my eyes narrowed. "Did he get you to do it?" I bit the words out.

"Max . . ." Tate said, and I heard the tenseness in his tone.

"Shut up, Englishman. Let her talk."

Bianca shook her head furiously. "It wasn't me. I promise. That night at the library I was with Felix, but we were having problems. I went to the restroom, and when I came back he was talking to Cyndi. They were whispering, and I couldn't hear what they were saying, but I heard Sunny's name. I stormed off, and I don't know what happened after I left them—but I can imagine. I overheard him talking to Cyndi in the stairwell a few days ago. They were laughing about it." She twisted her face, tears falling. "I'd never do that, Max. She could have been hurt."

She had been hurt! She'd fallen off a goddam cart. What if she'd broken her neck?

I ran both hands through my hair. "Why are you telling me this now? Why not as soon as you knew about the basement?"

Her face caved in on itself. "Because I *love* him. I kept thinking we were going to get back together—but last night he told me he was done with me for good." Fresh tears came.

I stood and paced around the room, my head a mess. Bianca didn't give a shit about anyone but herself and the only reason she was tattling was because she was miffed at Felix.

What had I ever seen in her?

Whatever. I couldn't focus on her.

But Felix?

I was going to kill that fucker.

In the background I heard Tate dealing with Bianca, talking to her and edging her toward the door. She kept apologizing for coming over early, saying that she'd been up all night wrestling with what to do.

I barely noticed.

I walked to the bathroom and turned on the cold water at full blast and splashed my face. Wiping it off with my hand, I glared at myself in the mirror.

Tate came to the open door, his voice calm. "She's gone. You okay?"

I gripped the edges of the sink and looked at him. "I could let the daisy thing go. And the car—it's just money, and I know he wants me to get mad. But locking her in a fucking basement? Hell no." I tied my hair up in a man-bun.

Tate frowned. "What are you going to do, mate? Do I need to call Coach?" I heard the worry in his voice, and it reminded me that he needed this game too. It was his senior year, and with the draft coming up, every single play counted toward making your stats look good. I rubbed my face.

I could tell Coach, but at this point there was no proof, and I'd seen his reaction already. Maybe Coach didn't want to believe it. Maybe Coach needed this win so bad he was past caring what happened off the field. Plus, it was hearsay and he'd tell me he couldn't do jack about that. I had to come up with how to handle Felix. And it had to be good—good enough that I didn't lose the game or get kicked off the team.

I got in the shower and let the hot water wash over me while I mulled it all over. I couldn't come up with any scenario where I came out smelling like roses.

One risky move and it could all go up in smoke.

THE NIGHT AIR was crisp and cold with not a cloud in the sky, perfect for a game. I felt loose and ready after letting one of the trainers work on getting the kinks out of my shoulders. The only rule I needed to follow to keep my cool was to pretend I didn't want to rip Felix's head off. Fool him. I stared off into space and zoned in on the game and what was waiting for me. I imagined the opposing players, their weaknesses, and how to beat them. I visualized every play, every hit I might get, and every touchdown pass I was going to throw. I used every single trick Coach had taught me.

Felix waltzed in, his beady eyes assessing me as he walked by. I waved, making him start before picking up his pace and going to his locker.

He opened it and froze.

I smiled behind my hand, even as Tate shot me one of his warning looks. Okay, okay, he'd talked me down from beating the shit out of Felix, but that didn't mean that I couldn't fuck with him.

I knew what he saw. My pearl-handled knife stuck in one of his practice jerseys. I'd practically shredded the material. It had taken me getting here early and picking his lock—*payback's a bitch*—but I'd managed.

It was a far cry from my eighty thousand dollar vehicle he'd ruined, but it made me feel better.

He'd thought he'd make me crack; but I was in control. *I had to be.*

On the other hand, I was taking a hell of a chance that he wouldn't run straight to Coach, but I had my lie all ready to go.

I'd lost my knife a while back.

Maybe it belonged to some other player with an M initial.

Plus, this was the most important game of the season, and I was counting on the fact that if Felix did run his mouth, Coach wouldn't want to hear any shit before we took the field. Not to mention, we *were* the two best quarterbacks on the team. No way in hell would he bench us and put in a third-string player.

Felix shot a quick look over his shoulder, but I made sure to be cleaning my shoes, my expression easy going. Calm. I trash talked with the other players.

Later, Coach called us all together, and I was exceedingly polite when I asked if Felix could pass me a water bottle during the pre-game talk. He eyed me warily.

If I wasn't so angry, I'd be enjoying this.

We headed out to face Taylor University, one of the top-rated schools in the country.

The hometown crowd was insanely loud, homemade signs and cheers from every direction. I looked up into the packed stadium stands to send Sunny my two-fingers kiss, but she wasn't there. Neither was Mimi. I saw my dad, though, sitting in the seat he'd managed to find that was behind the two he kept each season. I'd told him when he said he wanted to come that he'd have to figure out a way to sit near Sunny because his seat now belonged to Mimi. *So where were they?*

I slowed my run, and the football player behind me bumped into me as we were running out, and I quickly stepped out of the way to let them pass. I jogged to the bench, my eyes searching the student section, thinking perhaps she'd decided to sit with Ash and Isabella, but then I remembered it was Thanksgiving weekend and they'd gone home to see family.

I felt off-kilter when the game started, especially when we got off to two false starts and a holding penalty.

At the end of the half, we trailed seventeen to three as we walked to the locker rooms. We'd had two missed kicks and I'd thrown an interception. Anxiety rode me hard.

You've been in tougher situations, I reminded myself.

My gut churned for another reason as I passed the empty seats where Sunny and Mimi should be.

Where was she?

chapter
THIRTY-FIVE

Sunny

IT WAS A few hours before game day, and I was taking a pregnancy test.

Yes, I was on the pill, but accidents were possible, and as much as we'd been together—

I stopped. *Don't go there, Sunny.* You're not pregnant.

The night before I stayed at Mimi's because she'd been under the weather. We'd watched some TV and had dinner together. Right before I went to the guest room to sleep, I'd recalled the comment that Max's dad had made about me being pregnant, and it dawned on me that my period was late this month. I'd barely slept, and this morning when the sun came up, I headed back home, stopping at Walgreens along the way to buy the most expensive test I could find.

The earliest pregnancy indicator on the market, the packaging promised. *Please let it be negative.*

I rushed inside the house and locked the door—as if I was afraid Max could sense what I was doing and suddenly appear. Stupid.

"It doesn't look good, Charlie," I said to the unicorn on the wall as I walked in the bathroom. He glared down at me. I imagined he'd say something like *What did you expect, idiot? It's Max-freaking-Kent. All you have to do is look at him and you get knocked up.*

Max.

God.

He would—I didn't know what he'd do.

Nausea rose in my stomach as I read the directions on the back of the box. I sat down on the cold tile in the bathroom, recalling how Bianca had told him she was pregnant. She'd lied but I could only imagine the fear he must have felt.

He might resent me.

And those were the words that pinged around in my head as I took out the white pieces of plastic and did my thing. I set it aside on the back of the toilet and waited.

A knock came at my front door, sending me in every direction. I scrambled to pull back on my skinny jeans and ran out of the bathroom in my sock feet.

Mimi stood at the door dressed in a roomy number seventeen jersey Max had given her, leggings, and her fake Uggs.

"Whatcha doing?" I asked, trying to play off my *I might be pregnant* face. I caught a glimpse of a yellow cab as it pulled away from the curb. She'd woken up this morning feeling better after a bout of bronchitis but was still determined to get to the game. "I was coming to get you later for the game, silly. You didn't have to waste your money and come here."

That had been our plan anyway.

She swallowed, and it was then I noticed the way her lips compressed.

"Mimi? What's the matter?"

She shook her head and brushed past me and into the house, and I followed her all the way to the den.

"Your father—his cousin just called me. He's dying. The doctors don't expect him to make it through the weekend. He asking to see you. He's home."

I found myself sitting even though I hadn't remembered doing it.

My lips went numb but I managed to move them anyway. "Why now?"

Mimi sat next to me. "I don't know. Maybe he wants to ask forgiveness. He is a preacher."

My heart dropped. Before my mother died, he'd been a decent father to me, but could I just forget all the bad? "Do I need to be there?" I couldn't think.

Mimi looked at me, her face set in gentle lines. "It's ultimately up to you, but perhaps closure would be good. He's all you have left. And it's his dying wish."

I sucked in a breath. "What about Max's game?"

She nodded, petting my head like I was a child. "I know Max. He'll understand."

I leaned into her. "Will you—will you go with me?"

She nodded. "I've no love for your father, but I'll go for you. Just you, sugar. I'll pack us some Long Island Iced Tea, too. Well, not for you since you'll have to do the driving." A sad smile crossed her lips. "I wouldn't mind visiting your mama's grave, too. I didn't go to the funeral."

I nodded. I got that. Part of me wanted to see it again—and my brother's.

I'd left so many things behind.

For three years, I'd shoved everything from North Carolina into a dark box and focused on being the person I wanted to be. But now, perhaps it was time to face my past. I stood, my head fuzzy as I stumbled toward the hallway. "I'll pack."

chapter
THIRTY-SIX

Max

W E MARCHED ON the field for the second half, the smell of popcorn and beer filling my senses. I checked the stands. Still no Sunny.

Back in the locker room, when Coach had taken a restroom break, I'd snatched my phone to see if she'd sent me any texts. She hadn't. I sent her one.

Where are you? Worried.

She hadn't replied, but then I'd had to put my phone away when halftime was over. I didn't care about the appearances; I just wanted her to be okay.

Resolving to get back in the game, I slapped Tate on the back. "Dude. I'm throwing you the ball all damn day and you better catch it and hang on. We're gonna win."

He nodded, a gleam in his eyes. "Bloody hell, I like your pep talks."

"Let's do this," I called out as we lined up. Several agreeing murmurs came from my guys. The ball snapped, and I connected a gorgeous pass to Tate, who ran a route straight to the end zone. The crowd went nuts.

At a time out, I grabbed water from one of the boys and sat on the bench with Harley, the offensive coach. He walked me through some possible scenarios of the Taylor defense.

Felix approached although I pretended to barely notice. "I see your fiancée isn't in the stands. Wonder where she is, Kent? You think she found someone else?"

Now that I'd scored, I felt more in control. "Don't be such a baby, Felix, just because you aren't playing in the biggest game of my career. Fuck off."

His ears reddened. "I hope we lose this game."

I shook my head at him and smirked. "You will say anything to make me blow up. Guess it really doesn't matter anyway. The police will handle you."

His eyes narrowed. "What lies are you spouting?"

"I know what you did in the library to Sunny. Bianca told me. I skipped campus police and went to the Atlanta PD today and told them everything. Hell, I hate my father, but I even took him with me." I forced a laugh. "Everyone loves him, you know . . . big famous NFL player and all. The cops were more than willing to listen to us. He even signed a few autographs. They're waiting for you just outside the stadium because I asked them to let you be part of the team—just in case I got hurt."

Part of that was true and part of that was utter bullshit. I had gone to the police, but the cops weren't waiting for him. They didn't have enough evidence . . . yet.

I smiled a shit-eating grin, enjoying the shock on his face. "See ya." I jogged out on the field for another run.

We started off at the fifty, and when I saw the double coverage, I sidestepped, took an opening in the defense, and ran like hell, the sound of the crowd louder the further I went.

Touchdown! I tossed the ball in the crowd and a fan caught it.

I glanced up to Sunny's seats and kissed my fingers—out of habit— but she still wasn't there.

Let it go, Max. She's okay.

I concentrated on the next possession. We lined up, the ball was snapped, and like perfect choreography, I looked down the left sideline and connected with Tate for a twenty-yard pick up. Another pass to the tight end put us within thirty yards of a touchdown.

We moved the ball further down the field.

But we had to score to win. Time was ticking.

I caught the snap, looked down the center, and saw Tate wide open. I sailed it through the air, and he caught it on the ten and ran it in for the final touchdown.

The noise in the stadium was deafening. Confetti went everywhere. The marching band cranked up our fight song.

My heart raced as I looked at the scoreboard and watched as the seconds counted down. Three, two, one . . .

I tossed my head back and yelled my victory into the now darkened sky. *That's for you, Mom,* I whispered into the chilly air.

Like a horde, players and fans swarmed the field, jostling each other. It was an assault of flashbulbs, reporters, and the other team coming to congratulate us.

Someone nudged me in the back, and I turned around. *Felix.* He whipped his helmet off and held it with a tight grip. "Were you serious about the police?" His eyes darted around the stadium.

"Hell yeah." I slapped him on the back. "Can't go to the NFL if you're in jail, asshole."

Hardness grew in his gaze, and I could tell he was getting ready to mouth off.

Fuck that. I ignored him and turned away.

This was my team. *My moment.*

Someone shoved me from behind, causing me to stumble into a lady reporter who was busy getting her mic out. Mortified, I quickly regained my balance and apologized. Once I made sure she was okay, I flipped around, expecting to see some random person. It was Felix. Again. He curled his lip as people milled around us.

I just stared at him. He'd always been the instigator in our run-ins, yet infuriatingly cool when I'd been the one to react.

But now, he was the livid one, his taut stance practically begging me to come at him.

I wasn't stupid.

I read that asshole like a weak defensive line.

He was itching for me to hit him. He wanted me to fuck up. This was his last opportunity to ruin my chances at a Heisman.

I smiled at him. *Who knew that keeping my cool would feel so fucking good?*

Fast as ever and always looking out for me, Tate popped up next to me. He looked from me to Felix, taking in his clenched fists and red face. He took him by the arm and forcefully directed him to the sidelines. I watched as they disappeared slowly.

I refocused and met the bewildered eyes of the reporter who had obviously not seen anything since he'd been hidden behind me. Thank God. I didn't need any media drama. "Sorry about that. I can throw a ball but apparently I have two left feet."

She blushed and laughed, saying something about too many people and how she was glad to catch my fall. She waved her camera guy over and once he set up, she put her mic in my face. "What are your plans after the big win tonight?"

Clarity drifted in, *and fuck*, did it feel good.

Sunny. I needed her.

I couldn't exist without her in my world.

I smiled at the reporter, a genuine one, feeling lighter than I had in weeks. "I'm going to kiss my girl."

I just had to find her first.

chapter
THRITY-SEVEN

Max

"I T'S ON TV again," Tate called from the den. I jogged out from the bedroom and came to a halt in front of the blaring television.

It was Tuesday, and I was still riding high from our win. The only thing missing was Sunny. As soon as the game ended, I'd grabbed my phone and found the reply she'd sent me. Her dad was dying, and she and Mimi had headed there so she could say goodbye. I worried for her, missing her like hell and wanting to tell her everything going on with me, but I was waiting—albeit a bit impatiently—until I saw her.

"Check it," Tate called, pointing at the TV.

A Sports Center Special Report was on, showing the last play of Saturday's game. The head anchor, a burly fellow who'd played college football for Tennessee, spoke to the camera. "And later tonight at six, we'll be live at the Downtown Athletic Club in New York for the Heisman Finalist announcement." A picture of me came on the screen. I swallowed.

He continued, "Max Kent has been the front-runner most of the season, but he and the Tigers stumbled mid-season. He finished strong in the win against Taylor University, and I'm sure he's on the edge of seat wondering if he made the cut." The reporter sent a knowing look to his co-anchor.

"That's right," another sportscaster chimed in. "Plus, it looks like he might be headed to a national championship after the win against Taylor. Saturday was his best game of the season . . ." the voice drifted off, going into details about other games over the weekend.

Tate went to the kitchen and came back with beers, handing me one as he sent me a cocky grin. "Here's to tonight and the end of an era. No matter what happens, I couldn't have picked a better person to have this run with."

"Cheers, my friend, and ditto that." We clinked bottles, and I took a swig.

I leaned against the doorjamb, my eyes going to Sunny's house across the street. When I'd called her this morning, she'd been rather curt, busy with packing so they could leave as soon as the funeral was over. I was thankful Mimi had gone with her. We'd talked everyday she'd been gone, but she'd been off. Her dad had died on Sunday, and she was busy, handling the funeral and visiting with distant relatives.

She also said she had something to tell me, but she wanted to do it in person. I already knew what it was, but for the life of me, I couldn't ask her about it.

I went to my room and pulled the blue and pink packaging from my nightstand drawer and stared down at it. It was wrinkled and dented from the nights I'd cradled it in my hands. I'd been wrestling with what it meant since I'd found it in her house on Sunday after the game. She'd called and asked me to use the key she'd given me after the daisy incident to double check her lights and locks because she'd left in such a hurry.

She'd left the light on in the bathroom, and I found the empty box— with no test strip. Of course, she'd probably taken it with her.

I came out of the bedroom and headed to the kitchen to eat some of the catered food my dad had sent over. Our countertops and kitchen table were covered in sandwiches, fancy deli meats, dips, chips, and a plethora of other snacks. Two kegs were outside by the fire pit, also courtesy of my dad, just waiting for guests to show up later when we had our party that Tate insisted on.

Dad had even bought us a new eighty-inch big screen TV. Two guys had arrived this morning and set it up outside under the covered porch, so we'd have plenty of room for the players, coaches, and anyone else we wanted to watch the live show in the backyard.

Yeah. My dad was trying.

Buying me things wasn't going to make a difference, yet we'd had a slight bonding moment when he'd gone to the police department with me. Just today he'd called to let me know that the police had sought out an interview with Bianca, but she'd left school unexpectedly. Bullshit. She just hadn't wanted to squeal on Felix. He'd probably gotten to her and convinced her to keep her mouth shut. She wasn't a reliable witness.

On the other hand, Cyndi and Felix had been questioned by the police, but according to my dad's contacts, they'd denied any involvement in the library incident. As of now, everything we had was hearsay. Whatever. I wasn't going to worry about it. Not today. Somehow, someway, Felix would fuck up.

As for my dad, it would take time and a shit ton of patience to build a relationship with him. Anything was possible, I guess.

"When does Sunny get here?" Tate asked from the kitchen where he was cramming pepperonis in his mouth. "I hope she makes the show."

I grinned. "Tonight. You gonna string more lights up for her?"

Dude had gone nuts on the decorating, even calling some of his favorite groupies to come over and help him get the backyard situated like he wanted. Tiger football banners, twinkling lights, and an assortment of tables and chairs now dotted the area.

"Maybe," he chuckled. "I didn't think we'd get it done in time, but it looks great. I'm glad the weather warmed up." He made a funny face. "Bloody hell, I'm a good decorator."

I agreed.

A few hours later, the house was packed. About fifty people, most of them players and coaches, roamed around the den and outside. I got nervous, watching all the smiling faces as they came in the door. If I didn't get a nod as a candidate, I'd be embarrassed while everyone watched.

I drank another beer and waited, my eyes bouncing to the bay window every few minutes so I could see if Sunny had arrived. I rechecked my phone. The last call I'd gotten from her had been two hours ago when they'd stopped for gas.

"Ten minutes 'til show time, folks. Time to head outside," Tate called.

Following him, we went outside where people crowded around the big screen. Tate turned up the television with the remote, pulled Kiki down onto his lap, and sent me an excited smirk. "It's on, mate!"

The swing of headlights came from across the street just as the announcers came on inside the New York Athletic Club. A well-dressed sports anchor began the show. "Welcome to the live coverage of the Heisman finalists where five players will be chosen to represent the best of the best in college football. In one week, one of those five will hold the golden trophy . . ."

"Where you going?" Tate called as I stood to walk to the edge of the yard. "You're gonna miss it!"

I waved him off, checking to see if I saw the Camry.

It was her. She'd gotten out of her car, and I watched her slim figure open her trunk to pull out her overnight bag. She wrestled with it, finally freeing it, and then pulled it to the sidewalk that led to her steps. She glanced up and our gazed locked.

My heart jumped.

My hands shook.

My body hummed at the thought of seeing her again.

I pushed the gate open that led to the front of the house and walked over to her.

chapter
THIRTY-EIGHT

Sunny

WE FINALLY ARRIVED in Atlanta.

I dropped an exhausted Mimi off at her apartment. After carrying in her things and walking through her place to make sure all was well, I gave her a hug and thanked her for being with me for the trip.

She cupped my face with wrinkled hands and kissed me on the forehead. "It meant everything to me. Being with you. Seeing your mama's grave. You handled yourself like a lady, hon. I'm proud of you."

I nodded, my throat clogged, recalling the visit.

Leaving Mimi at a hotel, I'd headed up the curvy road to his house, my head in jumbles, not knowing what to expect.

What I got when I walked in the door was a host of memories—good and bad.

Walks in the woods. Happy times around the piano. Family dinners. Then my mom left us and everything changed.

The house reeked of loneliness, and I wasn't surprised. After my mom, he'd never even glanced at another woman.

He lay reclined on a hospital bed, sleeping from his medication, his face and body shrunken. I knelt down next to him and waited for him to wake.

His eyes opened at two in the morning. With a slight turn of his head, his gaze found mine.

At once, I was glad I came.

Because no matter his demons and the darkness they'd caused, he was my father.

I hadn't known *how* it would feel to look at him again.

But I had no hate for him. *How could I?* That emotion was too destructive. Too ugly.

And I wouldn't allow it to be part of who I was.

I was saying goodbye and I was going to mean it.

He wasn't able to speak. Instead he pulled his thin hand out from the covers and showed me a crumpled postcard. His eyes were tremulous and watery, pleading with me.

Feeling confused, I took it, flipping it over to read. Scrawled in my sloppy nine-year-old handwriting was a card I'd dropped in the mail to him from summer camp, a sappy little message from a daughter that told her daddy how much she missed him.

So long ago when we'd been a real family.

And he'd kept it.

My stomach clenched.

Stunned. That's how I felt.

"I forgive you," I said, my heart aching.

For him. For me.

For a family that had cracked right down the middle.

Relief flooded his face as if a burden had been lifted. He closed his eyes and wept.

The rest was a blur. He'd passed a few hours later. I sat with him alongside my cousin who'd been caring for him and a hospice nurse.

Mimi's voice brought me back.

"You going to talk to Max, right?" she asked as I made my way out the door. "He loves you, ya know. I see it. Only one man ever looked at me the way he does you and that was my husband."

"Of course. Now get some rest." I waved goodbye, got in my car, and drove home.

And now there he was—coming across the street, looking ridiculously gorgeous in jeans and a black T-shirt. His hair flowed around his shoulders. My Viking.

It may have only been a few days apart from him, but it felt like a lifetime.

I let go of my luggage, sucked in a deep breath, and prepared myself. *What was going to happen to us?*

"Sunny," he called, his eyes full of questions as they roamed my face. He came to a halt in front of me. "I'm so damn glad you're back where you belong."

I nodded, feeling anxious and trying to shake it off. We had so much to talk about. "I just got in. It was a long trip."

"But you're here now."

"Yes."

A loud cheer came from his house, and I looked over his shoulder, taking in the line of cars and the glow from the lights in his backyard.

I started. *Oh.*

I looked back at him. "Max! The announcement . . . I'd almost forgotten. Are you a finalist?"

He shrugged broad shoulders. "I don't know."

My mouth parted. "You don't know? Why not?"

His gaze zeroed in on mine. "Because I wanted to see you. Everything else can wait—even the Heisman."

My heart skipped a beat.

"I've thought about us a lot . . ." he said, sticking his hands in his pockets. "I guess we should talk."

"Yeah."

"I found your pregnancy test. I—I guess that's what you wanted to tell me. Right?"

My eyes widened. What? How had he—

"I found it when you asked me to make sure you'd locked up. The only thing missing is the test strip."

Oh. I nibbled at my bottom lip, picturing his reaction. "I packed it with my stuff when I was getting ready to leave. I took the test and then Mimi showed up to tell me about my dad. Things got nuts."

He reached out a tentative hand and caressed my cheek, but let it fall as if he didn't know quite what to do with me. "It's not your fault. You were on the pill, but we were going at it like crazy."

I sent him a small smile, recalling several of those moments. "I'm not pregnant. If I had known you'd find the package, I would have told you sooner, but I was waiting until we were together so we could discuss things."

A myriad of emotions flitted across his face, but I couldn't pin them down. "It would have been okay if you were," he said softly. "We can handle anything. You and me."

I glanced up. "You're not upset at the close call? Even after Bianca . . ."

"You are *not* her. You're trustworthy and beautiful and the person I want to be with."

My stomach fluttered. God. I needed to hear these words. I needed *him*.

He continued. "I freaked, sure, but I was never angry. I was worried about *you*, but I didn't want to bring it up with everything else you had going on." His hand lifted again, this time more confident as his fingers glided into my hair and tugged me closer to him. "Let's put the baby scare aside. I'm sorry I roped you into being my fake fiancée—no wait—I can't say that because I don't know if things would have turned out like this."

"Like how?"

"I love you, Sunny."

Such simple words. Words I needed.

My insecurities slipped away and elation flew over me. I put my hands on his shoulders. "Say that again."

His blue-green gaze searched mine. "I love you. I have for a long time. I was scared it would screw up my game, but life is crystal clear now. It's just taken me a while to wake the hell up." His voice was fierce, almost gruff in the delivery. He swallowed once and then twice, the lines of his throat moving. "Since the night I pulled you out of that car and brought life back to you, you gave life to me." He looked at me certainty. "You're mine. You always will be."

"It's about time you told me, Quarterback," I said, my voice thick. "I love you so much. You're everything to me. You were meant to be mine since the night you saved—"

His lips stopped my words.

We kissed in the street, our arms tight around each other.

I was never letting him go.

Another cheer, louder this time, came from across the street, and I glanced over his shoulder.

Tate appeared on the edge of the their property, the streetlight illuminating the little smile he wore. He yelled out. "Hey, Sunny! Glad you're back! Sorry about your dad."

"Thanks," I said softly.

He looked at Max. "Dude. I know you're in the middle of making out, but they called your fucking name! You're one of the finalists! We're going to New York! *You're fucking in.*" He whooped. "There's people waiting to congratulate you, mate. Just, um, whenever you two get done with all the mushy shit."

I laughed as he walked away.

"You should go back over there," I said. "They're all waiting. I need to freshen up and unpack anyway."

He laced our fingers together. "I'm not going anywhere without you. In fact, I have a surprise for you."

He tugged me toward his house, and I followed my heart skipping. *Had I ever been this happy?* Ever? No.

We popped into the party through the back gate and the entire place erupted in cheers. Max garnered backslaps and congratulatory man hugs. His dad embraced him. Isabella and Ash ran up to me and asked about my trip. He kept me firmly by his side the entire time, refusing to let my hand go. I didn't mind.

Ten minutes later, much to my surprise, he announced we were leaving. Most begged him to stay, except for Tate and Isabella who seemed to be in on the surprise.

"Where are we going?" I asked as he led me to his car, which had brand new tires on it. I didn't ask about Felix. He'd told me most of what had happened and no way did I want to bring him up when this was our moment.

"You'll see," he said as he tucked me in the passenger side, and once again I was reminded of that first day when he'd given me a ride to class. I grabbed his hand, tugged him to me and kissed him hard. My hands squeezed his face and poured everything I had bottled up for the past few weeks. Our mouths clung. Hot and fast.

He growled under his breath. "You keep this up and we won't be going anywhere."

He drove out of the parking spot, and a few minutes later we pulled up to the Leland football stadium.

I quirked an eyebrow as he parked. "You know it's closed, right?"

"Cookie, please. I know people. This is my turf, and if I want it opened, they're gonna open it. See, the lights are even on."

We got out and walked into a brightly lit stadium. He led me to the entryway to the stands and over to his Dad's season seats. The very same place where I'd watched his games.

"You just can't get enough of this place, can you?" I teased.

He just shrugged. "Will you sit down?"

I did.

He knelt down in front of me—and my heart flew away.

I couldn't breathe. "Max?" Only it came out as a wheeze.

He gazed at me with tremulous eyes, his face as serious as I'd ever seen it.

"I asked you to marry me here, and it nearly messed everything up. I used a fake ring that my best friend picked out."

I swallowed.

He eased the engagement ring he'd given me off my finger, slipping it in his pocket.

He pulled a small black box from his other pocket. "But this . . . this is a ring that I picked out yesterday. I searched every jewelry store until I found the perfect one. The idea that you might be pregnant had nothing to do with me buying it. Maybe that was another reason I didn't ask you about that test strip. I wanted *this moment* to be about us—nothing else." He paused. Our eyes locked. "I love you, Sunny Blaine, and I want you to marry me. For real." He opened the box, revealing a heart-shaped diamond ring.

I gasped. It was huge. It was beautiful. It was *mine*.

With sure hands, he slid it on my finger and looked up at me. "For the rest of my life, I want you. Forever."

The butterflies in my stomach went crazy. I nodded. "Yes, yes, yes."

He pulled me to my feet and kissed me under the lights of a quiet stadium.

There was no Jumbotron. No cheering fans. Just us.

It was everything.

He was everything.

We were everything.

EPILOGUE

Two years later . . .

MAX JUMPED IN our king-sized bed like it was a trampoline and stuck his cold feet against my naked back. I yelped, smacked him on the arm, and wiggled away from him. "Stop it, Quarterback! I haven't had coffee yet."

"I haven't had you yet," he growled and turned me over to my back, tickling my ribs as he rubbed scruff down my chest, kissing and nuzzling my stomach.

I laughed at his antics, which turned passionate as he went lower, his mouth finding the curve of my knee, the sensitive area on my hipbone. He ran his fingers around my back, idly tracing the lines of one of my scars. He paid special attention to them.

"I've never been this happy," he murmured against my neck.

Deep contentment coursed through me. "I know. Me too."

I thought back over the past two years. He'd won the Heisman and a National Championship. Then, we'd gone to New York for the draft where he'd been the number one pick for the New York Giants. I took a second to gaze out of our high-rise window overlooking the Manhattan skyline. With his signing bonus and a monetary gift from his dad, we were living in an upscale area with tree-lined streets and adorable coffee places.

After graduation, we'd gotten married in Atlanta. It had been a relatively small affair with our closest friends and family. Isabella had been my bridesmaid, and I'd worn the fishtale dress I'd tried on.

Now, I worked part-time at a dress shop that made up-cycled clothing. One day I wanted my own boutique, but for now, I was enjoying being with Max.

Life was perfect.

As far as Felix went, he hadn't been picked up in the draft.

Oh, how Max had loved that.

When it came down to it, Felix didn't have the talent. We'd heard he was a used car salesman in Florida. After much discussion, Max and I had mutually decided to put him behind us and let the past go.

We didn't spend time thinking about him.

We had too many good and *real* things to focus on.

He kissed me again. "You've got that dreamy look on your face. Whatcha thinking about?"

"You."

He grinned. "I am pretty damn dreamy."

I poked him in the ribs and he collapsed against me, his naked body gliding against mine. The air thickened around us, heat building. It never took much for us to be hot for each other.

He touched me, his hand coasting down between my legs and dipping inside. He kissed me, soft and then hard, his tongue sucking on mine.

My need ramped up. I cupped his ass, pulling him in closer, wet and ready. "Hurry," I murmured.

Lifting my leg over his shoulder, he said my name with reverence and slid inside.

I arched, my body accepting all of him.

"I love you so much," he ground out as he made me his.

I kissed him.

Our lives were just beginning.

Max . . . us . . . Fate had divined our love.

Since the night we'd met on that shore, an invisible thread connected us.

I didn't understand the *hows* and *whys* of our meeting, but life isn't nearly as complicated as we make it.

Sometimes there really is a bigger plan.

Sometimes there really is that *one person*.

Sometimes true love finds you no matter what.

The End

Continue on to enjoy the first two chapters of Dirty English, a Wall Street Journal Bestseller

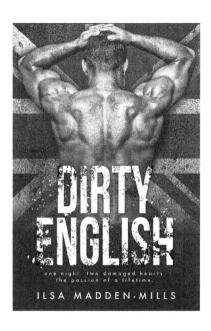

PROLOGUE

A STABBING PAIN IN my temple.

Fat and swollen lips.

A throbbing tenderness between my thighs.

Why did I feel like I was dying?

Muddled images flashed in my head, but nothing connected or made sense, just a big black hole of nothingness. Thanks, vodka.

The ache seemed to spread across my face. I groaned. *Had something hit me?*

Nausea curled as I got my bearings in the dark. Bit by bit, I figured out I was sprawled cross-wise on a bed that wasn't mine.

A small hotel room came into focus.

Careful to move my head slowly, I gazed around, taking in the battered nightstand and a rickety desk that had seen better days. In the corner of the room lay the beaded clutch purse I'd borrowed from my best friend Shelley for prom. Okay. *But where was she?*

My last memory was dancing in the gym. Maybe on top of a table?

My eyes went around the room.

Threadbare navy curtains.

A bed that reeked of stale cigarettes and body odor.

A bottle of Grey Goose.

My stomach lurched at the memory of that bitter taste sliding down my throat, and I swallowed to keep the bile down.

Was this a hangover?

I didn't know. I had nothing to compare it to.

Snippets of the night came in vivid clips.

Dinner with my boyfriend, Colby, and my friends Shelley and Blake at an Italian restaurant in downtown Petal, North Carolina. Lots of giggling. Colby sneaking in his flask so we could spike our drinks. Dancing under twinkling lights at the prom in the Oakmont Prep gymnasium. Getting in Colby's Porsche to head to the lake for an after-hours party.

No memories of the lake came to me.

Colby, though, I remembered him urging me to drink, pushing the bottle at my mouth on the way to prom and then later as we drove to the lake. *Don't be a pussy, Elizabeth. Drink it. Let's rule the world, babe.*

Rule the world was his thing. He was invincible, and I guess since his father was a Senator of North Carolina, he believed it. Being part of his inner circle, especially being his new girlfriend, made me feel like I was freaking royalty.

My tummy still fluttered from winning prom queen to his king. On stage when they'd set the sparkling crowns on our heads, he'd turned to me and told me he loved me. Crazy and giddy happiness had filled my heart. He loved *me*. The girl from the wrong side of town. The girl without a real family. The girl who was nobody.

I'd waited for someone to love me like that my whole life.

More flashes from the car came and I groaned.

I remembered the second sip. Third. Fourth.

Things got hazy.

God, I couldn't remember.

Colby giving me a little white pill.

Did I take it?

It was all so fuzzy.

Pink, sparkly sequins dotted my hands and I gazed down at them on the bed. My dress—the one I'd scrimped and saved to get by waiting tables at the local diner—lay in scattered pieces around me. My body was on display with my breasts hanging out.

I whimpered and tried to cover them, but my arms were too sluggish. Panic ate at me—and then an awful realization hit. The material had been ripped from bust to hem, the delicate spaghetti straps torn off. My underwear lay twisted around my ankles and spots of blood dotted the coverlet below me.

For a millisecond my brain refused to accept what was plain as day, but when reality finally settled in, horror pooled in my gut.

My hands attempted to move but only fluttered around my body.

Red marks. Bruises. Scratches. Teeth marks.

No. No. No. This was all wrong. This wasn't supposed to happen tonight.

Whispers came from a corner of the room. Colby.

My eyes found him standing shirtless in the bathroom, his back to me as he talked on the phone.

Pieces of his conversation came to me.

"She's out of it, man . . . like an animal in the sack . . . popped that cherry . . ."

His words hit me like a tsunami, and my breath snagged in my throat. I struggled to regain my equilibrium—to focus—lying to myself that this whole episode was a figment of my imagination.

Colby grunted. "I don't think she'll be able to walk for a week." A pause, and then he burst out laughing at something the other person must have said.

Something fragile inside me cracked and split wide open.

A sound tore from my throat, low and primitive, and his eyes swiveled to me.

I flinched, every muscle in my body jerking in revulsion.

"Gotta go." He hung up and stalked toward me, stopping at the edge of the bed to stare down at me with ice-blue eyes. A flash of annoyance crossed his face as his gaze skated across my body. "You made a mess."

Being from the trailer park, I'd had more than my share of scuffles with boys who wanted my attention and girls who wanted to boss me around, so I knew how to kick ass. Right then every nerve ending in my body wanted to jump up and claw his heart out piece by piece with my nails. He'd done this to me.

Rage burned inside, but I couldn't move.

My voice came out thin. Reedy. "You hurt me."

I struggled to sit up but collapsed backward.

He watched me dispassionately as I flailed around on the bed, letting the moments tick by, escalating my fear.

My tongue dipped out to lick dry lips.

He scooped up his white dress shirt from the floor, careful and steady hands buttoning it up, and that gesture, it said everything. He pulled on his pants and checked his sandy hair in the mirror. He wasn't drunk at all.

"What did you give me?" I pushed out. "Why?"

"Don't play games, sweetheart, you begged for it. *This* was consensual." He twirled his fingers around the bed, a look of derision on his face. "Whatever I gave you, you took it without asking."

"No, that's not true." *Had I?*

"Oh yeah, and you were the best lay I've had in months. Well worth the time I spent on you." He bent down until his eyes were level with mine. "Don't be telling lies about what happened here. No one would believe you anyway as drunk as you were. Still are. I'm sure there're photos and videos from the prom to prove it." He laughed as if hit by a sudden memory. "Damn girl, you were crazy in the gym, dancing on the tables and yelling at people. Chaperones tossed us out, babe. If I didn't know better, I'd think you were a bad influence on me." He cocked his head. "That's what I'll tell everyone at least." He brushed at some lint on his trousers.

I shook my head. *No.* I was the good girl who'd scored the highest in her class on the SAT. I was the girl who volunteered at the local animal shelter—and not just for service hours. I didn't get thrown out of parties. I barely got invited to them.

He pushed hair out of my face, his fingers trailing down my cheek.

I flinched and jerked away as far as I could. "Don't touch me."

"Ah, and here I was hoping you'd be ready for another round." He chuckled, his hands fiddling with the ring I'd made for him a few weeks ago, a sterling silver band with our initials etched on the inside with a heart between them. I'd spent hours on it, engraving the letters and then fashioning the metal until it was perfect. I'd even used some of my college savings to buy the butane torch and tools necessary to make it good enough for him.

"You said you loved me." I hated the weakness in my voice.

His lips quirked up. "I tell all the girls I love them, Elizabeth. You just took a little longer to give me what I wanted."

A strangled noise came out of my mouth.

He sighed and zipped his pants. "Don't be upset. We both wanted this."

No, no, no.

He twisted his ring off and twirled it between his fingers. "I guess you'll be wanting this back now." He tossed it on the nightstand and it made a tinkling sound as it hit the wood, spun off, and fell onto the floor.

He checked his appearance in the mirror one last time to straighten his jacket. "Well, I have to go, but I'll see you at graduation in a few days. Later, babe."

And then he walked out the door, shutting it softly behind him.

Thank God.

I sucked in a shuddering breath, my lungs grasping for more air.

To make sense of what had happened.

An hour went by. Another one.

Memories flashed like a horror movie you didn't want to watch but couldn't stop. Colby carrying me in the hotel and placing me on the bed. Ripping my dress. Groping at my legs. Hitting. Shoving. *Pain.*

I'd tried to say no, but the words hadn't come.

I'd tried to move, but I couldn't.

My body had been a frozen statue, and he'd moved me where he wanted. Twisted me. Ruined me.

I held myself together and watched the minutes tick by on the digital clock as my alcohol-soaked brain struggled to make my body move again. In tiny increments, I slid my legs down until they touched the floor, my toes clenching into the cheap, fuzzy carpet. Groaning, I forced myself to sit up and then immediately fell. I crawled until I got to my purse in the corner of the room and found my phone.

Panic drove me.

Any minute he could come back in here and do it again.

My hand shook as I pushed 911 but froze when the nasally voice of the operator came on.

"You've reached 911. Do you have an emergency?"

Shame. Guilt. Remorse. *Truth.*

Had I asked for it?

Was this my fault?

I panted, the throbbing between my legs reminding me of my sin.

"Hello? Do you have an emergency? Do you need assistance?" The voice was more insistent.

"No," I croaked and ended the call.

I gazed down at my ruined dress. Who'd believe a girl whose father was in prison—if he even was my father—versus the wealthy son of a senator? I was white trash, a small town girl lucky enough to get a scholarship at the prep school down the road.

Nausea rose again, more violently this time, until the contents of my stomach spewed out everywhere.

The smell of alcohol made me sicker.

Mocking me. Telling me the cold hard truth. I'd had a part to play in this scenario.

I clutched my chest, my heart hurting. Broken.

My muscles screamed.

My head banged.

I was done. Dead. Cold. Even my skin wanted to crawl away.

The sun crept up in the sky, the rays curling in through the dirty curtains. Dawn, a new day, but I'd never look at the sunrise the same.

Clarity happens to all of us when our heart jumps ship, and mine was no different.

Something dark slithered around inside me, crawling into the crevices of my soul and suffocating it. Everything I'd believed about myself . . . about who I was . . . about *love* . . . unraveled, turning into something dark. Dirty.

Love is a knife that cuts out your heart piece by piece, feeding it to the boy you love.

Broken in more ways than one, I vowed to never fall again.

My body caved in on itself as I wept.

CHAPTER 1

Two years later

Elizabeth

SWEAT DRIPPED DOWN my neck as I tucked blond hair behind my ears and groaned in the hot sun. It was Friday afternoon in Raleigh, North Carolina, and the only day I had to move into my new apartment before junior year started on Monday. "Welcome back to Whitman University," I muttered as I pulled yet another box out of the trunk of my beat up Camry.

For only being twenty years old, I'd accumulated a lot of stuff.

Most of it consisted of jewelry making supplies and books except for my furnishings, which I'd inherited from Granny Bennett when she'd passed this summer. A beige and green plaid couch, a kitchen table with ducks painted on the top, an old bedroom suite, and a collection of crocheted doilies in various colors was my inheritance from her. Not exactly Ethan Allen, but it had a certain style.

"Your apartment looks like an eighty-year-old cat lady lives here," Shelley called down to me as she popped her head out of my apartment to peer down over the railing at me. My bestie since prep school, she was a privileged rich girl, a sharp contrast to my own wrong-side-of-the-tracks upbringing, but she'd been there for me through everything. Even Colby. Her red hair had gotten fuzzy in the humidly, but it didn't detract from her prettiness. She pinched her nose and made a scrunchy face. "And it kinda stinks."

"Stop your complaining and get your butt down here to help. I'm melting in this heat," I said.

She snorted and made her way down the metal stairway. "You and your fair skin. If you'd get out of the house now and then, you might get some color. But no . . . all you do is study and work at the bookstore.

You probably have more colors of highlighters than you have dating prospects. Not to mention, you go to the library so much people think you work there."

I grinned. "I'm not that bad. I see people in class. I even talk to them sometimes."

She lowered her head at me. "Get real. If it wasn't for me forcing you to go out with me—like tonight—you'd hole up here and eat ramen noodles for the rest of your college career."

"Meh, sometimes I eat pizza."

She sent me a smirk and grabbed one of the boxes at my feet. We waddled back up the staircase and came to a stop at apartment 2B on the second floor. A two-bedroom with a balcony and a bathroom, it felt like a mansion compared to the dorm room I'd lived in all last year. I was on the corner and facing the setting sun, and I only had one neighbor on my left, 2A.

As if on cue, the thump of loud rap music blasted from next door.

I listened. Was that Eminem?

"That's loud and obnoxious," Shelley said. "Maybe it won't be as quiet here as you think."

I tried to be optimistic. "So? It's two in the afternoon, not two in the morning."

"They're just moving in, too," she noted, nudging her head at the pile of boxes sitting outside the neighbor's door, which I noticed was slightly cracked. She indicated the pile of books in one. "Looks like a nerd. Yuck. And here I was hoping you'd win the jackpot with a hot neighbor."

Making sure the new neighbor was nowhere in sight, I leaned over and hurriedly rifled through some of the titles: *The Great Gatsby, Wuthering Heights.* "Hmm, someone likes the classics. English major, maybe?"

She rolled her eyes. "Boring. What you need is a sexy neighbor who likes to have great monkey sex."

I shook my head at her. "See, you say 'monkey sex' and all I can think of are hairy animals in bed. Gross."

She huffed in a teasing kind of way. "Whatever. It's like every time you see a hot guy, you have FUCK OFF tattooed on your head."

Colby had been a hot guy and look what that had gotten me.

I shrugged, swallowing down those memories. "So? I don't want to fall for anyone. Ever. Love hurts. Remember?"

"Yeah." She nibbled on her lips, a hard look growing on her normally smiling face. She was remembering the hotel and the devastation that had followed. She'd been the one to pick me up that morning and take me home. The kind of girl who fell in love at least once a month, she was under the impression that if I could just meet the right one, then all would be well and I'd have my happily ever after. Crock of shit.

"Don't worry about me, Shelley. I'm good, okay? I don't need a guy in my life to make me happy. All I need is you and Blake—and the occasional hookup." Blake was my other best friend from Oakmont Prep who'd come to Whitman as well.

She smirked. "Your sex rules again?"

I nodded.

Here's the thing. I'd had sex since Colby. Plenty of times. The events of that night didn't ruin my sexuality, only my trust in men. So a year after Colby, I halfheartedly propositioned a guy from my science class and asked him to come back to my room. Connor had been his name, and I'd seen him checking me out more than once when we had a lab together. That day, he'd looked at me like I'd suddenly grown two heads—me having a reputation as a bit of a bitch when it came to guys flirting with me—but he'd been eager. We'd walked back to my dorm room, and while the sex had been horrible, a furtive and awkward encounter, it proved that Colby had not won.

He was *not* the last person to touch me.

My body was my own.

So was my heart, and I planned to keep it that way.

After that, sex got easy—as long as I was in control. Over the past year, I'd made it into a game with strict rules. Pick an average guy who wasn't popular or rich or too good-looking. Make sure he wasn't taken. Make sure he didn't drink or do drugs. Make sure he wasn't an escapee from the local insane asylum. Have sex. Never speak to him again. End of story.

It was about control. My choice. My rules.

I had to initiate the first move, and I had to be on top. Most importantly, I had to be in my own bed and around my own things. Sex with me was tame by most standards, I suppose, based on some of the crazy stories Shelley had told me about her adventures. But I didn't care. If they wanted me, then they'd follow my lead.

"Maybe I'll join a nunnery."

She grinned. "You don't look good in black."

"True."

"And you aren't even Catholic, goofball."

"Again, true." I smiled back widely. I didn't mind her teasing me. It was better than pity.

I moved past her and we went back into my apartment to unpack. I pulled out a picture of me with Granny on her front porch the day I left for Whitman freshman year. Most days, it hurt to look at that photo, to see the skinny girl in the picture with the saggy jeans and wrapped wrists. But it was the last picture I had of Granny and me together, and that was worth something to me no matter how hard it was to be reminded of my foolish mistake with Colby. I set it on the coffee table.

We finished putting the dishes in the kitchen cabinets and then moved to the bedroom where she helped me arrange my closets. Later, we ventured into the extra bedroom, which was more like a tiny storage room. This was university housing and the apartments were notoriously small, but I managed to fit my jewelry supplies and a twin bed in there.

But I hadn't made any jewelry in two years. The metals I'd once loved to shape and mold had become a metaphor for my own stupidity in love.

Shelley fiddled with one of my drawing pads, a pensive look on her face. She darted her eyes at me and then back at the boxes against the wall.

I steeled myself for her questions.

"When are you going to get serious about your jewelry? What are you going to do when you graduate in two years?" She opened the book and flipped through the pages. "Besides, I really need a new necklace. Something with a butterfly. Or a heart." Her face softened as she looked up at me. "Remember the little friendship medallions you made us when we were fifteen—"

"Shelley, I'm not talking about this. I can't make jack right now."

She cocked her head. "Are you just going to give up on your dreams because you made a ring for Colby? It's been two years, yet he's still dictating your future. It's fucked up. At one time *this* was all you wanted to do—design and create. Do you honestly think you'd be happy in some job where you can't make something beautiful?" She sighed, a resigned look on her face. "I mean, you use sex with guys to say you're past him, but you're not. Not really. You're still punishing yourself for something that's not even your fault."

It was my fault. I'd been drunk. I'd taken his drugs. Willingly.

The familiar shame settled in my gut. I blinked rapidly. "You weren't in that hotel room. You know nothing."

She bit her lip. Nodded. "You're right, I wasn't, but I saw you afterward. I took you home and took care of you until your mom got back from Vegas. I know how wrecked you were. I—I just love you, that's all."

I exhaled and paced around the room, setting things out, arranging them. We'd gotten too serious. "Besides, butterflies and hearts are worse than tramp stamps. *If* I made you a piece, it would stand for something big."

She grinned. "Like what?"

"Maybe your phone number on something since you give it out so much to guys."

She pretended to be pissed but then giggled. "God, that is so true. I'm a slut."

We laughed. "Come on, let's go get the rest of my stuff." We made our way back outside my apartment and stood in the breezeway. I sighed as I looked out over the parking lot. I still had several more boxes to bring up before I could even think about relaxing.

She poked me in the arm. "Hey, I have an idea. Let's go meet your neighbor."

I shook my head. "No, it's move-in day, and I'm sure they're just as busy as we are."

She ignored me and tiptoed over to the door. Instead of knocking, she pushed the cracked door open and peeked inside the darkened apartment.

"I don't see anyone. Maybe they're in the back on the balcony." A grin crossed her face. "Which gives us plenty of time to be nosy." She bent down and riffled through the boxes outside, pulling out a cap with a Union Jack flag on it, a pair of men's athletic underwear, a pair of men's black Chucks. She went a bit crazy, pulling out fingerless boxing gloves—*that was interesting*—and a collection of postcards from London.

"Oh, your neighbor is definitely a guy. And hung." She held up a box of condoms. Super-sized and ribbed. Triumph gleamed in her eyes. "Magnums, baby. Score," she sang out.

My eyes scanned the door to make sure no one saw us. "Put that stuff back before they come out here. Are you insane?"

"Yes."

I groaned at her obvious disinterest in being caught, but I couldn't help venturing closer. I did want to know more about my neighbor who read the classics and listened to rap music.

She tapped her chin, eyes coasting over the contents. "Even with the musty books, he's not a terrible combo. I'd do him."

"You'd do Manson."

She laughed.

I snapped the postcards out of her hand and tossed them back where she'd gotten them. "Step away from the box, or I won't go to the Tau party with you tonight or wear that silly dress you spent an hour hemming last night." Shelley was a fashion major and took all sewing projects serious. I was her number one model.

She sent the box a forlorn look and pouted. "Fine, you win. Party pooper."

"Huh. You need me to keep you in line. You never would have survived freshman English if I hadn't been yelling in your ear every morning to get up."

She agreed—a little too easily—and we moved back inside and went to sit on the balcony.

"What's that you have?" I asked later, noticing a brown book she kept pressed against her side.

She glanced down with a feigned look of surprise. "Oh this old thing?

I got so wrapped up in your new place, I must have forgotten to put it back in the box."

Right. I narrowed my eyes. "Really?"

She got a giddy expression on her face, ignoring my sarcasm. "Okay, you got me. It's Jane Austen's *Pride and Prejudice*. I snitched it from your neighbor. I mean, it's your favorite book because your name is in it." She let out a dramatic sigh and pressed the book to her heart. "Don't you see? It's fate. You and the boring neighbor dude are meant to be."

I shook my head. Sometimes she was too much. "That's it. No more silly romantic movies for you. I don't even know why we're friends. I'm revoking our friendship as of now." I snatched the book out of her hands. An old hardback with gold lettering, it was an older printing, perhaps even valuable.

What kind of guy hangs on to a book like this?

The kind that believes in love, my heart whispered.

I cracked the book open and turned the pages until I found the chapter where Mr. Darcy describes how he fell in love with Elizabeth Bennet: *I cannot fix on the hour, or the spot, or the look, or the words, which laid the foundation. It is too long ago. I was in the middle before I knew that I had begun.*

Sappy drivel. I snapped it shut. "I love lots of books. It's called reading, you know. You should try it."

"No need. I have my looks." She preened and flicked a strand of hair over her shoulder. "Where are you going?" she called as I marched through the living room and toward the front door.

I held the book up in my hands. "Hello! To return what you stole."

She threw her arms up. "It accidentally got stuck to my hand, I swear! There's a difference!"

"Uh-huh." I walked over to the neighbor's, but the door was shut, and the boxes were gone. I put my ear to the door, but all was silent.

The sudden blast of music from a car in the parking lot made me jump.

I leaned over the breezeway railing that overlooked the parking lot and searched below until I found a rugged-looking black Jeep with the top off. The Beastie Boys song "Fight for Your Right" reached my ears. I blinked. Damn, it was loud.

The driver was a bulky guy with a black Union Jack hat pulled low over his brow, blocking his face from me, leaving only the ends of his brown hair showing as it curled around the sides. A pair of aviators rested on his nose. Even from here, I saw broad shoulders and taut, muscular forearms as he shifted gears on the manual transmission. I even caught the flash of tattoos on his arms but couldn't make them out.

Mystery neighbor? It *was* the same hat from the box.

I found myself leaning over further, arching my neck to see more of him.

Something about a big dude that read *Pride and Prejudice* made me breathless.

In my head earlier, as we'd gone through the boxes, I'd pictured my neighbor as more the Harry Potter type, a geek with black-rimmed glasses and a shy smile. *Wrong, wrong, wrong.*

Before he pulled out into the traffic, he turned and glanced back at the apartment building, his shielded eyes seeming to zero in on me. His car idled as he looked at me, and even though there were quite a few yards between us, I felt the physical weight of his stare.

I inhaled sharply, goosebumps making the hair on my arms rise up.

Had he seen Shelley going through his things? Shit.

The book! I looked down to see it was still clutched it in my other hand. *Dammit.*

Feeling ridiculous, I tore my eyes off him and backed up slowly until he was out of my vision. I propped the book up against his door and bolted for my apartment.

"Who was that?" Shelley asked as I flew in the door.

I shook my head. "It wasn't Harry Potter, that's for sure."

Dirty English is Available Now

books by
ILSA MADDEN MILLS

Ilsa Madden-Mills' books are ALL standalones!

BRIARWOOD ACADEMY
Very Bad Things
Very Wicked Beginnings (prequel)
Very Wicked Things
Very Twisted Things

Dirty English
Filthy English

ABOUT THE AUTHOR

WALL STREET JOURNAL best-selling author Ilsa Madden-Mills writes about strong heroines and sexy alpha males that sometimes you just want to slap. She's addicted to dystopian books and all things fantasy, including unicorns and sword-wielding females. Other fascinations include frothy coffee beverages, dark chocolate, Instagram, Ian Somerhalder (seriously hot), astronomy (she's a Gemini), and tattoos. She has a degree in English and a Master's in Education.

Sign up here for her newsletter to receive a FREE Briarwood Academy novella plus get insider info and exclusive giveaways! I never spam! I love to send out freebies, do prizes, and early excerpts!

www.ilsamaddenmills.com/contact

For more information about the next book,
please visit my social media sites:

www.ilsamaddenmills.com
www.amazon.com/Ilsa-Madden-Mills/e/B00F277DE2
www.facebook.com/authorilsamaddenmills
www.instagram.com/ilsamaddenmills
www.twitter.com/ilsamaddenmills
www.goodreads.com

ACKNOWLEDGEMENTS

THERE ARE SO many fantastic people in the indie world that made this journey possible. Please know that my gratitude in no way lessens as the list continues.

For my husband who has stood by me every step of the way. You and me, babe, against the world.

For author Lisa N. Paul—thank you for all the giggles and lunch dates that we've never had in person—except for the grits! We had grits together. Most of all thank, you for being my dear friend and being there every single day. Let's go smoke.

For author Tia Louise, my twin brain, my signing buddy—thank you for the friendship, advice, and encouragement. I can't imagine a unicorn without thinking of you. Someday, my friend, we will ride one together.

For all the girls in FTN, you are BAD ASS, and I appreciate each and every one of you! Thank you for all the sarcastic memes, funny comments, and most all, the love.

For the girls in Tribe who have encouraged me and lifted me up. I'm here for you, and all you have to do it ask. Mwah.

For Rachel Skinner of Romance Refined, my awesome and sweet editor who is extremely tough on content and exactly what I need.

For Julie Deaton—thank you for proofreading and helping me polish.

For CA Borgford of Type A Formatting for doing a phenomenal job with formatting.

For Miranda Arnold of Red Cheeks Reads: my wonderful and talented PA. HOLLA! So happy we connected through our love of *Very Bad Things*. Thank you for being a go-getter for me. Race to the end, baby!

For the admin girls of Racy Readers: Erin Fisher, Tina Morgan, Elizabeth Thiele, Miranda Arnold, Stacy Nickelson, Sarah Griffin, Heather Wish, Lexy Stories, Pam Huff, and Suzette Salinas. Thank you for your constant support, ideas, and love.

For the ladies of The Rock Stars of Romance who worked tirelessly and answered all my questions and offered advice: Lisa and Milasy . . . you are the best!

For Jenn Watson with Social Butterfly PR, you are amazing! Thank you for holding my hand.

For my Ilsa's Racy Readers Group (Unicorn Girls): you may be last on this list, but you are the BEST. You picked me up when I got knocked down and made me laugh. Thank you all for every shout out and each review you posted. Thank you for sharing a part of yourself in our group.